AFTER PEARL

A NICHOLAS BISHOP MYSTERY

STEPHEN G. EOANNOU

sfwp.com

Library of Congress Cataloging-in-Publication Data

Names: Eoannou, Stephen G., author.
Title: After Pearl / Stephen G. Eoannou.
Description: Santa Fe, NM : Santa Fe Writers Project, 2025. | Series: A
    Nicholas Bishop Mystery | Summary: "1942. War rages in Europe. Pearl
    Harbor still smolders. And alcoholic private eye Nicholas Bishop wakes
    up on a hotel room floor with two slugs missing from his .38 revolver.
    The cops think he's murdered lounge singer Pearl DuGaye, mobsters think
    he saw something he shouldn't have, and Bishop remembers nothing…"
    —Provided by publisher.
Identifiers: LCCN 2024041366 (print) | LCCN 2024041367 (ebook) |
    ISBN 9781951631475 (trade paperback) | ISBN 9781951631482 (ebook)
Subjects: LCGFT: Thrillers (Fiction) | Novels.
Classification: LCC PS3605.O16 A69 2025 (print) | LCC PS3605.O16 (ebook) |
    DDC 813/.6—dc23/eng/20240906
LC record available at https://lccn.loc.gov/2024041366
LC ebook record available at https://lccn.loc.gov/2024041367

Published by SFWP
369 Montezuma Ave. #350
Santa Fe, NM 87501
www.sfwp.com

For my sisters, Carol and Sue.

*Thanks for letting me tag along to that
little red-brick library when we were kids.*

Chapter 1

Nicholas Bishop named the one-eyed dog Jake even though she was female. Jake seemed like a good name for a pup missing an eye. He couldn't remember where the mutt had come from. When he awoke on the floor of his room at The Lafayette Hotel, she sat close by, giving him a single-eye stare. Strong odds said he stole the dog. She didn't weigh much, maybe ten pounds, easy enough to scoop under his arm as he staggered home.

He struggled to a sitting position and waited for the room to stop teetering. Vertebrae ground together as he rolled his head, hoping that would end the pounding between his ears. It didn't. He massaged his closed eyelids. The corneas felt swollen beneath his fingertips. Jake watched all this, never once taking her eye off him.

Bishop took inventory when the world righted itself. Rubbing his chin, whiskers whispered against palm. He tried to guess how long it'd been since he'd shaved. Two days? Three? His shirt cuff was dirty and frayed. He pushed it higher on his arm. The Bulova was still on his wrist, the crystal cracked, hands frozen at 2:30. His pewter-handled cane was on the floor next to an empty bottle of Four Roses. The pain in his right foot stabbed sharper than usual. He wondered if it would swell when he unlaced his shoe. No memory of reinjuring it came to him. He patted his suitcoat and felt his wallet in the inside pocket and the .38 Detective Special holstered near his heart. The wallet was empty. There were four slugs in the snub nose. Not six. He sniffed. It'd been fired.

He crawled to bed and pulled himself on the mattress, not bothering with his clothes. Jake hopped up, circled twice, then settled by the footboard, keeping her eye on Bishop as if her doubts about him were increasing now that he was conscious.

Memories were slivered as he tried to recall when he had fired the gun:

Day drinking at The Kitty Kat.

The revolving bar at The Chez Ami.

Perfume.

A blonde.

A car ride.

No recollections about a one-eyed dog or gunshots.

He checked the .38 again. Who had he fired at? Had he hit them? Killed them?

The ringing phone was an ice pick to his ear. The only way to stop the pain was by answering.

"Hello," Bishop said, his voice raspy.

"Coppers."

It took a heartbeat for the desk clerk's voice to register. The line died. When it did, Bishop slammed the receiver into its cradle and swung his legs to the floor. The world again tottered. He swallowed bile until his swollen eyes teared. His damaged foot bore weight but every metatarsal sent ripples of agony with each step. He retrieved his cane and hat from the floor without toppling, something he considered miraculous, and felt grateful to the angel or demon in charge of keeping crippled detectives upright.

The hallway was deserted. He limped to the stairwell before the elevator full of cops arrived at his floor. Bishop didn't mind talking to the police, but he wanted to know what they were after before he did. He was certain it had nothing to do with a stolen dog but everything to do with two fired slugs. Guilt, thick and dark, oozed through him but he couldn't tell if it was old remorse or something new.

It was slow going down the stairs. He couldn't outrace the fattest cop, not with his 4-F foot. He gripped the railing and leaned on the cane as he eased down each step, moving like a man much older than thirty. Jake waited on the landing, tilting her head as if to listen for shouts or thunderous feet descending from the floors above. There were none.

Was Buffalo's Finest tossing his room, rifling through drawers, pulling suits from hangers, checking pockets for…what? His gun? He wished he could walk into The Allendale Theater, buy a dime bag of popcorn, and watch the last few days of his life projected on the silver screen, certain it would be more informative than any newsreel.

When he reached the ground floor, he pushed open the fire exit and was blinded by sunshine reflected off the sidewalk and car fenders.

So, it's afternoon, he thought. But was it Monday or Tuesday? Bishop raised his hand to shield his eyes. He didn't see his Packard anywhere.

Benny The Junkman stood by the hotel's dented garbage cans. His cart was loaded with the day's salvaged items—bundled rags, andirons, dresses, blouses. The clothing looked newer and of better quality than what Benny usually found. Bishop wondered if they'd been pulled from clotheslines. Unlike the mean drunks and meaner children who tormented him, Bishop knew Benny wasn't stupid. He'd left the best part of himself in the Argonne still fighting that battle two decades later. He spent his days pushing his cart through the streets, crisscrossing Buffalo, searching for discarded treasures. His body passed through alleys rummaging for things to pawn, but what remained of his mind was mired in that burning forest surrounded by the dead and dying. Still, Benny sometimes saw and heard things that were real:

A woman got her purse snatched on Genesee Street.

There was a new girl, a real doll face, working at the Michigan Avenue brothel.

A big card game was going on above The New Genesee Restaurant.

He would whisper these truths to Bishop, and the shamus would pay for the information—a quarter, fifty cents, maybe a buck—even if it had nothing to do with the case he was working. Other times Bishop asked him to keep an eye out for a certain car or dame—nobody paid attention to a junkman lingering on a corner, just like no one had paid attention to a fifteen-year-old Bishop when he'd started working the streets. The information that Benny provided that was relevant to Bishop's investigation was worth a fin or more—a fortune to a rag collector. Benny was still the good soldier, putting the mission first, and most times getting information the gimpy detective needed. Jake sniffed the junkman's unlaced army boots.

"Benny, what do you know? What do you hear?"

Benny turned from the garbage pails and squinted as if trying to pick Bishop out of a crowd of gathering ghosts. Recognition registered in stages from the top down—brow wrinkled, eyes widened, mouth curved to a smile. "I didn't know you had a dog, Bishop."

"You see her, too?"

The junkman wasn't sure how to answer.

"Have you seen my car, Benny? The Packard?"

"Your car?"

"The green convertible."

Benny looked around the hotel alleyway and down Ellicott Street. "There's no green car here, Bishop."

"Keep your eyes open for it, all right? You know which one it is, don't you? Let me know if you spot it."

"You think someone stole your green car?"

"It's probably parked in front of The Kitty Kat or The Chez. Hopefully, it's not in a ditch somewhere."

"Why would you leave your car in a ditch, Bishop?"

"For safekeeping," Bishop said. "Say, you hear anything about a shooting or why the cops are looking for me?"

"I haven't heard about those things."

"Okay, maybe it's nothing. But if you hear something or find my car, you come tell me. If I'm not here, leave a message with Corbett at the front desk."

Benny saluted, his hand slicing the air as sharp as it had in 1918.

"Good man. Carry on," Bishop said, and the junkman resumed rummaging through the garbage pails.

It was a four-block limp to The Kitty Kat to hunt for his car. Bishop wasn't sure he could make it. He was considering sticking out his thumb when Lieutenant Darcy rounded the corner. His face, flushed pink from the heat, broke into a wide grin when he saw Bishop.

"Rats are always in alleys, but I found a weasel. You think you can outrun the law with that crippled foot, Bishop?"

"I'm not running, Lieutenant. I'm walking my dog."

"That's a dog? It's in worse shape than you."

"Me and Jake aren't morning people."

"Morning people? The day's half done, Bishop."

"Time flies."

"Not in prison it don't. Which is where you're headed, draft dodger."

Bishop winced and hoped it didn't show. "Is sleeping late a crime?"

"No, but murder is. What do you know about Pearl DuGaye, smart guy?"

"Never heard of her. Who is she?"

"A singer from The Chez Ami gone missing. We found her purse not far from here. Cleaned out, of course, except for one thing."

"Trolley fare?"

"Your business card." Darcy pulled out the card and read, "*Bishop Investigations. Civil. Criminal. Missing Persons Located. Licensed and Bonded.* Who the hell would bond a coward like you?"

Bishop took off his hat and ran his fingers through his hair. "When did this DuGaye woman go missing?"

"Saturday."

"What's today?"

"Thursday."

Jesus.

Darcy wiped his face with a handkerchief. "Funny you never heard of her. Not only was your card in her purse, I also got a revolving bar full of people at The Chez Ami who saw you two together. They say you weren't exactly acting like brother and sister."

"You ever seen my sister, Lieutenant? She's a looker."

"I wouldn't put it past you. I wouldn't put anything past a guy who sticks his foot in front of a moving taxi to keep out of the army. Were you working for DuGaye or just working her?"

"I honestly can't say, Lieutenant," Bishop said, wondering if she was blonde.

"If she hired you to protect her, it looks like you did your usual swell job. Speaking of which, how's business?"

"It pays the light bill."

"Not at your office it don't. Heard you had to close that down. Got rid of that good-looking secretary, too. Lucky Teddy Thurston must be rolling in his grave."

"I work out of The Lafayette now. Teddy would be fine with that."

"The hell he would. Only whores work out of hotels. Funny how business dried up on you. I guess folks who lost husbands and sons on December seventh and at Bataan don't want to hire a chicken-shit Jap lover. Makes me wonder why DuGaye hired you. She must be as shady as Fat Ira. I read you work for him these days."

"I hear you work for Joey Bones. Have been for a long time."

Darcy took a step forward and jabbed a finger at Bishop. "Listen, you crippled shit. If this Pearl DuGaye shows up dead, I'm pinning it on you. I got a nice frame already picked out."

"Pleasure talking to you, Lieutenant, but I'm late for an appointment."

"With which bottle?"

"Say hello to Joey for me."

"Watch out for taxis, Weasel. Wouldn't want you to have two crippled feet."

Bishop caned his way down Ellicott as Jake trotted ahead. The sun was hot on his neck. He could smell bourbon seeping through his pores. His stomach cramped and he wondered when he'd last eaten, uncertain he could keep anything down if he ate now. Guilt weighed on him, its cause remained unclear.

* * *

There were a few day drinkers at The Kitty Kat. They sat at the long oak bar nursing bourbon and looked up when the door opened, their rummy eyes red. Empty stools separated them, leaving each alone to sip until mercy kicked in. A radio behind the bar was tuned to the Bisons' game, Detroit's Double A affiliate. Roger Baker was calling the action. No one paid attention. The Bisons were an uninspired team. They swung their bats and ran the bases as if waiting for their induction notices. Their best players had either been called up by the Tigers or Uncle Sam or enlisted after Pearl Harbor. Everything had changed after Pearl.

When the door shut behind Bishop, a sadness crept into him. He never liked being sober in a bar during the day. Night's dimness forgave a tavern's flaws. Lowered lights hid chipped paint, shadows masked stained walls, cigarette haze obscured the faded faces around him. Whisky made it tolerable. Sobriety and daytime's unforgiving light burned those illusions away and it was all revealed—the chips, the stains, the washed out and washed up. Sorrow always filled him.

Bishop's stomach clenched again. The Kitty smelled of spilled beer and burning cigarettes. Maybe a drink and a smoke would settle him. Maybe a few more drinks would drown the sadness. The bartender, a thick man wearing a stained apron, stared at him with folded arms; a toothpick slid from one side of his mouth to the other. Bishop sat at one of the stools. His foot had swollen during the walk down Ellicott. He could feel it ballooning inside his brogan.

"Hello, Frank. What do you know? What do you hear?"

"I know you shouldn't be in here, Bishop. Charlie don't want you around."

"Charlie always wants me around," Bishop said, and outstretched his arms. "I add to the atmosphere."

"Not after Saturday you don't."

Bishop lowered his arms. "What happened Saturday?"

"You don't remember?"

Bishop remembered showing up around noon and ordering Four Roses to celebrate. He had closed that adultery case for Fat Ira, getting clear photos of their client's husband, a Buffalo councilman, coming and going from The Blue Dolphin Inn with a tall brunette. He even got a few action shots between the curtain gap—the brunette's long legs wrapped all the way around—worthy of the extra prints he had kept in a file for himself. Ira had paid him well. He remembered buying drinks and playing the juke box—*Chattanooga Choo Choo, Jersey Bounce, A String of Pearls.* There may have been dancing, or as close to dancing as he could manage. Had he imagined it? He hadn't danced since before the accident. He'd been happy Saturday—hadn't he?—and had only planned on having a few.

"Tell me what happened," he said.

"You went crazy, Bishop. Swinging your cane like DiMaggio. You're lucky you didn't kill that Irishman."

"What Irishman?"

"Jesus, don't you remember anything? That big-headed lug at the end of the bar was riding you about your foot, kept saying you stepped in front of that taxi on purpose to dodge the draft. Next thing I know, you're choking up and swinging away, smashing glasses and bottles off the bar like hanging curveballs. Booze and glass was flying everywhere. Some dame got a shard in her eye and had to go to the hospital. Then you started taking cuts at that that big-headed Mick and screaming you weren't no draft dodger. You're lucky you fell over before you killed him. If your cane's handle had connected with his skull, you'd be sitting in jail right now and not even Fat Ira could help you."

Bishop vaguely remembered swinging, losing balance, falling. He thought it'd been a dream. He often dreamed of falling. Perhaps those dreams were memories.

"You got to learn to walk away when people ride you, Bishop," Frank said. "That lug's son is missing in the Pacific. He's got a right to be angry. This war's gonna be a long one. There'll be more dead sons and folks won't be happy seeing you limping around and dancing while they got gold stars hanging in their windows. Things are going to get worse for you."

Bishop dug out a quarter. "Gimme a beer."

"You don't listen. Charlie don't want you here. Go get cleaned up and dry out. Let Charlie cool off. Maybe after a while he'll let you back."

"One drink, Frank."

"One drink but not for you. Look at the way that mutt's panting." He poured water into a coffee cup and pushed it across the bar to Bishop. "Give him that and then get out before Charlie gets back."

"It's a she," Bishop said, taking the water. "Her name's Jake."

"Jesus, I hope you never have to name daughters."

Bishop set the cup down and Jake lapped it up like there was nothing she needed more at that moment than a drink, just like everyone in The Kitty Kat.

"Was I with a blonde Saturday?"

"Not in here you weren't."

"Who was I dancing with?"

"Your cane, Bishop. You were dancing with your cane."

* * *

There was no sign of the Packard on Ellicott or Genesee Street. His foot hurt too much to walk to Oak and look for it there. He and Jake stood in front of The Kitty Kat in the building's shade, trying to remember the last time he'd seen it. If he was to place a wager with Joey Bones, he'd bet large it'd been after dark and a blonde was driving, the wind whipping her hair, perfume scenting the night. He couldn't remember where they'd driven. While he tried conjuring her face from the fog of lost days and blurry nights, Fat Ira pulled to the curb. He leaned across the front seat of his Hudson to talk to Bishop through the rolled-down passenger window. The lawyer had come by his nickname honestly. His face was cheek and jowl, hanging flesh that rippled in waves. His suits never fit. They were either large and billowing or tight and constricting. Today's pinstripes parachuted around him. He weighed three hundred pounds on a slim day and wheezed when he talked. Bishop's mentor, Ted Thurston, had been the opposite: blade thin and always wearing custom suits with an inside jacket pocket designed to hold a gun. Lucky Teddy had never liked shoulder holsters.

"Bishop, where've you been?" Ira asked. "I've been looking for you."

"I've been around."

"I've got work for you." He opened the door, and Jake leapt in and settled in the backseat. "You got a dog? I'm glad you finally made a friend."

Bishop pulled the door shut behind him. Ira liked the Hudson because it had a roomy interior to accommodate him. Bishop liked it for the same reason. He didn't like the fat man pressing against him, especially in summer.

The gear shift was on the column and Ira put it in first, easing from the curb and down Genesee Street. "You don't look so good, Bishop. Your color's off. I've only seen gray skin on corpses."

"Summer colds are the worst," he answered, scanning the lots for his Packard. He flexed his leg, grateful to be off his foot.

"You don't smell too good either."

"The dog needs a bath."

"Dogs don't smell like booze," Ira said, glancing at Bishop to see if he was listening. "You got to start taking care of yourself."

Bishop pulled out cigarettes. "You got a job for me?"

"Yeah, another cheating husband case."

"Christ."

"Don't be that way," Ira said, steering around a corner. "Adultery is your specialty. You're a genius at creeping around. Nobody peeks through windows like Nicky The Weasel."

"Don't call me that."

"You'll like this case. It's society people. I know how much you enjoy taking them down."

"I enjoy taking their money." Bishop lit his smoke and flicked the match out the window.

"Well, these folks have plenty. At least she does. Her husband's an artist."

"What kind?"

"The starving kind until he met her. She's quite a bit older and wealthier from what I hear."

"You haven't met her?"

Ira looked at his watch. "We're meeting her at my office in ten minutes. We'll get the skinny then."

"Raise your rates if she's wearing a lot of jewelry. Double them if they look real."

"We've had this conversation before, Bishop."

"Listen to me this time."

"Everyone gets charged the same," Ira said.

"That's why we'll never be rich. Swing by the hotel so I can clean up before I meet this dame."

"No time. We'll tell her you were working undercover in the slums."

"Maybe I was. I work other cases besides yours."

Ira laughed. "No, you don't. Not anymore."

Bishop shot twin streams of smoke through his nostrils. "You don't know everything, fat man. I landed a missing person case today. A singer named Pearl DuGaye. Ever hear of her?"

"DuGaye? Sounds like a burlesque dancer, not a singer."

"No fans or feathers for her. She sang at The Chez Ami. She's legit. Pretty sure she's blonde."

"What do you think happened to her?"

Bishop rubbed his eyes. "Don't know. Hoping she's not stuffed in a missing car with a couple of slugs in her. I was on my way to The Chez when you picked me up."

"Let's talk to this wronged wife first, then you can chase after your blonde."

"Are you sure this wronged wife's rich?"

"I'm beginning to think you're only in this for the money."

"I have certain habits to feed," Bishop said, wishing he'd brought his flask.

Chapter 2

Fat Ira's name was gold lettered on the plate glass window:

Ira Weiss, Esquire
Attorney At Law

Two scales of justice, also gold, flanked either side of the lettering. *Jude*, two feet high, had been black painted over his name. His chin trembled as he stared at it. Passersby wouldn't meet his gaze. They hurried on, their eyes darting from the office window to the three-hundred-pound man balling his fists then to the ground ahead of them.

"A busy street like this and nobody saw?" Ira shouted, pivoting and glaring up and down the sidewalk.

Bishop touched the glass. His fingertips blackened. "Still wet," he said.

"In the middle of the *day* and nobody stopped them?" Ira thundered.

Cars slowed as drivers took in the scene. A balding man in a gray three piece peeked out of the insurance office next door.

"You didn't see anything either?" Ira yelled at him. "Neighbors for all these years and you did *nothing?*"

The man ducked inside. Bishop leaned on his cane and wiped the glass, moving his arm counterclockwise, smearing paint over the lawyer's name with his sleeve. Ira was reflected in the window. He quieted, the yelling replaced by loud wheezing and soft curses aimed at everyone on the block. Bishop remembered sitting in Ira's office on December eighth drinking homemade schnapps. They'd been listening to news trickling in from Hawaii and the Philippines, none of it good. Ira had been quiet then, too, telling Bishop about *Kristallnacht* and relatives in Cologne who no longer answered letters. Bishop wished he'd listened more carefully that night, but the schnapps had been smooth and strong, lulling him into a haze until Ira's voice and the news reports had married to static.

He gave the window one more rub then stepped back to inspect the mess he'd made. *Jude* had transformed into a black swirl, covering most of the gold lettering, the paint like a spreading stain intent on covering everything—the lawyer's name, justice scales, the entire building—its ugliness obliterating all.

"That's the best I can do. Maybe wait until it dries then call a window man to fix it."

Ira, still wheezing, dug keys from his pants pocket. His hand shook as he unlocked the door. A ceiling fan circulated warm air, hinting at the discomfort inside. Ira reached for the pushbutton light switch as Jake rushed in and claimed a spot under the fan. She was panting hard again. The storefront was cramped with furniture. A mahogany desk was fronted by two mismatched chairs. Behind it, Ira's leather wingback tilted to one side, damaged by years of bearing his weight. A trio of wooden file cabinets stood against one wall and a row of barrister bookcases lined the opposite one; binoculars rested on a stack of birding guides. Along the walls hung his framed law degree and colored illustrations of goldfinches, mourning doves, magpies and mockingbirds. The inside temperature was as uncomfortable as it'd been on the street.

Ira strode to his desk and pulled the city directory from the bottom drawer. He began flipping pages. "I'll need a gun," he said.

"For what?"

"Protection."

"It was probably a kid, Ira."

"Yeah, some kid wearing jackboots. Can you get me a gun?"

Bishop thought of his strapped .38 and its missing slugs. If the cops found that DuGaye woman filled with holes, Darcy would check his piece to see if the bullets matched. For all Bishop knew, they might.

"You can have mine," he said, the words coming out easier than they should have. "I've got others."

"Thank you." Ira picked up the candlestick phone from his desk and dialed, turning his back to Bishop.

The detective pulled the revolver from its holster and wiped it down with his shirttail. He stepped forward and placed it on the desk.

"Thank you," Ira repeated, then spoke to the window painter on the other end of the line.

"I'll get cleaned up before the wife arrives," Bishop said, and headed to the small bathroom in the back of the office, the door marked *Private*. There was a wood-framed mirror above the pedestal sink.

He couldn't look into it.

* * *

Bishop wanted to raise their rates as soon as Elizabeth Brandt walked through the door. She wore a tailored suit, the shade of dollar bills, with a brimless hat pinned in place. Dangling earrings reflected light. He couldn't tell if they were sterling or platinum, but the emeralds looked real. A matching necklace and bracelet completed the set. Standing straight in heels, padded shoulders back, she walked with finishing school grace. To Bishop, it seemed possible she could balance an entire set of encyclopedias on her head without crushing her hat. Slim lines creased from the corners of her eyes and mouth, small fissures in a heart-shaped face. She was one of those women he would sometimes spot across the room at a party or nightclub, cigarette holder in one hand, champagne coupe in the other. The kind of woman who would never talk to him unless she needed a husband tailed.

She sat opposite Ira and crossed her legs, a small clutch in her lap. Bishop had a weakness for dames with a set of pins like hers. He took the chair next to her and tried not to stare. He was in shirtsleeves, his hair finger-combed as best he could. He'd shaved with Ira's razor, his cheeks smooth and pink with borrowed bay rum. His empty holster and paint-smeared suitcoat remained in the bathroom. Bishop propped his cane against the desk and gave in, drinking in her legs with a long glance.

When introductions, handshakes and small talk had ended, Ira asked, "What makes you think your husband is being unfaithful, Mrs. Brandt?"

"A wife knows," she answered, ignoring Ira and turning toward Bishop.

"Do you know who the other woman is?" Ira asked.

"I assume one of his models or students," she said, addressing Bishop.

"Your husband's a painter?" Bishop asked.

Her green eyes flicked from his rolled sleeves to his stained tie. A nostril flared, as if the first whiff of him reached her. "He's an artist, Mr. Bishop, not a fence painter. But yes. Lately he's been working in oils again."

"Has he done this before? Slept with his models?"

She held his gaze until he felt like he needed to apologize. "Yes. He painted my portrait. That's how we met."

"I see."

"Meyer told me an artist needs to know his subject completely in order to capture them on canvas."

Bishop didn't break eye contact. "If that line worked once, he'd probably try it again. I would, and I don't paint."

"Could you describe your husband for us, Mrs. Brandt?" Ira asked.

"I brought a photograph."

She opened her pocketbook and Bishop craned to see inside: compact, handkerchief, gold lipstick case, a thick fold of bills. He leaned back and nodded at the fat man. Ira shook his head. She pulled out a photo with scalloped edges and handed the picture to Bishop.

There was something familiar about the man in the snapshot. Dark curls, longer than the fashion, touched ears and shirt collar. The nose was narrow and straight, the skin smooth, a face that had never been punched. Bishop wanted to change that, but he wasn't sure why. He guessed Meyer was fifteen years younger than his wife, maybe more.

"How tall?" he asked.

"Five eight."

"Your height, then." He glanced at her legs.

"In heels, yes."

"Weight?"

"His is one fifty. Mine's none of your business."

"One fifty? Is that even healthy?" Ira asked.

Bishop held up the photograph. "Can I keep this?"

"Certainly."

"You mentioned that Meyer may be having an affair with a model or a student," Bishop said. He tucked the photo in his coat pocket. "Where does he teach?"

"The Art Institute on Elmwood Avenue. He has a studio there as well. That's where he spends most of his time, or so he says. They're having their annual exhibit of faculty and student work. The opening is tomorrow night. You should attend, Mr. Bishop. That way you can observe my husband in his element. I'm certain his mistress will be there."

"I've never been to an art opening."

"You'll need a jacket and clean tie. And a bath."

"I'll see what I can do."

Jake barked at the door, looking at Bishop over her shoulder with her one eye.

"Somebody needs to go out," she said.

"You take care of that while Mrs. Brandt and I discuss fees and expenses," Fat Ira said. Her mouth pinched into a line.

"Yes, the rates *do* need discussing," Bishop said, arching an eyebrow at Ira. He grabbed his cane and limped to the door. Jake's tail wagged faster as he approached. Outside, as the dog sniffed a lamppost, Bishop found a bent Chesterfield in his shirt pocket. He leaned against the doorway, keeping weight off his throbbing foot, and lit the cigarette. The smoke calmed his stomach and jittery hands.

Across the street stood a red brick building. Apartments and walk-up offices filled the higher floors. A grocer, a milliner, and Krieger & Son Hardware were at street level. Bishop eyed the hardware store, wondering if they stocked black paint and if any had been sold within the hour. Even with the sun reflecting off the store's window, he could see someone staring at him from inside, their frame and shoulders narrow. Maybe Krieger's son. He stepped back when Bishop waved.

A maroon Caddy was parked in front of Ira's office. The whitewalls were wide, the rims red, the interior wood and leather. The top was down, and Bishop hobbled closer. The bench seat was pulled close to the steering wheel. He set the time on his cracked Bulova to the clock embedded in the walnut dash. Keys dangled from the ignition. He rested a hand on the soft seat and snuck another glance at the hardware store. The window remained empty.

"Are you a car aficionado, Mr. Bishop?" Elizabeth asked, walking out of Ira's office toward the Cadillac.

Bishop turned to her. "I like things I can't have. Is she yours?"

"Yes, a birthday present to myself. Perhaps not the most practical gift with gas rationing coming."

"It's not practical to leave the keys in a beauty like this either. Somebody could have misplaced their own car and been tempted to take yours."

"Did I leave the keys? I must've been in a hurry to speak with you and Mr. Weiss."

"I wanted to ask you about that," Bishop said, rubbing his chin, his hand trembling. He hoped she didn't notice.

"About what?"

"Why Ira? Hand-made suits, brand new Fleetwood. You could afford the best divorce attorney in town. Why hire a storefront lawyer like him?"

She took a step closer. "There's where you're mistaken, Mr. Bishop. I didn't hire a storefront lawyer. I hired *you*. You just happen to work for one. I never would've considered hiring him if it wasn't for you."

"I'm flattered, but there are better detectives in this town than me. A lot better and plenty of them. How do you even know about me?"

"I read about you in the paper. The councilman's affair was quite the story."

Bishop's body trembled. He needed a deep drag off the Chesterfield before answering. "That made the news?"

"Every edition. Timothy Flynn has written a series of articles about it. Didn't you see the headlines?"

"I must've missed those. I've been undercover."

"It's the scandal of the year, especially since they're calling for his resignation. After I read about you, I made some inquiries. You have quite the reputation."

"Yet you still hired me."

"I hired you *precisely* for your reputation. My husband is smart and sly, Mr. Bishop. I'm afraid he's had practice sneaking around. He's always up to something. You'll need to live up to your moniker to catch him."

Bishop frowned. "Moniker?"

"Nicky The Weasel."

"I'm not particularly fond of that nickname."

"I'm not particularly fond of gossip. If Meyer is having an affair, we need to keep this scandal out of the papers."

Bishop leaned against the Cadillac, hoping that would stop the twitching. "I can't control that."

"But you can be discreet."

"I can try."

"I expect you to do more than try."

"You and Ira didn't talk very long," Bishop said, certain Ira didn't raise their rates. He doubted he even tried.

"I couldn't wait to get out of there."

"Oh?"

"It was stifling in that office."

A rusty pickup pulled behind the Caddy. *Huffman Painting* was stenciled in red on the door. A blockheaded man with square shoulders and squatty legs hopped to the ground. He wore faded coveralls and stood in front of Ira's office with hands on hips, staring as if the paint-smeared window was the damnedest thing he'd ever seen.

"What happened there?" Elizabeth asked.

"Someone painted *Jude* on the window."

Her face darkened. "*Jude?*"

"German for Jew. Probably some kid. I doubt it'll happen again."

"Do you think the police will catch them?"

"They won't even try."

"Well…" She let her thought trail off as she glanced across the street and then faced him again. "Are you heading anywhere, Mr. Bishop? Would you like a ride?"

Bishop imagined the Cadillac's soft seat cupping him, the smooth ride, Elizabeth's legs working the pedals to the transmission's rhythm. He could see her calf flexing in her silk stocking as she pressed the clutch. All he had to do was say yes and open the car door. Who knew where that ride would lead? Maybe they would stop for a drink—a cold Campari and soda at some outdoor café or perhaps chilled wine at The Lafayette's bar. From there it was a short elevator ride to his room and the bourbon on his nightstand. Then he remembered who she was and what he was and pushed those thoughts away.

* * *

The shakes began in earnest in the taxi. Bishop's left hand quivered first. He covered it with his right and hoped the tremor would pass, but both were trembling in a few blocks. By the time the taxi parked in front of Giancarla Alessi's duplex on Seventh Street, Bishop had difficulty handling the cab fare Ira had lent him.

"You okay, pal?" The cabby asked, taking the money from Bishop's jittery palm.

"Aces," he answered, struggling with the door handle. When he got it open, Jake hopped out first. Bishop shoved his right hand in his pocket to hide it and gripped his cane as best he could with his spasming left. He couldn't hold the handle firmly and was unsteady on his bum foot.

Giancarla lived in the upper apartment with her mother. Her grandparents lived in the bottom flat. Like Bishop, she had never known her father. An only child, she was raised with strict old country rules, but she was more American than Italian and tended to rebel. Hammett and Hollywood forged her idea of detectives and planted the idea of her becoming one. When she saw the ad for a secretary at Bishop Investigations, she arrived a half hour before the office opened, picked the lock with a hairpin, and was seated at the desk typing when Bishop arrived. He'd hired her on the spot for her initiative. Her legs weren't bad either.

There were five steps leading to the porch. To climb them, Bishop had to tuck his cane under his arm and pull himself up with both hands by the wrought iron railing. By the time he reached the upper step, alcohol was leaking from his pores. He pushed the upper apartment bell.

"Gia," he said, when she opened the door. "What do you know? What do you hear?"

She didn't unlock the screen but just crossed her arms and took it all in—the disheveled hair, the paint-soaked sleeve, the one-eyed dog staring at her.

"Christ, you look like The Little Tramp with your cane and that mutt."

"She's my guard dog."

"Not a very good one, is she? Why are you here, Bishop?"

"I miss you."

"Then you shouldn't have fired me. Let's try again. Why are you here, Bishop?"

"I didn't fire you. You quit."

"You stopped paying me. What was I supposed to do? Work for free? I'm no volunteer."

"I need a little time to get back on my feet. Then I'll rehire you."

"Get back on your foot, you mean. God, you look awful. Are you going to fall down?"

"There's a betting chance."

"You better come in because I'm not picking you up if you fall." She unhooked the screen door and held it open. Bishop managed the one step into the hallway, wanting to brush against her but making sure he didn't. The stairs leading to her apartment looked like Everest.

"God, you can't make it, can you?"

"It might take a while. I'm a little shaky. Must've been something I ate."

"All that rye didn't agree with you. Come into my grandparents' apartment. They're at Mass with my mother."

"Why aren't you with them?"

"Because you led me astray."

She took his elbow and helped him inside. He sat in the closest chair, his hands jerking in his lap. Jake lay at his feet, her chin on her front paws.

"Do you have the suitcase?"

"So that's why you're here."

"You still have it, right?"

"No, I hocked it for thirty-five cents," Gia said, sarcastically, her hands on hips. "Of course, I still have it. It's in the basement where Mother won't find it."

"Could you get it?"

"Are you going to be all right? It looks like you're going to shake right out of that chair."

"I'll be fine. I need the suitcase."

"Give me a minute. And don't do anything stupid—like die."

"I'll be smart."

"That'll be a first."

Bishop closed his eyes. He'd dozed but a hand would tremble, or arm jerk and he'd awaken. He wondered when he had his last drink. His body was telling him it was time for another.

She returned with a green alligator suitcase, the initials 'NB' stamped in gold near its handle. She set it on the couch.

"Hand me the key," she said. "I'll open it."

"It's on the same keyring as my car keys."

She stared at him.

"And I've temporarily misplaced both my car keys and my car."

"Christ, Bishop."

"You have the extra set?"

"Upstairs. Let me get it."

She returned with a ring jangling with keys. The smallest was for the suitcase. She unlocked both silver clasps and pushed open the valise.

Teddy Thurston had taught him about the get-away bag, and Bishop knew the contents without looking: a full change of clothes, shaving kit, an envelope stuffed with cash, a modified Colt .45 called The Fitz Special. A bottle of bourbon was tucked inside for medicinal reasons. A matching suitcase with identical contents was stored in the Packard's trunk, wherever that had gone. He hoped that was the only thing in the trunk.

"You running, Bishop?"

"I can barely walk. I just need the gat and the greenbacks. Maybe a little bourbon."

"Why don't you take a bath? I'll put the suitcase in the bathroom."

"Pour me a drink first."

"That's not a good idea."

"Just one. I'll help with the shakes. Hair of the dog."

"When have you ever stopped after one?"

"Today. Starting now. I got to stay sober. I'm working three cases."

"Don't lie to me."

"I'm not. I have a missing person case, an adultery case, and a lost vehicle to locate. Two of the three may be related."

"Any of those paying jobs?"

"The adultery case, but I have a vested interest in the others."

"Go take a bath."

"One drink."

"When's the last time you had a meal?"

"I know I had breakfast Saturday."

"Jesus, Bishop."

"Silver dollar pancakes for fifty cents at The New Genesee. Silver dollars on your plate, silver dollars in your pocket."

"Why do you still go there?"

"For the pancakes."

"It's not healthy."

"It's flour and egg."

"You know what I mean. I'll make you something while you soak."

"Hand me the bottle."

"One drink, then a bath."

"You're a doll, Gia."

"I'm a sap, Bishop."

She went to the kitchen and came back with a fruit jar.

"Three fingers," he said.

She poured two.

"That's why I fired you. You don't listen."

"You didn't fire me. I quit. And you're re-hiring me when you get back on your foot."

"You working now?"

"I have an interview next week with The Pinkertons. Receptionist, but it's something."

"The Pinkertons? That's like playing for The Yankees. I hate the Yankees."

"The Yankees pay well. You don't pay at all."

Bishop struggled from the chair and gimped to the suitcase. He pushed the dress shirt aside, dug out the envelope, and shook out a twenty.

"You owe me more than that."

"This isn't back pay. I'm hiring you to be my driver. We've got to use your car, though. I'll pay for gas."

She raised a dark eyebrow. "You're taking me into the field?"

"You're just driving."

"Can I carry a gun?"

"You're just driving."

"You've never let me work a case before."

"Jesus, you're just driving. Hand me the glass."

Gia tucked the bill into her blouse; his eyes followed her fingers. She closed the suitcase and handed him the bourbon. "You better sip because that's all you get today."

"Since when do you make the rules?"

"Since you showed up at my door looking worse than your one-eyed dog."

* * *

Bishop soaked in the clawfoot tub. The mirror steamed, his skin pinked from the water. He'd ignored Gia's advice and downed the two fingers in a single gulp. The whisky had helped. His hands still trembled but not so severely. Another glass or two would have fixed him. He wondered where she had hidden the bottle and hoped she hadn't poured it down the sink. He could hear her in the kitchen opening cupboards, rattling pans, humming. Jake barked and she laughed. He could smell coffee percolating.

The water rose to his neck as he sunk lower in the tub. His back and shoulder muscles loosened. A calmness spread through him like morning bourbon. He closed his eyes. It was easy to imagine that this was his tub, his apartment, his Gia now singing along with the radio. Who wouldn't want this? The fantasy even came with the family dog, albeit a half blind one. There must be men living up and down Seventh Street who have a life like this, a home like this. Men who hadn't spent their last dime at The Kitty Kat. Men who knew where their cars were parked. Men who kissed their wives goodbye at the train station when their country called. Bishop opened his eyes. His feet rested on the tub's lip, the right a grotesque cousin to the left—swollen, toes angled. Another step or two and that cab would have struck him dead on, hurtling him forward until skull struck pavement. Maybe that would've been best.

Voices filled the apartment. They were quiet, at first, and in English, then grew louder and switched to Italian. Bishop didn't understand a single word but knew what they were arguing about. Gia's voice matched the others in volume and never wavered. A pot slammed against the stove. He guessed she'd done the slamming. Jake joined the quarrel, howling with her two cents. Bishop held a breath and slid beneath the water, the arguing muffled below the surface. If he had his way, he'd stay under until the bath cooled or his lungs burst, but he couldn't let Gia fight alone.

Exiting the tub was no easy task. He leaned as far back as he could, gripped the tub's sides and pushed. His arms trembled until he was sitting on the edge. The family fracas had shifted from kitchen to living room, farther from the bathroom but no quieter. The front door slammed. He was certain Gia's mother had retreated to her apartment, leaving her daughter to battle with her grandparents. Bishop swung his legs out of the tub, first his left then the right, and stood, almost losing his balance. He pulled the plug to empty the gray water from the bath, the gurgling drain adding to the apartment noise.

His open case sat on top of the toilet. He dried himself and dressed quickly. The suit was tan and double-breasted, his shirt crisp and white, the tie striped and Windsor-knotted. He ran pomade through his hair and combed it straight back without a part. Gia's voice rose an octave as he tied his two-toned oxfords, his swollen foot barely fitting. The Fitz was loaded and shoulder holstered, the suitcoat bump noticeable only if a wise guy was looking for it. Envelope money was transferred to his wallet and slipped inside his jacket. The cracked Bulova was still ticking. He fastened it on his wrist, hoping it was keeping time. The bathtub was ringed, but he didn't have time to clean it. He gathered his dirty clothes from the floor and folded them in the suitcase, latching it shut.

As he stepped toward the door, the mirror reflected what he'd once been, back when he'd walked into his office and found Gia typing, her hairpin dangling in the keyhole. The drinking had been manageable then, a steady intake that kept him sharp enough. He wasn't flush, but he could afford an office, an apartment, a car, and now a lock-picking secretary, who he saw long after she'd left a room. The casework had been varied then—insurance fraud, criminal investigations, background checks. Locating missing persons, searching for lost faces, became his specialty. Then the drinking became unmanageable. He began losing things—the apartment, the office, Gia. He lingered on his reflection before turning away. It felt like he was wearing another man's shoes. He blamed the discomfort on his swollen foot but knew better.

The Alessi family argument ended when he entered the living room, cane in one hand, suitcase in the other. Gia inspected him from his slicked hair down to his two-tones. She smiled. "You don't look like The Little Tramp anymore."

He nodded at her, noticing her fresh lipstick, her dark hair combed shiny, the light dancing in her eyes. He wanted to stare longer but forced himself to look at her grandparents. "Good afternoon, Mr. and Mrs. Alessi. Thank you for letting me use your bathroom. The plumbing is on the fritz at my hotel."

The grandmother raised her chin, sending her Roman nose in the air, before looking away. The grandfather waved the back of his mottled hand, dismissing him. Jake wagged her tail.

"Come on, Bishop," Gia said. "The food's ready."

The kitchen table was set for one. She brought Bishop a bowl of gnocchi, crusty bread, a cup of coffee, and a tall glass of water.

"No sauce?"

"Your stomach wouldn't do well with my sauce. You need something to soak up that poison. Eat some bread." Jake was face deep in her own bowl. "When's the last time you fed that mutt?"

"Her name's Jake and I've never fed her, as far as I know. I don't even know where she came from."

"Eat."

Bishop tried a forkful, unsure how his stomach would react to anything but liquor. At first bite he realized how hungry he was, how good the dumplings tasted, and ate with Jake's gusto. Gia poured a cup of coffee and sat near him. "Slow down or you'll get sick for sure."

"I didn't know you could cook."

"There's a lot you don't know about me."

The grandparents resumed arguing in the living room, Italian words ricocheting off the walls. Bishop cocked his head, his fork frozen between plate and mouth. "What are they fighting about now?"

"You."

"Still?"

"Again."

"Why?"

She took the handkerchief from his breast pocket and folded it into fingers. "You're eating their dinner."

Chapter 3

Bishop made Gia drive past The Chez Ami. The neon marquee wasn't lit in the waning afternoon light. Black letters spelled out:

CHEZ AMI

DINNERS • STAGE REVIEW • DANCING

NO ADMISSION • NO COVER CHARGE

A banner flapped beneath, announcing Tommy Valentine and His Orchestra were now appearing. A doorman stood at parade rest under the banner—feet apart, hands clasped behind his back, eyes straight ahead—as if he'd already been inducted. The revolving bar had opened at one, but dinner service didn't start until five-thirty. There were few cars parked on Delaware Avenue. None were the Packard. They circled the block, cutting down Tracy Street, turning north on Elmwood, then making a right on Tupper back to Delaware. Bishop's convertible wasn't parked on those streets either.

"Maybe the cops got it wrong," Gia said, pulling in front of The Chez Ami. "Maybe this Pearl DuGaye isn't missing. Maybe she stole your car and left town. You think she'd do something like that? Head to New York, maybe?"

"I have no idea. I couldn't even tell you what she looks like."

"It's tough seeing through the bottom of a whisky glass. All that amber and ice."

"I was in a nightclub. It was dark."

"They serve drinks there, Bishop. They don't develop film."

"What about her purse?" Bishop asked. "She wouldn't have left town without it."

"Maybe she lost it. Maybe it was stolen."

"Too many maybes. Wait here and let me see what I can find out."

"Wait here?"

"You're just the driver, remember?"

"Right." She opened the door, crossed in front of the car, and stopped on the sidewalk facing him. Her hip jutted. "You coming?"

He liked the jut. "A driver drives, Gia. That's all she does. That's where the name comes from."

"I'm a special kind of driver."

"You're special, all right."

He left the passenger side window open for Jake and limped to Gia. Placing a hand on the small of her back, he guided her to the dinner club's entrance, allowing himself to imagine that she was his. The doorman didn't greet them or move to usher them inside.

"Albert," Bishop said. "What do you know? What do you hear?"

"I know the lady can go inside, Bishop, but you can't."

Bishop spread his feet shoulder width, planted his cane between them, and leaned on the handle with both hands, bracing himself for what was about to come. "Why's that, Albert?"

"Why? I had to bum rush you out of here Saturday. Mr. Amigone said not to let you back in."

He could see Gia staring at him from the corner of his eye, but he wouldn't face her. "Let me talk to Phil."

"Mr. Amigone is busy getting ready for the early dinner crowd. He don't have time for you."

"Why did you escort him out, Albert?" Gia asked.

"*Escort* him? That sounds gentlemanly. I was no such thing. I grabbed him by the collar and belt and tossed him like a gutterpup."

"Why'd you toss him?"

"Mr. Amigone told me to. This fool was buying drinks for everybody. Expensive ones, too—champagne cocktails, extra dry martinis, enough bourbon to flood Kentucky, but that was mostly for himself. And when it came time to pay, Nicky The Weasel didn't have a dime. Shoot, he didn't even have a buffalo nickel. All he had was a big, long tab. Mr. Amigone was not pleased."

"Is this true, Bishop?"

"Sounds possible," he answered, wishing she'd stayed in the car.

"Possible? It's a damn fact," said Albert.

"So, it's not just me you don't pay," Gia said. "You told me I was special."

"Look, Albert, I'm sorry about Saturday. I wasn't myself. Let me settle up with Phil."

"Settle? Show me."

Bishop took out his wallet, fat with envelope money.

"I don't see nothing."

He tugged out a five and handed it to the bouncer.

Albert palmed the bill then stood aside. "You better not cause trouble," he said, reaching for the door. "I won't be careful of your foot if I have to toss you again. Not this time."

"I'll fix everything with Phil. I'll fix things with everybody."

"You better."

"Say, Albert, after you tossed me, did Miss DuGaye leave, too?"

"She surely did. Picked you out of the gutter and poured you into your Packard. You left together."

"I was driving?"

"Hell, no. You got to see to drive."

"She's a blonde, right?"

"Blonde? She's darker than me."

* * *

The usual daytime sadness didn't grip Bishop when he stepped inside The Chez. Fresh paint saw to that. A fire had ripped through the nightclub on Christmas. The owner, Phil Amigone, had remodeled and reopened in the spring. Everything gleamed. A bandstand with a backdrop of gold curtains dominated one end. Plush maroon carpeting covered the dining room, ending at the raised dancefloor in front of the stage. Tables draped with white linen and tented maroon napkins, the same shade as the carpet, surrounded the circular bar in the center of the club. Balcony seating crowned it all. Amigone himself had designed the gold deco bar, which moved almost unnoticeably, taking seven minutes to complete its rotation. Bishop was leery of the bar. Drinking in one place and then finding himself in another always unnerved him.

Waiters with spit-polished shoes were setting tables. Bow-tied bartenders wiped down glasses. Phil Amigone was talking to Tommy Valentine near the stage. Only a few men sat at the bar at this early hour. Joseph Bonesutto—Joey Bones—sat at a table with a wicker-wrapped Chianti and two of the Gospel brothers, maybe Mathew and Mark. Bishop could never tell them apart.

"Sweet Jesus, how drunk were you?" Gia asked, as they walked past Joey's table toward the bandstand. "You didn't even know Pearl was colored?"

"I'm missing parts of the last few days."

"Which parts?"

"The Saturday through Wednesday parts."

She stopped and grabbed his arm, forcing him to finally face her. He struggled to meet her gaze. "This isn't funny, and this ends today. The drinking, the benders, the blackouts. It all stops. I won't be your driver or secretary or whatever the hell I am if you don't quit. I won't stick around to watch you bourbon yourself into an early casket. It's me or the bottle. You understand?"

Bishop sucked in a breath and held it before exhaling and nodding. "Say it."

"I understand."

"Decide now so you don't waste more of my time."

"I'm not sure I can quit by myself."

Gia studied him, her eyes a hard brown. She didn't blink or look away. He could tell she was deciding something, mentally turning things over, weighing for the hundredth time if he was worth it. His hand shook faster.

"The Pinkertons will have to wait then," she said, squeezing his arm until it hurt.

Phil Amigone walked toward them, his lips pressing into a frown. He wore a dinner jacket with wide silk lapels, the jacket as dark as his expression. "How did you get past Albert?" he asked, loud enough for Joey Bones to turn.

"I came to pay up."

Amigone stopped in front of Bishop. He stood a head shorter than the detective, had black, receding hair, and thick eyebrows that collided when he frowned. His face and body were ovals, his neck non-existent. He looked every extra inch like a restauranteur who enjoyed his own menu. A pudgy finger jammed Bishop in the chest. "Most guys come the next day to pay what they owe. They don't show up six days later on a date like everything's jake."

"I'm not his date," Gia said.

"She's my chauffer. All the classy detectives have one."

"Where've you been, Bishop? More importantly, where's my money been?"

"I've been working a case."

"A case of bourbon is what I hear."

"I want to make things right, Phil."

"You wouldn't know right if it punched you in the jaw, which is what I want to do."

"You're not punching anybody," Gia said.

"Your chauffer has a mouth on her."

"That's not news. Forget about her. I've got your money."

"This is the last time. You hear me, Bishop? No more tabs for you. Starting today you pay upfront before a drink gets mixed. I'll make sure all the bartenders and waiters know. You got that?"

"I got it."

"You guys hear that?" he yelled at the bartenders. They nodded. "And what the hell happened to Pearl?" Amigone asked, turning back to him. "I haven't seen her since you two drove off together."

"What time did all that happen?"

"After ten. Said she had to stop at a friend's house."

"Did she say where?"

"Some place on Linwood. She never made it back for the midnight show like she promised. She'd been packing them in all week, too. People were coming to hear her not Tommy. Then she gets mixed up with you and my golden goose turns into a golden ghost. Don't think I haven't felt it in the till. You cost me money, Bishop."

"I'll find Pearl for you."

"Sure, you will. Nicky The Weasel, Master Detective. You should have your own radio show. Pay Nathan behind the bar before I change my mind and punch you in the jaw." Amigone brushed by Bishop, bumping his shoulder on his way to greet a dinner party.

"You make friends wherever you go, don't you, handsome?" Gia asked, walking next to him as he limped to the bar.

"It's a gift I have."

Nathan already had his tab waiting for him. Bishop's cheeks twitched when he saw the amount.

"Did you blow *all* your adultery money here?" she asked, looking over his shoulder at the bill.

"Maybe I left some in my car. Maybe I put a wad in the glovebox. I do that sometimes."

"Maybe I should give myself a promotion."

"Chief Chauffer?"

"Treasurer. Ira pays me. I pay the bills and put some in the bank. You get an allowance."

"You mean salary."

"I mean allowance."

"I'm working for you now?"

"You're on probation. We'll see if you pan out."

He reached into his wallet and counted out what he owed, leaving his billfold thinner. "Keep it," he said, pushing the money across the bar to Nathan. "For all the trouble I caused."

Nathan counted the money.

"You don't trust me?"

"Maybe a little less than Mussolini."

Bishop drummed his fingers on the bar to give his shaking hand something to do. He could smell beer being poured from the tap, watched oranges and lemons being sliced, saw a wine cork laying nearby. He imagined a fresh draft hitting the back of his throat, red wine on his tongue, the bite of lime following salt and tequila. Both hands trembled again. The dull throbbing behind his eyes grew to a headache.

"Are you all right?" Gia asked.

"You want a drink?"

She stomped her foot. "Jesus, what did you promise me five minutes ago?"

"I can't stop all at once. It's got to be gradual, or I'll be sick on the floor for days."

"I think those days have already started. You're flushed one minute and pale the next."

"Maybe you aren't such a good cook."

"Don't blame my gnocchi. You did this to yourself. One beer, but that's it."

"A beer for me and a Sidecar for the lady," he told Nathan.

"You know the new rules, Bishop," the bartender said.

He placed a bill on the bar then touched his forehead. How could he sweat and shiver at the same time? "I need some air. Splash water on my face. I'll be right back. Don't drink my beer."

"I ride Sidecars, honey. You know that."

He hobbled to the restrooms down the hall from the coat check, the pain in his head matching the pain in his foot. The men's room was marked with a silhouette wearing a top hat. The one on the ladies' door sported a flapper's cloche. Both looked blurry. The tapping cane echoed in the empty marble bathroom. He leaned it against the sink and opened the cold-water tap. His stomach felt untrustworthy. He didn't hear the men enter behind him as he bent over the sink and cupped his hands under the faucet. The first blow landed on his kidney.

Pain shot up his right side.

His mouth opened.

No sound came out.

No air went in.

The second punch landed on the other kidney. He caught a Gospel's reflection in the mirror as he fell. The third punch struck his temple, knocking his head against the sink, dazing him. Curled on the floor, he tried to gather his breath and clear his head. A pair of polished wingtips approached. The other Gospel stopped in front of him. He yanked Bishop by his pomade hair until he was kneeling.

"Mr. Bonesutto says to stay away from the councilman. You understand? Stay away and forget what you saw."

Bishop pushed words out a syllable at a time. "That case is closed."

"I'm not talking about him and that tall broad and you know it. Forget what you saw."

"What'd I see? I don't know what you're talking about."

"Sure, Weasel."

The second Gospel took two steps back and kicked Bishop in the stomach like he was punting a football. Gnocchi, bourbon, and bile splattered on the marble floor. Bishop doubled over.

"Don't make us come back and tell you again," he said, drawing back his leg and kicking him above the ear.

Bishop was sent sprawling, his head exploding in pain. A loud ringing sounded in his skull and black orbs floated in front of his eyes. The floor opened into a dark pool, and he fell in. He sank fast, being pulled deeper and deeper by invisible hands. It grew darker and colder as he plummeted and then the ringing stopped. The orbs inked over like blackout curtains had been drawn. He felt weightless, his limbs and torso, head and hands and crippled foot dissolving one after the other until nothing remained, until he had become nothing, not even a memory.

He didn't fight any of it.

Chapter 4

For the second time that day, Bishop woke on the floor. Instead of Jake, Amigone and Albert were staring at him. Gia was crouched by his side, her skirt riding above the knee, not a bad sight to wake to. He sat up, touched his head, and felt the swelling. His right side hurt more than the left when he breathed. The first punch always hurts the most. Overhead lights burned his eyes. The vomit smell made him want to heave again, but he refused to in front of Gia.

"I told this drunk not to cause trouble," Albert said. "Then I walked in here and found him passed out."

"I didn't pass out and I'm not drunk. I was knocked out."

"Who knocked you out?" Gia asked, brushing his cheek with soft fingers.

"A couple of Joey Bones' boys. The Gospel Brothers. I think it was Mathew and Mark. I get the four of them mixed up."

"They're not all brothers," Amigone said. "I think John's a cousin."

"I heard Luke isn't really Luke, either," Albert said. "They call him that because it fits. His real name's Samuel."

"Both of you shut up. Why'd they beat you, Bishop?" Gia asked.

"There's a line of guys waiting to beat him, doll," Amigone said. "I'm sure of it. I just don't know how many are ahead of me."

"Help him up. And I'm not your doll."

Albert and Amigone grabbed under his arms and hoisted Bishop to his feet. They let go but he wavered, so they each held a shoulder until he steadied. Gia handed him his cane.

"Have you ever thought of relocating, Bishop?" Amigone asked. "Move someplace new? Pittsburgh's nice."

"This is my city."

"Your city is kicking your ass in case you haven't noticed. And if you got trouble with the Evangelists, your days here are numbered anyway. Pick a place where nobody knows what happened to your foot. Tell them it was a birth defect. Things will go smoother for you. Nobody likes you, Bishop. Nobody wants you here. It's time to move on."

"That's enough," Gia said. She raised her chin and pointed it at Albert. "You, go back to guarding the sidewalk." Her eyes flashed to Amigone. "And you, get someone to clean this mess."

Amigone's oval face lit in amusement. "You telling me what to do in my own club?"

"Damn right I am. Now go." She pushed his chest with both hands.

Amigone backed to the door with arms raised as if she was pointing a gun. "I see who wears the pants, Bishop."

"Go!"

"Come on, Albert. Mrs. Roosevelt has spoken."

Bishop leaned against the sink and waited for the dizziness to pass. Vomiting was still a possibility. He could hear Amigone's laughter fade on the other side of the door. The men's room spinning slowed enough for him to take inventory. His wallet was still in his pocket, the cash untouched. The Fitz was holstered. No shots had been fired. The Bulova's second hand swept its cracked face. Overall, a much better accounting than the earlier inventory.

"What beef do The Gospel Brothers have with you?" Gia asked. "Don't tell me you owe them money, too."

"I have no beef with Mathew, Mark, Luke, or John. They were delivering a message from their boss."

"What message?"

"He wants me to stay away from the councilman."

"Rhielman? Are you still investigating him?"

"No."

"I don't follow."

"He must be up to something more than cheating on his wife. Something shady with Joey Bones. They told me to forget what I saw."

"What'd you see?"

A porter entered with a mop and bucket.

"Nothing I remember, but I'm going to find out."

* * *

Linwood Avenue was wide and tree shaded. Gothic Revivals to tricolored Queen Anne's lined the boulevard. Deep lawns, green and thick, stretched to sidewalks. The homes had servants' entrances and carriage houses and were built by families with Buffalo Blue Book names— Bartlett, Holmes, Lautz. Their children and grandchildren now lived in those homes while newer families with newer money moved in around them. Linwood remained a promenade as couples from lesser neighborhoods strolled and pointed to stained glass, gingerbread gables, brass doorknockers with faces of lions and gods.

Gia and Bishop walked, arms linked, blending with the others on the street. The sun hung lower. The wind blew off the lake, cooling the air. On any other day he'd feel like Rockefeller with Gia beside him, but they were halfway down the block, and he was tiring. The Gospels had beaten the strength from him. It hurt to breathe, to step, to move his head. His stomach hadn't settled. He wasn't sure if this was caused by kidney punches, booze, or lack of booze. Maybe he ate too much too soon, maybe the Italian food was too heavy. He was only certain that he wanted sleep. He pushed on, studying each house, hoping an entranceway or roofline would unearth a memory. His Packard was nowhere in sight. Jake ran ahead then back, investigating elms.

"Pearl had friends out here?" Gia asked.

"Evidently."

"You two hit it off right away, didn't you?"

Bishop didn't answer. He stopped in front a three-story brick mansion with cathedral windows. Rocking chairs, pushed by the breeze, were grouped in pairs on the wrap-around porch. Corbels and fascia were painted olive, the dental work a clean white. Potted begonias flanked the bottom step. The address—288—was marked in black numerals above the doorway.

"Is this the one?" she asked.

"I remember rocking chairs."

"Do you remember the house? The brick, the slate roof?"

"Just the chairs. *Those* chairs," he said, pointing with his cane. "All of them in twos like that. I remember rocking in one. I'm sure of it."

"Okay, then. What's next? We knock on the door?"

"Let's find out who lives here first."

"I think we should ring the bell and ask them what the hell happened Saturday."

"We need more information before we do anything."

"Let's break in. They may have Pearl tied up in the basement."

"They may also shoot intruders."

"Jesus, Bishop. What kind of private eye are you?"

"The cautious kind."

* * *

Gia's heels clicked on The Lafayette's terrazzo floor. She was holding Bishop tighter, and he leaned heavier on his cane as they navigated the lobby. All his aches—head, foot, kidneys—had combined into a single misery. He needed sleep. Deep, restive, restorative sleep, not the drunk's lack of consciousness. He hadn't slept in his bed since Saturday, as far as he knew. The sheets would still be fresh and soft, the pillowcase cool against his cheek. He imagined being curled around Gia, his face pressed into her hair, breathing in everything that's clean. He chided himself. He didn't deserve such fantasies.

Corbett stood behind the front desk, a mural of the Buffalo harbor looming behind him. The painting depicted freighters steaming by a skyline of grain elevators. The clerk acted as if he wanted to be on one of those ships or at least someplace other than the hotel. His body was a set of moving parts—drumming fingers, wrist turning to check the time, weight shifting from foot-to-foot. He glanced at the revolving door as if a promise was waiting on the other side. He hardly looked at Bishop when they approached, but his eyes weren't shy with Gia. Bishop wasn't sure if Corbett was his first or last name. He'd never bothered to ask.

"Corbett, what do you know? What do you hear?"

"I know you're a popular guy, Bishop."

"With the ladies?" Gia asked.

"No, first coppers came by and then a couple of gunsels right after."

Bishop touched his swollen temple. "They both caught up with me. Did the gunsels go up to my room?"

"Yeah, the hotel detective wasn't here to stop them."

"What about the junkman? Did he come by? Did he leave a message about my car?"

"No junkman, but your uncle stopped in a couple times."

"Probably wants to borrow money."

"Boy, he's passing the collection plate down the wrong pew," Gia said.

"About those coppers," Corbett said.

Bishop took out his wallet and placed a sawbuck on the counter. "I appreciate the phone call."

"We better find your car and the envelope in your other suitcase or you'll be broke soon," said Gia.

"If I find my car, I won't need a driver."

"We'll discuss that when the Packard turns up."

"Do you need anything else tonight, Bishop?" Corbett asked.

"Could you send ice to the room?

"You want a bottle as well? Four Roses?"

"Yes," Bishop said.

"No." Gia elbowed him hard.

"Ice will be fine, Corbett."

They walked toward the bronze elevator doors next to the brass mail chute. The ache in his kidneys increased with each step. They didn't get far. He heard his name called. Lafayette's assistant manager, Oliver Prine, hurried after them.

"Can I have a word, Mr. Bishop?"

Everything about Prine was straight: posture, tie, hair part. Bishop had never seen him without a crisp collar or creased trousers. His shoes always sported a new-bought shine. The Lafayette Hotel's assistant manager neither smoked nor drank. Bishop had once asked if he was a member of The Women's Temperance Society. Oliver hadn't laughed. Bishop couldn't remember him ever laughing.

"Oliver, what do you know? What do you hear?" he asked, trying to stand straighter and not sound like a man who'd gone days without sleep or sobriety.

"I need to speak with you in private."

"You can talk freely in front of Miss Alessi. She's my bodyguard."

"I sure have a lot of jobs for someone not on payroll."

"It's about your position," Oliver said.

"My position is currently vertical, but that can change at any time."

Oliver lowered his voice. "I meant as hotel detective."

"You're a hotel dick?" Gia asked.

"Not just in hotels from what I hear."

"What are your main responsibilities in that role, Mr. Bishop?" Oliver asked.

"Protecting the property, the guests, and the property of the guests," he said, by rote.

"Correct. Now explain to me how you can carry out those duties when you've been absent for nearly a week. Other security officers have been covering for you. They said you were ill."

"I was sick, still am, in fact. Take a close look at me and you can see that I'm not a well man."

"I can vouch for that," Gia said.

"I've been working on behalf of the hotel in a very delicate matter," Bishop said. "One of your guests had their car stolen last Saturday night. A very nice convertible. Almost paid for, too. A lovely shade of green. I've been tracking it down."

"Why haven't I heard about this?"

"I've been keeping it quiet. It could hurt business if guests don't feel safe parking their automobiles here. We don't want cops or reporters sniffing around, do we?"

"Of course not, but I need you here at the hotel when you're *scheduled* to work, not when you feel like it. Last night there were underage girls drinking at the bar."

"I assure you, Oliver, starting this evening those underage girls will get my full attention."

Gia elbowed him again.

"We expect better, Mr. Bishop. You're compensated very nicely here plus you have a room at very little cost. You're close to being both unemployed and evicted."

"I'll be working tonight."

"You'd better, and whose dog is that?" Oliver said, pointing. "You know the rules, Bishop. No pets."

He looked at Jake by his feet. "Must belong to one of the guests. Corbett needs to make sure they don't bring dogs with them. I think I saw a cat earlier."

"I'll speak to him, but the next time I see *you*, you'd better be sober and working."

"I'm painfully sober now, Oliver. I'll see you later," Bishop said, and pushed the elevator button. He watched the floor numbers light up on its sunburst dial above the door.

"Is Miss Alessi accompanying you upstairs? Unmarried guests are not allowed to entertain women in their rooms. You know that. It's part of your job to *enforce* that."

"I'm his bodyguard, remember?" Gia said.

"I don't feel safe unless she's around."

"Watch yourself, Mr. Bishop. I'm a patient man, but I can only look away so many times. And you?" he said, addressing Gia. "I know your grandmother. What would she say?" Oliver spun on his heel and walked in a perfect line toward Corbett to scold him about pets in the lobby.

"Well, that was fun," Gia said.

"It's a laugh a minute with me, kid."

"You used to make fun of hotel detectives."

"So, you're really coming up?" he asked, still watching the numbers, not daring to look at her.

"It didn't work out so great last time."

"The night was fine."

"The night was wonderful, but you were a heel in the morning."

"I'm a changed man, remember?"

"You better be," Gia said. "Heels run out of chances quick."

The brass door slid open. Bishop, Gia, and Jake stepped inside the car.

* * *

The door to his room was ajar. He pushed it open with his cane. The light switch was inside the doorframe; he reached for it. It was impossible to tell if the police had ripped his room apart by themselves or if The Gospel Brothers had finished the job. Suits torn from hangers were strewn across the floor. Drawers had been pulled from the dresser, their contents dumped in piles. Case folders had been rifled through;

photographs of philandering husbands in various stages of undress had spilled from them. Some were of women wearing nothing at all.

"They did a pretty good job tossing this place," Gia said.

"Looks like they enjoyed their work, too," Bishop said. A sinking feeling descended through him. The bottle of bourbon on the nightstand was missing. It must've walked off in a patrolman's pocket. It was going to be a long, dry night.

"Any idea what they were after?"

"The cops were looking for something to tie me to Pearl. I'm sure they came up bupkis. Based on the one-sided conversation with The Gospels at The Chez Amis, I'd guess they came for Councilman Rhielman's file."

There was a knock at the door. Gia opened it. A porter entered with ice. He was a kid, maybe eighteen, freckled and ginger haired. Surprise flashed across his dappled face when he saw a woman in the room.

"Patrick, what do you know? What do you hear?"

"Hello, Mr. Bishop. I brought your ice."

"Put it anywhere or throw it on the carpet with everything else."

He set the bucket on the desk next to an overturned lamp. "What happened in here, Mr. Bishop? This place is wrecked."

"Miss Alessi and I had a pillow fight and it got out of hand. Say, do you mind putting the mattress back on the box spring for me?"

"Sure thing, Mr. Bishop."

"A pillow fight? Is that why you asked me up here?" Gia asked.

"I thought you'd jump at the chance to take a swing at me."

"With your cane, maybe."

After the mattress was back in place, Bishop handed Patrick a silver dollar. "Tell the maid to get some rest. She'll be busy in here tomorrow."

"What's that supposed to mean?" Gia asked.

"You have a suspicious mind."

"With good reason," Gia said, over her shoulder as she crossed to the bathroom. She stepped on the pictures of naked women on her way.

"Have a nice evening, Mr. Bishop," Patrick said, shutting the door behind him.

"Thanks, Patrick," Bishop called, shrugging off his suitcoat and wincing. He unfastened his holster and placed it on the nightstand, then took off his tie and shirt. Gia returned with towels. She filled the larger one with ice and handed it to him. "Put that on the bed and lay on it." He did as he was told. The ice felt hard against his kidneys, and he struggled to get comfortable. She filled the smaller towel. "This is for your head. You got quite a goose egg there."

Bishop held it against the swelling. "Thanks."

She eyed his undershirt. "You look thin."

"I'm getting down to my fighting weight. The city directory is by your foot. Go to the street section and look up 288 Linwood."

Gia picked up the directory and sat on the edge of the bed. She flipped through the pages then ran a finger down the column before stopping.

"288 Linwood Avenue. Brandt, Meyer J. Brandt, Elizabeth Mrs."

Chapter 5

Bishop woke shivering. He didn't remember falling asleep. The ice beneath him had melted, soaking his mattress and undershirt. He sat up, head pounding, and checked his watch. 7:30. The drapes were open. Dusk. The Bulova might be running slow. Jake was curled at his side.

His room had been cleaned. Suits hung in the closet. Clothes had been refolded into drawers and drawers had been slid back into the dresser. Only his files remained scattered for him to sort. He switched on the righted desk lamp and read the note:

Now the maid won't have to come at all.

G

Gia had ordered him a roast beef sandwich. It sat on the nightstand. Bishop scraped the meat from the bread and set the plate on the floor for Jake. She jumped from the bed and gobbled the beef. Bishop limped to the toilet and pissed pink. The color stunned him. Were the kidney punches or bourbon responsible for the blood, he wondered? Maybe both. In either case, he wasn't sure what to do about it.

His wet t-shirt stuck to his back when he tugged it off. Twisting sideways in the mirror above the sink, first to the left then the right, he saw fist-sized bruises had blossomed on each side. Both were tender to the touch. The swelling where his head had knocked against the sink had subsided, the discoloration blending red to purple.

Something silver beneath the radiator caught his attention and his heart thumped. He used his cane to sweep out the dented flask and picked it up. It felt half full. A better man, he knew, would flush it with his pink piss. A smarter man would remember his promise to Gia. He unscrewed the cap and sniffed. Bourbon. Not Four Roses, something rawer, cheaper, something that would numb him faster. How had the cops, Gospels, and Gia missed it? Maybe they hadn't seen it. Maybe they didn't care. Maybe she had found it and left it as a test. He breathed in the rotgut again, thought of the long night ahead, scrutinizing guests or looking for prostitutes and pickpockets at The Lafayette bar.

He raised the flask and took a glorious pull, hating himself only after he'd swallowed.

* * *

Dressed in a blue suit, clean shirt and hand-painted tie, Bishop sat in a red leather lobby chair, the final edition of *The Courier-Express* folded across his knee. He had clear views of the front desk, the elevator, and the Washington Street entrance. The flask rested lighter in his jacket pocket. Despite the shooting pain in his kidneys when he shifted, an evenness buzzed through him, something he hadn't felt in a while, like when the Packard's gasoline and air mixture is perfect and the engine hums. He was certain his body ran the same way on bourbon and blood. The trick was getting the mixture right.

A well-dressed man and a poorer-dressed woman entered the hotel. A bellboy carried their mismatched luggage. Bishop knew they weren't married, at least not to each other. Corbett glanced at him from the front desk, and Bishop shrugged. Let them register as Mr. and Mrs. Smith and have their fun. Who were they hurting other than their spouses? Maybe the next time he saw this cheating couple it'd be through his camera lens. Sometimes life played out like that, and he got paid for his kindness.

He watched as the pair registered then walked toward the elevators, her step not as light or as excited as the man's. The bronze elevator doors parted, and Bishop thought of when he and Gia had first stepped through those doors, their fingers laced. He mustn't have been drinking that night because he could recall everything—her touch, her skin and her lips. Most of all he remembered how effortless it'd been, how their rhythms had matched as if they had done this before. He was certain it'd been the only time he'd ever smiled while making love. At one point, as they held each other, coupled but still, he'd felt like he'd found a place where he belonged and was wanted, needed. Then the sun rose, its first rays streaming through the opened drapes, melting away all that he was sure of and leaving behind the old fear. He pulled away before he could be pushed.

Benny The Junkman was five steps through the door before Bishop spotted him and was torn from his memories. The doorman was trying to stop him, but Bishop waved him off. He pushed up from the chair, kidney pain catching his breath, and gimped toward Benny. His foot was numb from sitting too long. If Oliver peeked from his office, it'd look as if Bishop were doing his job by preventing a street bum from entering the hotel. Through the glass door he could see Benny's cart on the sidewalk, empty except for the andirons. Bishop had no idea who bought that junk. Benny couldn't pawn it all.

"Benny, what do you know? What do you hear?"

"I know something."

"Do you know where my car is?"

"Where's your little dog, Bishop?"

"Guarding my room. Do you know where my car is?"

"The green one?"

"That's right."

"I don't know anything about your car. I know something else. Something you want to hear."

"Yeah? What's that?"

"Big poker game going on. Cards. High rollers."

Bishop pulled out a pack of Chesterfields and shook one free for Benny and then one for himself. A match sparked to life with a scrape of his thumbnail. He didn't care about a poker game. He wanted his Packard and whatever was in the trunk. "Cards, huh? Above The New Genesee again? That Greek will lose his restaurant if he isn't careful."

"Not there," Benny said, pleased he brought Bishop something he needed.

Bishop handed him the smoke. "Where then? The Buffalo Club?"

"Here."

"The Lafayette?"

Benny inhaled, shutting his eyes, holding the smoke. He released it before answering. "That's what I know."

"Fuck," Bishop said. "You sure?"

Benny nodded. "That's what I hear."

"Who's running it? Joey Bones?"

"I don't know that."

"What room number?" Bishop asked, watching Patrick, the room service waiter, step into the elevator balancing a covered tray in one hand.

"I don't know that."

"You know anything else, Benny?"

"That's all I know. That's all I heard."

Bishop peeled off some bills and handed them to him. "You did good, Benny. Make sure you buy something to eat with that money."

"I will, Bishop."

"You'll get more if you find my car."

"The green one?"

"That's right."

He made sure the junkman had left, then hurried as best as he could to the front desk. He spun the hotel register toward him and checked names, hoping one would stand out. None did, but enough Smiths had checked in to have a reunion.

The hotel had rooms on six floors. He'd have to walk every hall, sniffing for cigar smoke, checking for corridor lookouts. He'd start at the bottom and work his way to the top then down again, repeating the search until he found the game. Benny's information had better be jake, he thought. His foot would swell with all that walking. God knows what color his piss would be tomorrow. He struggled to the elevator. A car was waiting, and he stepped inside, telling the operator to take him to the second floor. When the door closed, he pulled his flask and took a long swig to keep his engine running right.

* * *

Bishop serpentined the second-floor hallway. He'd listen outside an even-numbered room then cross and put his ear against an odd-numbered door. Most times he heard nothing. Sometimes murmuring voices or squeaking boxsprings would reach him, but nothing that sounded like a roomful of betting men. His disposition darkened the further down the corridor he went. Gambling didn't bother him. He'd been known to wager on trotters at Buffalo Raceway or throw dice to make a buck or two between paying cases. He didn't care that an illegal card game was taking place. He'd grown up watching plenty of those. His Uncle Sal made sure of that. What worried him was that it was taking place in *his* hotel, and he might be out of a job if he didn't break it up before Oliver found out. Bishop didn't want his new bed to be Fat Ira's floor.

Patrick rounded the corner tucking a tip in his pocket. Bishop stopped him and filled him in on the card game. The boy hadn't seen anything unusual but promised to let Bishop know if he did.

"Make sure you tell the other waiters and bell boys to keep an eye out. You fellas see things before I do."

"I'll spread the word, Mr. Bishop," he said, and left the detective to snake down the hallway alone.

Bishop had the same luck searching the third floor as he'd had with the second. His foot ached. His kidneys throbbed as he climbed the stairs. He started doubting Benny's information. The gist of it was probably right. Chances are there was a poker game somewhere. And maybe the game *was* being held at a hotel, maybe even The Lafayette.

Or maybe not. Maybe Benny had heard wrong or gotten confused when a remembered artillery round exploded in his head. Maybe the game was being held at The Statler or The Lenox—though The Lenox might be jinxed since that dame was found dead in the alley. Gamblers tend to shy away from places like that. A dead woman's luck might rub off.

Benny could've gotten the *day* wrong. Maybe they wouldn't cut cards until tomorrow, or Saturday. Maybe he'd gotten *none* of it right, and there was no game at all. Maybe Bishop was limping from door-to-door for no reason.

But as he stepped into the fourth-floor corridor from the stairwell, he knew that the junkman's dope had been dead on the money. His Uncle Sal stepped out of Room 409 at that same moment. Bishop no longer needed to sniff for cigars or listen at keyholes. He'd found the game. He'd bet his whole stake he was right. There was no legitimate reason for Sally to be here. In fact, there was nothing legitimate about him at all. The older man stopped and lit a smoke, cupping the match as if there was an indoor breeze, and Bishop caned his way toward him.

Sal looked up as he waved out the match. Neither surprise nor happiness spread across his face when he saw his nephew. He dropped the match on the carpet and ground it with his toe to make sure it was out. "I was wondering when you'd find us. You're here earlier than I thought."

"What are you doing, Sal?"

"Entertaining friends."

"You have to entertain them in my hotel? This puts me in a spot."

"I know it does. I came by to talk it over with you a couple times, but you were never here."

"I've been working. I haven't been around much."

"Well, you're here now. I want to give you something. Think of it as a spot remover." He reached in his pocket and pulled out an envelope. He handed it to Bishop.

The door to Room 409 opened and a slender man in his early twenties stepped out. Bishop shoved the envelope in his pocket before the slender man noticed. Through the opened wedge between door and frame, Bishop could see into the room. Bottles—bourbon, brandy, rum—were lined on the dresser. Cigar smoke hazed the air. He didn't recognize most of the men. A few were fair skinned, crew cut, squared jawed. Bishop could see bulges under their jackets. Another man was tall with round glasses, wearing a suit that looked like he'd slept in it. The only person he knew was sitting with his back to the door. He'd trailed Councilman Rhielman long enough to recognize the stooped shoulders and friar hairline, even from behind. The door shut.

"Getting sandwiches," the slender man said to Sal, and eyed Bishop with a kind of disgust even he couldn't miss.

"Have we met, friend?" Bishop asked.

"We don't run in the same circle, *friend*," he answered, and walked toward the elevator.

Bishop tilted his head to the closed door and said to Sal, "Nice table. How'd you get it up here?"

"A couple of the boys carried it up the back stairs. Nobody bothered us. The hotel detective wasn't around."

"Who are those guys? How do you know them?"

"They're regular joes who were looking for a game. I arranged it for them. That's all."

"They don't look regular to me. That councilman is as regular as a knuckleball. You should go get sandwiches, too."

"Limp away, Nicholas. Buy yourself a bottle with that money I gave you. Take out that pretty Gia from your office. Show her a good time."

Bishop stared at his uncle, the dark eyes and straight nose mirrors of his own. They had the same thick hair, though Sal's had silvered at an early age. His uncle had an inch on him but was soft in the middle. Bishop knew there wouldn't be a bulge in his suitcoat. Sal had always been a knife man.

"Like I said, Sal, take it on the arches. There's a nice deli on Ellicott. The pastrami's sliced thin. You should leave within the next ten minutes. Your pals should go with you."

"My pals aren't the kind you should play detective with, Nicholas. Be smart. Go have a drink. Pretend you don't know anything."

"But I'm not smart, Sal. I took after you."

"I paid you. I warned you. That's all I can do. You break up this game, you'll make enemies."

"I've got more enemies than Hitler. A few more won't hurt."

Sal blew cigarette smoke out of the corner of his mouth. "You might be wrong about that."

* * *

Nicky The Weasel wasn't the type of house detective who would kick open the door and clear the room. He was the type who took the bribe and called the cops anyway. The elevator operator looked at him sideways as he sipped from his flask. When they reached the lobby, Bishop tottered to the front desk and made two phone calls. The first was to Lieutenant Darcy. The second was to *The Courier-Express*. After he hung up, he told Corbett to find Oliver and buy some Cracker Jack. The main feature was about to begin.

He lit a Chesterfield and wondered how much money was in the envelope.

* * *

The police paraded the handcuffed gamblers from the elevator. Sal was not among them. He must've taken his nephew's advice and slipped out for pastrami before the coppers arrived. Bishop, who watched the parade with Oliver, didn't care. Sal had raised him, or at least given him a roof over his head for a while, but it wouldn't have been the first time he'd watched his uncle led away in bracelets.

None of the men noticed Bishop except Councilman Rhielman. He glared at him, face flushed, teeth bared, a jagged vein bulging on the side of his bald head. The last time Bishop had seen him, he was on top of that brunette at The Blue Dolphin, slapping her hard between thrusts. Bishop smiled and waved. The councilman's vein bulged green. Guys like him made Bishop feel better about himself.

"How'd you uncover this?" Oliver asked, gesturing at the men being led away.

"Good detective work, Oliver. That's what you pay me for."

"I hate the publicity, but maybe this will discourage others."

"Maybe," Bishop said, knowing guys like Sal don't get discouraged. They get paroled early and pick up where they left off.

A flashbulb popped as Timothy Flynn, a reporter for *The Courier-Express*, snapped a photo of the gamblers being led away. He tried to get a comment from Rhielman, but the councilman was still leering at Bishop.

"How did a reporter get here so fast?" Oliver asked.

"Beats me. Those guys are uncanny."

Flynn was a Kitty Kat regular. He liked to buy rounds of gin, his favorite drink. When he'd had too many, which was often, he'd throw his arm around the shoulder of whomever was standing next to him and yell, "Have some gin with Timothy Flynn!" Bishop didn't particularly like gin, or the reporter for that matter, but he never refused a free drink. Both he and Flynn worked on crime's periphery, sometimes closer, and often did favors for one another. Bishop considered it a professional relationship, not a friendship, no matter how many rounds of Gilbey's Flynn had bought.

The reporter walked toward him when the last of the poker players had been shoved into the paddy wagon. Oliver whispered to Bishop to deal with the press "briefly and diplomatically," then hot footed in the other direction. He never wanted to be on record for anything. Let Bishop say something wrong and risk his neck.

Flynn half smiled as he approached Bishop, which was the best he could do. The left side of Flynn's face had been paralyzed by a clumsy forceps delivery. His eyelid drooped, the corner of his mouth downturned. Sometimes when Bishop had too much free gin mixed with Four Roses, he'd spot a stupidly smiling drunk at the bar, throw an arm around him and shout, "You have a half-assed grin like Timothy Flynn!" Sometimes Flynn laughed. Sometimes it looked like both sides of his face had been paralyzed by those forceps.

"Thanks for the phone call. I didn't see any other reporters here. Looks like I got the scoop."

"Happy to help," Bishop said, shaking his hand, knowing Flynn now owed him.

"Can you give me a quote or two for the story?"

"Make something up. Make me sound smart and diplomatic to impress my boss. Spell my name right."

"I'll make you sound like you're running for office. Rhielman's seat'll be open after this. First his affair and now this arrest? You can run for his spot."

"No, thanks. Politics is a step below house dick. And I thought that was rock bottom," Bishop said. "You mind if I get a copy of the photos you took? One each of those guys?"

"You starting a mug shot collection?"

"Something like that. I got a thing for faces. Maybe alarm bells will go off the next time they come in here."

"I'll send the pics over tomorrow. I got to write this up and get it to my editor. You want to meet later for a drink? Fighting crime must make you thirsty. Hell, trying to walk must parch you."

"I'll pass," Bishop said. "I'm on the wagon."

Flynn laughed, half his face frozen. "Jesus, Bishop, they serve drinks on that wagon? I can smell booze on your breath."

"That's lubricant to keep my pistons pumping. Say, you haven't heard of Nazis around here, have you?"

"In Buffalo? Christ, no. Have you?"

"Somebody painted 'Jew' in German on Ira's window."

"Probably kids."

"That's what I told him."

"Goose steppers in Buffalo would make a hell of a story, though," the reporter said. "A piece like that would get picked up by the wires. Get me some national attention."

"Let me know if you hear anything."

"You do the same. Our part for the war effort, right?"

"Sure."

"If you change your mind about that drink, I'll be at The Kitty around ten."

"Don't tempt me."

They shook hands goodbye. Flynn sauntered to the door, tipping his hat at two girls who didn't look old enough to be heading to the hotel bar. Bishop wanted to call out and ask the reporter if he'd ever heard of Pearl DuGaye, but he didn't want him sniffing after her, not until he found the Packard and made sure the trunk was empty. It was bad enough Darcy was looking for her, but Bishop was certain that the lieutenant couldn't find his own ass with either hand. He figured the chances of Darcy finding the missing singer were about the same. Flynn, who pursued headlines and bylines like a gin-soaked bloodhound, was a different story. So, Bishop didn't ask. Instead, he followed the girls into the bar. The taller one had nice calves.

Chapter 6

Fat Ira's window had been repaired. Smeared black paint had been removed, and his name retouched in gold. The plate glass had been washed for good measure. The door had been smashed, however. Bishop picked up Jake to protect her paws. He pushed open the door and held it for Gia. Broken shards crunched under her pumps. At the sound, the fat man whirled, the Detective Special in his fist, its muzzle pointed at her face.

"It's us," Bishop said, cradling the dog. Ira lowered the gun, still gripping it tight. Gia released a held breath loud enough to be heard.

"Look what those Nazi bastards did," Ira said. The drawers of all three file cabinets had been pulled out, their contents scattered across the floor. Law books had been yanked from the barrister bookcase and tossed to the ground. Ira's framed law degree had been cracked and hung at an angle. Nothing anti-Semitic had been painted on the walls.

"It wasn't Nazis," Bishop said.

"It was the same brown shirts who fucked my window," he said. He pointed to the street. "My neighbors *again* saw nothing."

"Joey Bones' men did this. Maybe Joey himself."

"Since when do I have problems with Joey Bones?"

Bishop set Jake down. She sniffed the strewn folders. "Since we worked the Rhielman case. His file will be missing. I'll bet my own money on it."

"How do you know?"

"They tossed my place, too. My Rhielman notes are gone."

"It took me awhile to clean up the mess they made," Gia said. "Dale Carnegie here never thanked me."

"I didn't?"

"No."

"Thank you."

"Too late."

"Why does Joey Bones care about Rhielman?" Ira asked.

"I don't know yet." Bishop told him about his run in with The Gospels at The Chez Amis. He left out the part about pissing pink.

"What'd you see that's riled them so much?" Ira asked.

"Nothing. Just him humping and slapping that brunette."

"Well, they think we know something. That might be enough to get us killed. Unless the Nazis get me first." Ira tucked the gun in his waistband.

"I'll look into it."

"Into what? Rhielman or Nazis killing me?"

"Both. I'll start with the brunette and see what she knows about the honorable councilman. Then I'll look for Nazis. Hopefully, I'll find them before they kill you."

"That would be nice." Ira said. He fingered the gun at his waist, then scratched his side seeming to relax a second. "And don't forget about the Brandt case. That art opening's tonight."

"Something's not right about that dame."

"You say that about me," Gia said.

"I mean it with her."

"She seemed quite taken with you, Bishop. She wouldn't even look at me when she was here," Ira said.

"You noticed that, too?"

"She only had eyes for you. Then she rushed after you when you took the dog outside. Hardly spoke a word to me."

"She said it was too hot in here. She didn't want to stick around. Plus, I'm charming," Bishop said.

Gia rolled her eyes.

"Listen," Bishop said. "I'm not certain about much, but I'm certain there's something off about Elizabeth Brandt. Trust me."

"She's upset, Bishop," Ira said. "Jealous. Hurt."

"There's more to it than her artist husband dipping his brush in a different can," Bishop said. "I was at her house the night Pearl DuGaye disappeared, but she acted like we were meeting for the first time when she hired us."

"You acted the same way," Ira pointed out.

"I was blotto. I didn't remember her."

"Maybe she was blotto, too."

"Her spring's wound too tight for that. She likes to stay in control."

"Maybe you're not as memorable or as charming as you think," Gia offered.

"Nonsense," Fat Ira said. "Nicky The Weasel makes an impression wherever he goes."

* * *

The brunette's name was Doris Slater. She worked for the Buffalo War Council. Her office was in City Hall's basement. Bishop and Gia were parked nearby. Jake lay between them on the front seat. Bishop scratched her ears. The hall's thirty-two stories loomed above them. Municipal workers—secretaries, mayoral aides, political appointees—streamed through revolving doors and down marble steps into the quitting-time sun. They spread out to trolley and bus stops and waiting automobiles. Others sat on benches, smoking, laughing, tilting faces sunward like flowers. Some lingered by The McKinley Monument, the towering obelisk guarded by sculptured lions memorializing the assassinated president.

"There are other doors," Gia said. "How do you know she'll come out the front?"

"She and Rhielman always used this exit when I was tailing them."

"Maybe she wants to avoid him. Their affair was splattered all over the newspapers, thanks to you."

"Flynn wrote the articles."

"Either way, I'd use another door. Actually, I probably would've quit and gotten a new job far from here."

"With The Pinkertons?"

"I hear they're hiring."

"There she is."

Doris was tall, shoulders above the other girls she walked with, even in flats. She wore a peach-colored dress that swayed with each step. Her legs went for miles.

"Pretty," Gia said. Bishop was sober enough not to answer.

Doris walked toward their parked car, and he angled his face from her as she passed. Gia reached for the door handle, but he touched her arm, her skin soft like he remembered.

"Wait," he said, and watched Doris sway in the side mirror. When she reached the corner, he said, "Now. Slowly." He left the window cracked for Jake.

Doris and her friends crossed Delaware Avenue to The Statler Hotel. Gia and Bishop trailed behind. "They must be getting a cocktail," Gia said.

"I'll buy the first round."

"As long as it's coffee."

They waited for traffic to pause as a man held the hotel door for Doris's group. "What's the play?" Gia asked.

"We stay outside and have a smoke 'til they get settled. Let the waiter bring their drinks. Then we enter nice and slow, like the three of us being there is a coincidence. We take a seat where she can see me."

"Then what?"

"We wait until she comes over."

"She won't do that. You spied on her. Took photos. You ruined her reputation. I don't know how she goes out in public. You're the last person she'd want to talk to. Believe me, I feel that way every day."

"She won't be able to stop herself. I haven't met a dame yet who'll pass up a chance to tell me what a heel I am. They go out of their way to educate me. Slapping's usually involved."

"This should be fun then."

"Be ready to duck. Sometimes they throw things."

Bishop offered his arm, and they crossed the avenue, his cane tapping out their rhythm. They stood outside The Statler and shared a Chesterfield. He could taste her lipstick on the cigarette. It was familiar, an unfinished dream he wished would return. She was standing close, their hands touching as they passed the fag. He tried to ignore her perfume by studying the passing faces, a habit that started as a teenager when he searched crowds for his mother who'd abandoned him. As he grew older, he imagined how she'd look as she aged. Her face fuller, lined. Her dark hair gray streaked or silvered like her brother Sal's. Maybe she'd dyed it to look younger. He hunted for his mother with blonde hair, or raven, or chestnut brown. He stared at women who were well-dressed, hoping she'd prospered after she'd abandoned him. He also stared at women wearing rags in case her fortunes had turned for the worse.

Never once had he searched for his father. He didn't know what to look for, owning neither photograph nor memory of him. Sometimes he dreamed of a featureless man or hallucinated one after heavy drinking.

Teddy Thurston took Bishop in after his father had disappeared, then his mother, and after Sal was sent away. Teddy had caught him trying to snatch his wallet, and instead of turning him in, took him under his wing and taught him things—like how to remember faces and not just look for them. He'd told him to focus on a few characteristics that never change—large ears, pointed chin—then look for anything distinctive like bent noses, cauliflowered ears, scars running across cheeks or necks. Notice where you saw them and the time of day, then file it all away in case you ever needed to go back and find the bastard again, he'd say. It would be a starting point. As Bishop stood in front of The Statler trying to recognize and store faces the way Teddy had taught him, he noticed men ogling Gia and gripped his cane tighter. She smoked like she didn't notice. The flask in his suit pocket next to the envelope weighed a hundred pounds.

"Come on," he said, flicking the butt at a man's head whose gaze had lingered on Gia too long. "They should've ordered by now."

The Statler's lobby bar was long, narrow, and windowless. The coffered ceilings matched the dark wainscoting. The lights were kept low. Sconces were shaded with green glass, muting the bulbs. Corner booths were dim with shadows, perfect spots to negotiate political deals and dark matters of the heart. The bar was filled with slick-haired men in fitted suits, lawyers and pols from City Hall and nearby firms. A few enlisted men in their summer service uniforms leaned against The Wurlitzer Victory jukebox, feeding it coins and making selections. Bishop recognized Bill Everett, the Statler house detective, lighting his pipe like he was Sherlock fucking Holmes. Doris's group sat at a table near the wall. They each had drinks and menus in front of them. They laughed like the war and Rhielman and missing lounge singers only existed in dime-store novels. Bishop chose a table in the center of the room and sat with his profile facing her. His chair was wooden, straight-backed, and hurt his kidneys. A waiter came over. Bishop ordered coffee and a Sidecar. His flask felt heavier by the minute.

"Don't look over," he told Gia. "She'll come by when she's ready. It might take her a drink or two to work up to it."

"You sound like your old self, Bishop. Almost competent."

"I talk a good game."

Everett paused at their table, puffing his pipe like a steam engine. Bishop could smell cherry tobacco. Bishop hated cherry tobacco.

Everett pulled the pipe from his mouth. "Hello, Bishop."

"Everett."

The waiter slid the saucer and cup in front of Bishop and placed Gia's Sidecar on a cocktail napkin.

"I'm glad you're drinking coffee," Everett said.

"I'm glad you approve," Bishop said. He gestured to Gia with an open palm. "This is Miss Alessi, my associate."

"A pleasure," he said.

"Likewise," she responded.

"What are you doing here, Bishop? Working?"

"Drinking coffee isn't work at all." He sipped from his cup. "See?"

"If there's going to be trouble, I want to know about it."

"Why would there be trouble? Does Miss Alessi look dangerous?"

"I feel dangerous," Gia said. "This is a new dress."

"Trouble shows up six drinks after you do. I don't want any on my shift. Finish your coffee and move along."

"I'm not trouble, but that pro skirt has misfortune written all over her." Bishop nodded to the prostitute standing between the GI's.

"Christ, when did she come in?"

"When you were asking if I take milk or cream."

"Goddamn it."

"It's cream, by the way."

"Shut up, Bishop," Everett said.

Bishop nodded toward the bar. "Say, how long has that bartender been skimming from the till? I'd check his front left pocket if I were you. Greenbacks disappear in there."

"Motherfucker."

"I thought a 1A dick like yourself would catch these things."

"Stick to coffee, Bishop, and mind your business." Everett clamped the pipe between his teeth and steamed toward the soldiers.

"Your powers of observation are impressive when you're sober," Gia said. "They always have been. Haven't seen those powers in a while."

"I still have them and owe them all to clean living. Plus, I hate that guy."

"What'd he ever do to you?"

"I don't quite remember, but I'm sure it was terrible."

Gia excused herself to use the restroom. Bishop waited until she was out of sight before pouring a healthy slug from his flask into his cup. He took a nip before returning it to his pocket. He felt someone staring, certain Everett would puff over to chastise him for sneaking liquor into the bar. But the burning gaze came from Doris's table. Bishop refused to look over. He stirred his coffee, sipped it, and brushed imaginary lint from his cuffs.

"Get ready," he told Gia when she returned. "She'll be coming over soon."

"How do you know?"

"If eyes could shoot bullets you'd be sitting with a dead man."

"You always find clever ways to stick me with the bill."

He heard Doris's chair scrape against the wooden floor when she pushed away from the table. His eyes remained on Gia, never turning until the tall woman was a foot away, towering above him like McKinley's obelisk.

"Well, look who it is. Nicky The Weasel," she said, a hint of a slur slowing her words.

"Why, Miss Slater. Hello."

"You *are* a weasel, aren't you? I mean, a real weasel. What kind of man does what you do for a living? Spying on people. Creeping around for money. Ruining lives," she said, looking as if about to spit. "Have you always been so weasely or is this something new?"

"It started when I was fifteen and became an operative. Old

habits are hard to break. Why don't you sit down and join us? I have something to discuss with you."

"*Join* you? You think I came over to socialize? I came over to tell you what a weasely bastard you are." Her voice had risen, and Everett took a step toward them, but Bishop waved him away.

"Lower your voice and sit down. As I said, I have something to discuss with you."

"Well, I have nothing to discuss with you, you rat weasel."

"55 Oxford Place."

"What?"

"55 Oxford Place."

"What about it?"

"Sit down and stop calling me weasel, and I'll explain."

She sat. Confusion and two rounds of drinks made her face slack. "How do you know that address?"

He pulled the envelope from his pocket and placed it on the table. "It's the same one written on this."

"That's addressed to my father."

"He lives at 55 Oxford Place, doesn't he?"

"You wrote him a letter?" She grabbed for it, but Bishop pulled it away.

"I'm not much for letter writing. I'm more of a telephone Joe. There's only a photograph inside."

"Of what?"

Bishop reached in his pocket and set a photo next to the envelope. It was a picture of Doris giving fellatio taken through the drapes at The Blue Dolphin Inn, her cheek dark where Rhielman had slapped her.

"You bastard!"

She reached to throw the Sidecar, but Gia caught her wrist. "Easy, stretch. I'm not finished with that yet."

Tears pooled then spilled down her cheeks. "Why would you send that to my father? What kind of monster are you?"

"The kind who needs information. You provide me some, and you keep the envelope. I want to know what Rhielman's up to."

Gia let go of her wrist, the skin red from where she'd squeezed. "I don't see him anymore. Those newspaper articles ended us."

"But you were with him for a while. You must know things," Bishop said.

"He doesn't talk about business."

"Sure, he does. He likes to brag. Share some pillow talk with us." Bishop leaned back, balancing the chair on two legs. "You'd like to hear some pillow talk, wouldn't you, Gia?"

"Depends who's talking."

Bishop turned to Doris. "What's Rhielman doing with Joey Bones?"

"Who?"

"Joseph Bonesutto. About this tall. Kills people. What business does he have with him?"

"I thought you were going to ask about the Germans."

Bishop tried to remain expressionless. The muscle in his left cheek twitched. He glanced at Gia, her face was as unreadable as his own. He threw out a prayer. "Don't play blonde, Doris. The Krauts and Joey Bones are working together. Everybody knows that."

"I don't know anything about Joey Bones."

"What about the Krauts then?"

"I don't know anything about them either. Robert and I never talked about those things."

"Judging from that picture, you don't get much of a chance to talk," Bishop said. Gia grimaced then pushed the photograph closer to Doris.

"Robert never told me anything."

"How do you know about the Germans then?"

"His wife was out of town. They came by the house. He thought I was sleeping, but I heard them."

"What'd you hear?"

"They were arguing. Robert was yelling at them for coming to his house. I don't know what they wanted. He said you could still be hiding in the bushes with your camera. That it was too risky for them to meet."

"He told them my name?"

"Nicky The Weasel."

"Everybody knows you, Bishop," Gia said.

He let it pass. "How do you know they were German? They have accents?"

"No, they talked American like us."

"Then how do you know they were Krauts?"

"Robert told them they were too stupid to be real Germans. That they were all going to jail if they kept making mistakes."

"Are they Nazis?" Bishop asked.

"Not all Germans are Nazis," Gia said.

"They're not all Boy Scouts either."

"I don't know what they are," Doris said. "I told you everything. I swear."

Bishop stared at her, his face and eyes as hard as he could make them. The silence grew painful. He slid the envelope and photograph to her. She grabbed them and stuffed them in her purse. He didn't speak until she stood.

"Sit down."

"I'm leaving," she said.

"I still have the negative," he barked. "Sit down."

She sagged back into the chair. "Why are you doing this? I've told you everything." She reached for Gia's hand. "Can't you help me? Can't you make him stop?"

"I can't make him do anything," she said, pulling her hand away. She finished off the Sidecar.

"You say you told me everything," Bishop said. "Maybe you did. Or maybe you lied. It doesn't matter, because you *will* get me more information about these Krauts."

"How? I don't know anything else."

"Get the information from Rhielman."

"I told you, I don't see him anymore."

"He'll start up with you again if you give him the chance. He enjoys slapping you around too much not to. And when you two start tangoing again, you get me the information I need."

"He's never talked about the Germans."

"Dig something out of him. Anything. A Kraut name. A Kraut address. You bring me a nugget and I give you the negative. You don't, Daddy gets a photograph. One a week. A different one every Monday. Special delivery. Different angles. Different positions. I got a whole roll. He'll see a side of his little girl he'll never forget. Understand?"

She nodded.

"Scram."

She stood, unsteady in her flats. Bishop waited until she took three steps before he called to her.

"Does your grandfather still live at 89 Riley Street?"

* * *

Bishop couldn't keep up with Gia because of his foot. He wanted to stop and take a pull from his flask but was afraid she'd drive away without him. She couldn't cross Delaware because of traffic, and he caught up at the corner.

"What's the matter with you?" he asked, grabbing her elbow.

She pulled free. "You were awful. That picture was awful. Hasn't that poor girl been through enough?"

"She's not a poor girl, and she's not in the church choir. She's mixed up with Rhielman and he's mixed up in something that stinks."

"You were cruel. Her father? Her *grandfather*? Jesus, Bishop."

"Detective work is a dirty racket. I'm not the Thin Man solving crimes in silk pajamas and you're not Myrna Loy."

"That wasn't detective work. That was blackmail."

"That was getting the job done."

"Well, I didn't like it."

"Then maybe you're not cut out to be a private eye."

She held up the car keys. "I'm just the driver, remember?"

"Then drive me to that art show."

"Fine. And you're not fooling me. I can smell liquor on you. How's that for being a detective?"

"I told you I couldn't quit all at once."

"And I told you it was me or the bottle. Seems like you made your choice."

* * *

Gia shifted gears like the transmission had wronged her. Bishop was used to angry women and kept quiet. Jake had climbed on his lap, and he petted her. The Buffalo Art Institute was a five-minute drive from The Statler Hotel. They didn't speak for a second of the ride. Instead, he smoked and stared out the window while they whizzed past shoppers going in and out of stores, and boys lined outside the recruiter's office. His head jerked when she stomped the clutch. He thought he spotted his car parked in front of The Deco Restaurant, but it was a different green Packard. Benny The Junkman stood on a corner showing a woman a silk blouse he'd pulled from his cart. He held the blouse by the shoulders with his forefingers and thumbs like a department store salesman, turning the blouse so she could see both sides. The woman was smiling and reached to touch a sleeve. Bishop wondered what he was saying to her.

The Institute seemed out of place, sharing the block with two beauty parlors, a dentist office, and a pool hall. Across the street was a busy barber shop with a shoe-shine chair facing the avenue. The board of directors were looking for a bigger, more permanent home with larger studio space, but the war had interrupted those plans. For now, the school was in a three-story house near the corner of Elmwood and West Utica. Gia braked hard when she pulled in front. "Out," she said.

"You're not coming in?"

"No."

"You have to."

"I'm just the driver. I drove. My part's over."

"You're my cover. We're here as a couple looking at art. I'll stick out if I was by myself. In this job, sometimes you have to do things you don't like."

She glared at him. "This must be one of those times," she said.

"We can pretend we're married. You got the angry-wife face down pat."

"What do you know about wives?"

"I had one once."

She shifted behind the wheel to face him. "I give. What's the punchline?"

"No punchline. There's nothing funny about ex-wives."

"You were married?"

"Yes."

"You never told me that."

"You never asked."

"She must have been a saint."

"She wasn't an angel."

"We're going to talk about this when I'm talking to you again."

"I may need a drink first."

"I may need one, too. I'll drink yours."

"So, are we going in?"

"I suppose. I'd hate to waste this angry-wife face."

"You could save it for the next time you're mad at me."

"I have others."

* * *

Artwork filled the first floor of the house. Watercolors, oils, and still lifes were hung on walls and propped on easels in the living room. Sculptures were set on pedestals in the parlor. The hardwood floors were dotted with dried paint and clay, remnants of the lessons and work between shows. There were few people inside the house, but none of them were Brandt or his wife. Most of the artists and guests had drifted to the backyard where it was cooler and where larger art pieces were displayed. Gia and Bishop made their way to the backdoor off the kitchen to join them. Bishop stopped by an oil painting displayed near the sink. It was unframed and depicted a man propped on pillows, nude to the waist, his curls and bedding disheveled around him, his face shadowed with beard and contentment.

"Looks like he had a good night," said Gia. "But this is something I'd stop to admire. I'm surprised you like this one. I had you pegged as a dogs playing poker type."

"That's our boy."

"Who?"

"Brandt."

He pulled out the photograph Elizabeth had given him and handed it to Gia. She looked from photo to painting and back again.

"You're right," she said. "It's him."

"Self-portrait."

"He's talented. You can tell what he got finished doing. I hope the girl looks as satisfied as he does."

"Read the painting's title."

She took a breath. "*After Pearl.*"

Chapter 7

The people mingling by the backyard exhibits were a mix of artists and Buffalo socialites. Bishop didn't like any of them. The artists stood by their work, gazing far in the distance while they smoked, pretending to be bored, hoping someone, anyone, would snap their photograph. The society people, on the other hand, were appropriately starched, powdered, and perfumed and made no bones about wanting their pictures taken. They waved anyone with a Brownie over and bunched together with arms around waists or thrown over shoulders, their smiles painfully bright to the recently sober. Bishop wanted to swing his cane at the lot of them.

"I hate these people," he said.

"But they're serving your favorite," Gia answered. "Lemonade."

"More reason to hate them."

"Good thing you brought your flask."

"What flask?"

"The one in your breast pocket. It doesn't take a Pinkerton to see the outline."

"That's for protection."

"From sobriety?"

"Bullets. It's shielding my heart."

"It protects your heart but ruins your liver. That's some flask."

"I'm very fond of it."

"Keep it in your pocket, mister."

"I have to," he said, lowering his voice. "Here comes our client."

"*That's* our client?" Gia said, eyeing her from head to toe. "Of course, she is."

Elizabeth Brandt glided toward them in slingback sage sandals with enough heel to make men turn and admire her calves. Her cocktail dress was the same color as her shoes and front buttoned to a V-neck. Bishop decided that a woman who could fill a dress like that deserved to be unbuttoned slowly and carefully, but then his hand tremored and he wondered if he could work the buttons at all.

"Put your private eyes back in your head, shamus," whispered Gia. "You're supposed to be working."

"I'm admiring the artwork."

"I'd slap you, but I don't want to make you cry in front of your client."

"Mr. Bishop," Elizabeth said, as she approached. "You look bathed and are wearing an unspotted tie. I'm impressed—and more than a little surprised."

She offered her hand and Bishop took it. "I always cleanup for art openings," he said. "May I present my triggerman, Miss Gia Alessi."

"Are you expecting trouble?"

"I like to be prepared."

"Perhaps you are wiser than I thought," she said, and turned to Gia. "It's a pleasure meeting you, Miss Alessi."

"Likewise."

"Have you seen my husband, Mr. Bishop? Have you spoken with him?" Elizabeth asked.

"Not yet. We did see his self-portrait in the kitchen, though. He certainly knows how to capture a moment."

The left corner of her mouth curled downward. "Doesn't he."

"An interesting title, too, *After Pearl*," Bishop said. "Is Pearl your nickname, Mrs. Brandt?"

"I don't have a nickname."

"You can have mine. I don't like it much."

"From everything I've heard, Mr. Bishop, your nickname suits you perfectly."

"That's the part I don't like. If Pearl isn't your nickname, who is she? Is that the name of one of his students or models? A neighbor, perhaps?"

"I don't know. Now, if you'll excuse me, I'm being waved over for a photograph," she said, looking past Bishop to a group of society women and returned their wave. "We probably shouldn't be seen talking anyway. There's cake and lemonade by the tree. Enjoy the show."

Bishop watched her walk away, marveling how well her heels worked her calves.

"That was a quick exit," Gia said.

"Didn't sound like she wanted to talk about Pearl, did it?"

"Why would she hire you if she already knew about her?"

"For my photography skills."

"Something's not right."

"I told you that dame was off."

"There he is," Gia said, lifting her chin toward Meyer Brandt. He was leaning against the refreshment table, talking to a girl who looked a few years shy of legal. Her right eye was partially covered by a fallen wave of red hair. He said something to her, and she laughed. "He's more handsome in person than in his portrait."

"That underage Veronica Lake thinks so," said Bishop.

"For a kid, she has good taste."

"That guy's like Joe Louis. Young, old, doesn't matter. He takes on all contenders."

"That ginger won't know what hit her."

"You'd better go save her."

"Saving you is a full-time job. I don't know if I have the energy to save anybody else."

"Go meet him. Introduce yourself," he said, nudging her toward Brandt. "Tell him you love his self-portrait."

"I *do* love his self-portrait. I'd buy it, but my boss doesn't pay me."

"Get him talking about it. It shouldn't be hard. He's a ladies' man, or at least he thinks he is. He'll start blabbering to impress you."

"You're pandering me? I thought we were supposed to be married."

"We have a very unconventional marriage. We're practically French. Find out what you can about Pearl."

"What if he won't bite? Maybe he likes them young with peek-a-boo haircuts and won't be interested in me."

"Then he's either stupid or blind."

"Is that a compliment?"

"It's a fact. He has scotch in his cabinet older than her. Go find out about Pearl."

"This should be fun."

"Not for me it won't."

"Good," she said, and headed toward the lemonade. She walked with an extra roll to her hips. Bishop wasn't sure if it was for his benefit or Brandt's.

Brandt spotted her as she approached. The artist drank in each step like she was Four Roses in heels. The urge to punch him in his unpunched face swept over Bishop again. Gia poured herself a lemonade, eyed the apple cake as if she was deciding to take a piece, and didn't turn toward Brandt until he spoke to her. Then she smiled, her eyes and face brightening, and the underage Veronica Lake was forgotten.

Bishop pulled out his flask and tipped longer than he should've.

* * *

He wandered among the watercolors and charcoal sketches, pretending to admire the art while he scanned faces. There wasn't a colored person in the crowd, not that he'd expected Pearl to be there. No one was paying attention to Gia and Brandt except he and Elizabeth, who stood with a group of people and watched as Gia took the artist's arm and strolled toward the house. As they neared the backdoor, a slender man stopped Brandt, leaned close, and whispered in his ear. Brandt nodded once, then continued inside. The slender man had a boyish face. Bishop recognized it. He made his way to the side gate, and the detective hobbled after him, keeping his distance. The pain from his kidneys had eased into a dull ache across his lower back. The slender man slowed once to light a cigarette but didn't look twice at anything propped on an easel.

The side gate opened to an alley, and he stopped outside, the cigarette cupped between his forefinger and thumb. He slouched against the post with his other hand stuffed in his pocket. Bishop lingered by a bust of Medusa, certain that not all the snakes at the Art Institute were made of clay. He waited to see if Brandt would appear in the alley. But Brandt didn't join him. No one did. Instead, Bishop's green Packard pulled up and the slender man took a final drag then flicked the butt away before slouching into the passenger side. One of the Gospels, maybe Mark, was behind the wheel.

"Since when do weasels like art?"

Bishop turned as his car drove off, his teeth gritting. Lieutenant Darcy stood by the Medusa, sweating in civilian shirtsleeves and a tie. "You don't strike me as a connoisseur yourself, Lieutenant."

Darcy pointed to the bust. "That's my daughter."

"You're Phorcys?"

"What?"

"You're daughter's Medusa?"

"Jesus, are you drunk?" Darcy asked. He gestured to the statue again. "She sculpted that, you crippled mug."

"That's hard to believe."

"You don't think I could have a talented daughter?"

"I didn't think you could have a daughter at all. How did you get a woman to sleep with you?"

"Keep cracking wise and I'll crack your head right here."

"Have you found that singer you were asking me about? What's her name? Diamond something?"

"Pearl DuGaye. And, no, I haven't found her. You must have buried her deep."

"And those gamblers you arrested at my hotel, who were they?"

"I ask the questions, Weasel. Not you."

"But I'm curious, and I did give you that tip. That was a nice picture of you in the *Courier*, by the way. Your daughter must've been proud. Those gamblers weren't from around here, were they? I didn't recognize any of them except Rhielman."

"One mug was from Jersey. The rest New York City."

"What were they doing here?"

"Playing cards in your hotel."

"That's a long way to come for a poker game. How does Rhielman know them?"

"Christ, Weasel. They were playing cards together. He probably doesn't know them at all. Leave the guy alone."

"You still holding them?"

"Everyone made bail."

"Who paid?"

"None of your business. What do you know about Pearl DuGaye?"

"Nothing. I thought her name was Diamond."

"You're a lying weasel."

"Why are you looking so hard for a colored girl, Lieutenant? You and Jimmy Crow always struck me as pals."

"I'm doing my job, Weasel."

"You giving a damn about a missing Black singer…hell, *any* missing Black girl…doesn't seem like you at all. Who's making you look for her? Joey Bones? Councilman Rhielman? Why do they care?"

Darcy took a step forward, his face flushing, his fists balling. "Listen, you 4-F motherfucking alcoholic cripple—"

The Lieutenant was stopped mid-sentence by his approaching daughter. She looked old enough to buy Bishop a drink and shared the same fair skin as her father, the kind that blotched in the heat. Unlike him, she was frail with hollowed cheeks. She wore simple clothes— black trousers, despite the temperature, and a matching peasant top. Bishop thought she may have made them herself. Her eyebrows were thin and her gray eyes too big for her face. The combination made her look jumpy. "Daddy, is everything all right?"

"Your father was telling me how proud of you he is, Miss Darcy," Bishop said. "And with good reason. Your Medusa is aces. I'm curious, though. Did your father pose for you, or did you work from memory? That fat snake in the middle looks exactly like him."

The corners of her mouth curled a fraction.

"Get out of here, Bishop. Get out of here now," Darcy said.

"I was about to, as a matter of fact. I have to see a woman about a nude. Congratulations on your work, Miss Darcy, but watch out for snakes. This place is lousy with them."

Bishop hobbled back to the house. He spotted Gia alone under a shade tree sipping lemonade. She smiled when she saw him, her face flushed.

"What did you learn from Brandt?" he asked, when he got to her.

"I learned I have excellent bone structure."

Bishop stared at her.

"My cheekbones and jawline, my chin. All strong and pronounced."

"So, he thinks you're pretty." He dug out a pack of Chesterfields and shook one loose for her.

She pulled it from the pack. "He wants to paint me."

"The only way for him to truly know his subjects is by sleeping with them."

Bishop struck a match for her, and she leaned in. "You have a dirty mind," she said, after blowing smoke out of the corner of her mouth.

"His wife said that about him. She posed for him."

Gia passed the cigarette to him. "She has excellent bone structure, too."

"Her tibias are especially nice," Bishop said, and took a drag. "What'd you learn about Pearl?"

"I asked him why he named his painting *After Pearl,* who she was."

"What'd he say?"

"He said all women are pearls."

Bishop rolled his eyes. "Jesus."

"I know. I almost laughed in his face. He thought he was quite charming."

"I'd like to punch him," he said. "Before you entered the house, a slender man, a kid, came up and whispered in his ear. Did you hear what he said?"

Gia took the cigarette from his hand. "No. And Myer didn't say anything. He only nodded."

"Myer?"

"That's his name, Bishop. Who's this thin man?"

"An errand boy. He was with that crew that was gambling at The Lafayette. They sent him for sandwiches, so he didn't get pinched with the rest of them."

"What's he doing here?"

"I don't know but your boyfriend Brandt is tied to the gamblers, Pearl, and Joey Bones now."

Gia arched an eyebrow. "Joey Bones?"

"I kept an eye on the kid after you love birds disappeared inside the house. One of The Gospels—I think it was Mark—picked him up in my Packard."

"You're kidding."

"The last person who drove my car that I know of was Pearl DuGaye."

"After you were thrown out of The Chez Amis for skipping on the tab."

"I was on the delayed payment plan. The Packard may tie Joey Bones to Pearl."

"This Pearl gets around."

He took back the cigarette and flicked the ash. "And one more thing. While you were letting Brandt inspect your bones, I ran into Lieutenant Darcy."

"He's mixed up in all this, too?"

"I don't think so. His daughter is one of the artists here."

"He reproduced?"

"I was shocked, too. He told me the Lafayette gamblers were from downstate. That skinny errand boy might be, too."

"You'll need to talk to your uncle."

"We can see him in the morning."

"Meyer's sketching me in the morning."

"And you wonder why I drink."

"You told me to get close to him, Bishop. I got close to him."

Chapter 8

Bishop woke sweating. His undershirt stuck to his skin. Sweat stung his eye, and he knuckled it away. The flask lay opened on the nightstand. He grabbed it, shook the last few drops in his mouth, then threw it against the wall. Jake jumped and growled at the foot of the bed. It would be easy to call down for a bottle. They'd send one up, despite the early hour. Being the hotel dick had its perks. A few glasses would stop the shakes, sweats. A couple more would dull the ache in his kidneys and foot. By then he might be able to look in the mirror.

He reached for the phone. The switchboard operator answered, and he asked to be connected to TR2-5556. The party line rang, two shorts and a long. He knew the phone was in the hallway. It would take a bit for someone to get to it. The candlestick phone shook in his hands. He needed to piss and wondered if it'd be pink. Gia answered. Her voice deep, raspy, in use for the first time that morning. Bishop kept silent. She said hello, louder, into the mouthpiece, into his ear. He felt it in his groin. He closed his eyes and tried to picture her in her nightgown, the light behind her, hair mussed from sleep. The image was so clear he was certain he could caress it. He heard a click and knew her Seventh Street neighbor had picked up the party line and was listening. Gia swore in Italian. He wasn't sure if she was cursing him or the neighbor. He hung up the phone but held onto her image as long as he could.

* * *

Bishop stood in front of The Lafayette, wishing he'd ordered that bottle. The city was too much already. Traffic was too loud, the sunlight too bright. A woman passed him on the sidewalk. Her perfume watered his eyes. He thought of Gia getting ready to meet Brandt—brushing her hair, applying makeup, picking out something to wear for him. Bishop lit a Chesterfield. The smoke he drew into his lungs didn't calm him.

He waved down a cab and stepped back when it pulled to the curb. He didn't mind riding in taxis, but watching the yellow paint and chrome fender approach always unnerved him. It was so easy to step in front of one. Or be pushed. Sometimes when nodding off on a barstool he'd see a Checker or a Yellow hurtling toward him and he'd jerk awake. Sometimes he'd scream. Sometimes there were tears. People around him would laugh and say he needed another drink, and one would be pushed in front of him. Except the other drunks. They didn't laugh. They understood. They'd turn away, stare into their glasses, and wait their turn.

If Bishop had two working feet, he'd have walked to The New Genesee Restaurant. But he didn't, so he and Jake climbed inside the taxi for a three-minute ride. The cabbie wasn't interested in conversation. Maybe it was too early for chit-chat. Maybe small talk wasn't included in the small fare. Maybe the hackie didn't like dogs in his cab. All were fine with Bishop. He didn't feel like talking either. He took a long drag off the Chesterfield and blew smoke out the open window, not bothering to look for his Packard.

The cabbie let him out at the corner of Oak and Genesee. Bishop waited for the light to turn and stared at the building across the street. The New Genesee Restaurant occupied the ground floor, apartments were above. As always, his gaze drifted to the second-floor center window to his boyhood bedroom. At least it was his room for a while. Uncle Sal had won the building in a poker game and let his unwed sister and bastard nephew live in the smallest apartment. Bishop grew up with muffled conversations and cooking odors—frying onions and bacon—seeping through the floorboards. On nights his mother went out, he wouldn't sleep and would stare out that center window watching passing cars and passing people. He'd watch cops and drunks, whores and hustlers. He saw sidewalk fistfights and couples holding hands. He'd watch the men below and pick one to be his father, always choosing the tallest or the one with the broadest shoulders.

The rhythm of the street became his own rhythm. He knew the time by the milk delivery and when the grocery opened across the street. He knew when the bars had closed because the restaurant would become busy and loud a few minutes later. Uncle Sal had called it the 'floor show'. That's when he'd listen for his mother's footsteps, hoping she'd come home, hoping she'd be alone.

Bishop had liked looking out on Genesee best during a heavy snow. Shops would close early, the owners and clerks hurrying to real homes. The street would grow quiet. Nobody would walk or yell under his window. If a car passed, the tires would be muffled by fallen snow. Streetlights and store displays glowed for him alone on his perch. There would be no sound from the restaurant—no laughter, no kitchen noise, no customers. On nights like that he felt he was the last one left in the world.

Sal let Bishop stay in the apartment after his mother ran off with some horn player from Cleveland. Moving from town to town, club to club, and living out of a suitcase was no life for a kid, she'd told him. She'd come back for him when he was older. Until then, Uncle Sally would take care of him. She'd promised.

Every few days, longer if he was in jail, Sal would check on him. Bishop was allowed to go down to the restaurant three times a day for meals. He'd sit at the counter, legs swinging, and could order anything off the menu, including dessert; Sally would settle with the owner, Tamis, at the end of the week. Faye was his favorite waitress back then, always fussing over him, making sure he finished his food, and slipping him an oatmeal cookie when Tamis wasn't looking. She was pretty, with auburn hair and emerald eyes. He thought of her as his only friend, the only one who might really care for him.

Sometimes Uncle Sal would have card games in the apartment and Bishop would have to stay in his room. He'd crack the door and watch the men play as the living room fogged from cigarette and cigar smoke. The game could last for days, the players changing as one crapped out and another took his place. Through that cracked door Bishop felt as if he were spying into the world of men, filing away everything he'd seen and overheard. Once he watched Uncle Sal pull a knife on a man accused of cheating and he'd held his breath until the man left the money on the table, backed away, and Sally lowered his blade. He remembered Faye coming up after her restaurant shift to make extra money in what was once his mother's bedroom. Part of him had wanted to scream at her, part of him had wanted to be with her.

When the poker games ended, Bishop would empty ashtrays, sweep floors, and take the garbage to the alley. He'd keep the occasional forgotten liquor bottle and learned to drink bourbon sitting alone in his window watching it snow, wondering if this was the night his mother would return. Most days he went to school because it was better than being alone. The days he didn't go, he was sick from bourbon.

When Bishop was fourteen, Sal lost the building to Tamis, a Greek who knew cards better than he knew the English language. It was the last bet Sal had made during a long night of bad bets. Bishop watched it from his doorway.

"That's the way it goes, kid. Sometimes Lady Luck's a cunt," Sal had said afterwards, then told him to pack his things.

After that, it was a series of hotels when Sal was flush, flop houses when his pockets were light. When Sal moved in with a woman, Bishop slept on a couch if he was lucky, the floor if he wasn't. Sometimes he dreamt of his mother, sometimes of a faceless man.

He was on his own for good when Sal was sent away to do an eight-month stretch in county, and the woman they were living with said she had no obligation to him and pushed him out the door. Bishop was two weeks shy of his fifteenth birthday.

He leaned on his cane as he crossed the street and entered the restaurant. The New Genesee smelled of frying eggs and cigarettes like it always did in the morning. He nodded to Tamis behind the counter, and Tamis nodded back. If Tamis ever felt guilty about evicting him when he was a kid, he never showed it. He frowned at Jake but didn't say anything to Bishop about the dog trailing at his ankles.

The current crew of waitresses was too young to remember when he'd lived above the restaurant and looked at him like any other customer they hoped was a generous tipper. Faye had stopped waitressing years ago. Bishop wasn't sure what happened to her, but he had a pretty good idea how she was making her money these days.

Sal sat at the last table in the restaurant facing the door as he always did. Bishop knew what he was eating for breakfast before he slid into the opposite chair. Jake sat his feet.

"Silver dollars on your plate…," Bishop started.

"…silver dollars in your pocket," Sally finished.

"Don't you ever get tired of pancakes, Uncle Sal?"

"Who gets tired of silver dollars?"

"Not your downstate friends who got pinched at my hotel. I'm sure of that."

Sal leaned back in his chair. He removed the napkin tucked in his collar and wiped syrup from the corner of his mouth. "I haven't met anyone who doesn't like silver dollars or gold dollars or paper dollars for that matter. What are you doing here, Nicholas?"

"Can't I surprise my uncle and have breakfast with him?"

"Only if you want something. What's with the mutt?"

"She follows me around. Leaving her alone in a hotel room doesn't seem right."

A dark-haired waitress with olive skin stopped by their table. Sal asked for the check. Bishop asked for coffee. She was younger and prettier than Faye had been. She could have made a lot of money working out of mom's old bedroom, Bishop thought, and then hated himself for thinking that. She didn't say anything about Jake being in the restaurant.

"You should eat something," Sal said. "You look sickly."

"Allergies are bad this year."

"You should stay away from roses."

"I'm working on it."

"Good. You should stay away from those downstate boys, too. They play rougher than cheating husbands and the hotel hookers you're used to. They'd break your other foot for fun."

"How'd you get mixed up with them?"

"Why you asking? No good's gonna come from nosing around those guys."

"I'm curious. I like to know who the players are."

"I don't know much about them. Joey Bones said they were in town for business and asked me to put a game together. Get them a straight dealer, hard liquor, and some good-looking broads afterwards. He wasn't happy the game got pinched."

"Breaks my heart he was disappointed. What kind of business are they in?"

"They didn't say, I didn't ask. That's how you live to be an old man like me. You don't ask questions. You need to learn that."

"You're not old, Sally. You just look old. And it's my job to ask questions."

The pretty waitress dropped off the check and the coffee. Neither spoke until she walked away.

"Who invited Rhielman to the party?" Bishop asked.

"He showed up with the guy from Manhattan. I don't know how they know each other."

"Tell me about the skinny kid."

"What skinny kid?"

"The one who went out for sandwiches."

"Him? He's a nobody. A flunky. Wants to be a gunsel when he grows up."

"He got a name?"

"What's this all about, Nicholas? The cops broke up the game. You got a couple nice quotes in the paper and a probably a pat on the head from your boss. It's done. Stay away from them."

"What's his name, Sally?"

"I used to worry you'd drink yourself to death but if you keep sniffing around these guys, you'll be dead long before that."

"You've never worried about me. Not once. Tell me his name."

"Krieger."

* * *

Fat Ira's smashed door had been boarded, the broken glass swept away. A Star of David had been black painted on the plywood. Bishop's stomach clenched and it had nothing to do with alcohol. He touched the star before pushing the door with his cane; Jake nosed her way in.

"Ira, it's me. Don't shoot."

When no shots rang out, Bishop shoved the door wider, waited. He stepped inside. The office had been straightened. Files had been returned to cabinets. Books were again lined in Barrister bookshelves. The law degree had been straightened but the frame hadn't been replaced.

Ira lowered the gun. "Still think it was kids?"

"When did this happen?"

"It was there when I came in this morning."

"The paint's dry."

"Have you looked into these fucking Nazis yet or are you too busy chasing your missing blonde?"

"It turns out she's a little darker than blonde. I did find out that Rhielman is mixed up with some Germans, though. Not real Krauts. Downstate Krauts. Jersey. New York City. I don't know if they're Nazis."

"Mixed up how?"

"I don't know yet. Might be nothing but they're the only Germans I've stumbled across."

"What's your next move?" Ira slipped the gun in his waistband. "Rhielman certainly won't talk to you."

"I'm going to see a man about some paint. Keep an eye on Jake for me. I won't be long."

Bishop left Ira and shuffled across the street to the hardware store. The bell above the door tinkled when he entered. An older man stood in front of a drawer trying to match a nut to a bolt. A customer watched over his shoulder. Bishop pegged his age around fifty. The sleeves of his white dress shirt were rolled above the elbow, revealing thick forearms. His neck strained against his buttoned collar. A brown leather smock covered his barrel chest. He looked like a man who'd spent his life hoisting lumber, not selling it by the foot.

"Erik," the man called. "Customer."

Bishop made his way to the paint section and studied the cans behind the counter. Erik strolled from the backroom and Bishop let his eyes sweep over him. He wore a white shirt and matching brown apron like his father. His shirt sleeves were rolled down, his arms as thin as the rest of him. Must be built like his mother, Bishop thought, and stared at his shirt cuffs. Erik glared at him with the same disgust he had when he saw Bishop outside the poker game at The Lafayette.

Bishop grinned. "Hello, Erik. Remember me?"

Krieger glanced at his father, but the older man was still searching for a nut that fit, muttering that it was an odd-sized bolt and that he'd have to check in the back. He walked to the storeroom. His customer drifted to the corner to look at rakes.

"Never seen you before, pal," he answered, once his father was out of sight.

"No? Last time I saw you, you were driving around in a stolen Packard. A hell of a nice car, too. Before that you were fetching sandwiches. That refresh your memory, *pal?*"

Krieger placed both hands on the counter and leaned forward, pressing his face close. "Like I said, I've never seen you before. Why don't you buy some paint or get the hell out?"

"Sure, kid. Maybe I was mistaken. All you punks playing George Raft look alike. Give me a quart and a brush."

"What color?"

Bishop grabbed his cane with both hands and pressed it hard across Krieger's wrists, pinning him to the counter. His face twisted in pain, but he didn't cry out. "The same color that's on your right shirt cuff, Erik. What color would you say that is?" He pressed harder against bone.

Krieger didn't answer. His cheek muscles twitched.

"No guesses? I'll help you out since you're either slow or blind. That's black paint on your cuff. Nazi black. How'd it get there?"

He spoke through clenched teeth. "How do you think? I sell paint."

"Yeah? Who'd you sell black paint to yesterday?"

"I don't know. Some guy."

"What'd this guy look like?"

"I don't remember. He had a forgettable face. Never seen him before."

Bishop leaned all his weight on the cane and this time Krieger cried out. "I get the feeling you're lying to me, Erik. I hate when people lie to me. I don't think you sold any black paint yesterday. I think you took some from the backroom and painted a Star of David on my friend's door. Or maybe you got some on your cuff when you painted his window a few days ago. If I'm right about either of those things, and I'm betting that I am, I'm coming back here and breaking both your skinny wrists, do you understand me? And if I'm in a bad mood or hungover that day or had a fight with my secretary, I'm breaking a couple of your fingers to make me feel better. I'm partial to thumbs. You getting all this, *pal*? Is it sinking in, or do I have to talk slower?"

"I'm getting it."

"Good. Here's another news flash. If anything happens to my friend, I'm blaming you. If another window gets smashed, if anything else gets painted, if he trips crossing the street, I'll be looking for you. And when I find you, I'll beat you bloody with this cane. I've done it before and I'm getting good at it. Now get that paint and brush like a good errand boy before I lose my temper."

Bishop released him and took a step back from the counter, cocking the cane in case he had to swing. But Krieger didn't lunge. He straightened and rubbed his already bruising wrists. "You're going to pay for that. You're going to pay."

"I got news for you, sunshine. I'm not even paying for the paint. You're picking up the tab."

"You're dead, Weasel. I promise you. You're dead."

"Ah, Weasel. So, you do know me."

The old man came out of the backroom holding the bolt with a nut grooved halfway up the shaft. "Everything okay, Erik?"

"Sure, pop," he answered, still rubbing his wrists. "Just getting this man some paint."

Chapter 9

After Bishop had painted over the Star of David, Ira dropped him off at The Chez Amis with Jake. The club hadn't opened yet, so Albert wasn't at his post. No cars were parked in front. A new banner hung beneath the marquee announcing that The Johnny Martone Orchestra was appearing this week featuring singer Darlene Beauville. Girl singers with fake French names must pack them in, Bishop thought. He hoped this one had a better fate than Pearl.

The door to The Chez Amis was unlocked and he dragged himself inside with Jake leading the way. Chairs were stacked on tables. Stools sat atop the bar. A porter vacuumed the dining room's maroon carpet, the Kirby's whine the sole sound in the place. Another porter was changing a lightbulb near the stage.

Amigone, dressed in tan pleated pants and a green shirt without a tie, pushed through the swinging kitchen doors holding a fistful of invoices. His oval face sagged into a frown when he saw Bishop. He ran fingers through his receding hair. "Jesus Christ, Bishop. You can't bring a mutt in here."

Jake was sniffing the carpet, searching for crumbs the Kirby had missed. "I thought you were an animal lover," Bishop said.

"If they're medium rare." He slapped the invoices against his thigh. "What the hell do you want, Bishop? The bar doesn't open until one. Go find bums passing a bottle in an alley. You'll fit right in."

Bishop leaned on his cane, gripping the handle tightly so his hands wouldn't shake. "I need a favor."

Amigone tilted his head back and laughed, the loose skin under his chin shaking. "You got a nerve. You skip on a bill and then come in here with that walking fleabag and ask for a favor? The Gospels must have kicked your melon harder than I thought. And don't even think about asking for a tab again. That troop ship sailed, but you wouldn't know anything about troop ships, would you, Weasel?"

"A tab would be much appreciated, but what I need is Pearl DuGaye's address."

Amigone's dark eyes narrowed. "Why? That canary flew off somewhere. Nobody's seen or heard from her since she left with *you*. I still owe her money from last week and she hasn't come in to pick it up. She's gone."

"Don't you think it's odd she hasn't come in for her pay?"

"Singers, musicians. They're all odd. It's like working with children. The only thing worse is dealing with drunken gimps who think they're Sam Spade. Especially first thing in the morning."

"So, where'd she live? You hired her. You must have her address written down in your office somewhere."

"Jesus, Bishop. You spend one night with the broad and you're mooning over her? Chasing after her? Christ, no wonder she took off. You probably scared her."

"I just need an address, Phil. It's not going to cost you a dime to give it to me."

"Fine. If it'll get you and that mongrel out of my restaurant. She was renting a place across from The Colored Musicians Club on Broadway. Some dump up on the third floor."

"See? That wasn't hard. It was an easy favor."

"Do *me* a favor and get the hell out of here."

Bishop saluted with his cane and left with Jake trotting beside him. The sun was already beating down when he stepped outside, promising another sweltering day. He missed his Packard and knew he'd have to steal it back from The Gospels soon. Then he was afraid he'd have to deal with the body in the trunk, if there was one. And he was afraid there was. Benny stood across the street showing a man a watch. He held the watch to the man's ear to hear the ticking. The man nodded and reached for his wallet.

Bishop waved down a cab, taking a few steps back when it pulled to the curb.

* * *

The Colored Musicians Club was on Broadway near Michigan. Before his foot was crushed, Bishop liked to go to the club on Sunday nights for the open jam sessions. He'd sit at the end of the bar and drink cheap beer and sneak sips from his flask to save a few bucks. Musicians and singers, both white and Black, would fill the stage and play for the joy of it. Bishop would close his eyes and soak it in, letting the notes and chords take him where they wanted. He'd been back once since the taxi had run him over, but the stairs leading to the second-floor club were too narrow and steep for him to climb.

As the cab approached Michigan Avenue, Jake stood on her hind legs, her front paws pressed against the window facing away from the club. Her tail whipped back and forth as she whimpered. When the taxi came to a stop and Bishop opened the door, she leapt into traffic and darted across the street. Tires screeched as drivers slammed brakes to avoid hitting her. An old teamster with gray stubble covering his cheeks leaned out his truck and swore as Jake made it to the sidewalk. She ran to the orange brick building with arched windows across from the club. A sheet-metal works occupied the street level, but Jake raced directly to the entrance leading to the apartments on the upper floors.

Bishop waited for a break between cars and doddered after her. The door to the apartments was unlocked. Jake raced up the stairs as soon as Bishop pulled it open. There were no names taped to the mailboxes in the vestibule, so he hobbled after the dog. Nothing, not the stairs, not the green-painted walls, nor the hanging bare bulbs, looked familiar. He was certain he'd never been in the building, until he reached the third level. He could hear water dripping. The hallway reeked of marijuana and urine. The combination was pungent and hit him hard. He knew he'd smelled this place before. A reefer-smoking sax player lived at the end of the hall next to the shared bathroom. Bishop didn't know how he knew that.

Jake was scratching at an apartment door that faced the street. He hushed the dog and pressed his ear against it. No sounds came from inside, but he knocked anyway. Nothing stirred on the other side. He glanced over his shoulder before pulling out a thin screwdriver and pick from his suit pocket. He inserted the screwdriver into the keyhole before easing in the pick. The lock was old and simple, but his hands trembled enough that he struggled. Jake whined as Bishop worked the pins. When the lock finally gave, he pocketed the tools and pulled out The Fitz, cocking it before pushing open the door.

Jake shot inside, barking. Bishop let the door swing wide before following. The apartment was hot, the air stale. There wasn't much to the apartment, just a single room with a kitchenette and a Murphy bed folded into the wall. The place was deserted, so he holstered the gun and shut the door behind him. A combination of fear and excitement rippled through him, the way it always did when he was undercover or had broken into someplace to search it, knowing that at any moment he could be caught or arrested or find an elusive clue. He felt his pulse and breath quicken and a keen alertness switch on as if he were aware of every sight and sound and smell within the room, such an opposite sensation compared to the dull alcoholic fog that'd grown so familiar.

If the cops had been through the apartment before him, they'd left it tidy. Music magazines—*Dance Band Album, Song Hits, Downbeat*—

were stacked on the coffee table, *Variety* propped up a wobbly leg. An afghan was folded on the couch. Jake lay on top of it, a woman's sock in her mouth. Bishop opened the closet. Clothes hung on evenly spaced hangers, including three sequined evening gowns—a red, a yellow, and black one. Stage clothes, he thought. An empty hanger hung next to the black gown. A man's and woman's robe shared the same hook on the back of the door. He searched the pockets of the man's terrycloth. They were empty except the nub of a charcoal pencil. Wigs, one red, another black, sat on the shelf above the hangers. There was room for a third. He sniffed a blouse for lingering perfume. The Saturday night car ride came back to him.

He shut the closet and walked into the kitchenette. Jake hopped off the couch and followed, still carrying the sock. Two cereal bowls— one yellow, one turquoise—sat in the corner on the floor. The yellow one held water. Bishop could see the line where it had evaporated. The turquoise bowl held food scraps and ants. Jake sniffed both bowls. On the counter was an empty bottle of Four Roses and three lowball glasses. Pink lipstick smudged one of the rims. Bishop took it all in as if seeing it for the first time. Then he heard a shotgun being racked. The sound was sharp and sudden like a hard slap. The combination of fear and excitement that'd been coursing through him was jolted with a quick dose of adrenaline. He raised his arms, still holding his cane in his right hand. Everything inside him quivered.

"Turn around. Slow."

Bishop couldn't turn quickly if he'd wanted. The pressure on his foot when pivoting made him grimace. He worried about toppling. He recognized the Black man pointing the .410 at his chest from The Colored Musicians Club, except there he'd held a saxophone, not a shotgun. Bishop didn't know his real name. Everyone called him King.

"I should shoot you right now," King said.

King stood over six feet tall, his shoulders and arms tensed in his strapped undershirt. His eyes were bloodshot and dilated, black in a pool of red. He wore tuxedo pants but no shoes. Bishop thought he looked capable of squeezing the trigger.

"Why would you want to shoot me, friend?" Bishop asked, trying hard to keep the fear from his voice.

"Some people just need killing," King said. "Where's Pearl?"

"I don't know. I'm trying to find her."

King closed an eye as if aiming. "Last time I saw her, she was with you."

"Where was that?"

"Right here, asshole," he said, his voice raising. "Don't play dumb or your hair'll be on the walls."

"I don't remember much from that night. I'm trying to fill in the blanks."

"Yeah, you were a mess. Wouldn't stop drinking, though."

Bishop nodded at the .410. "Why don't you put that cannon down and fill me in on what happened?"

"Why don't you kiss my ass?"

"Can I at least put my arms down and lean on my cane before I fall over?"

King hesitated before allowing Bishop to lower his arms. He kept the shotgun centered on his chest.

"So, Pearl and I came back here Saturday night?"

"Shit, you really don't remember," King said. He lowered the shotgun a hair.

"That part of the evening is a little hazy."

"You're hazy."

Bishop shrugged. "No argument there. What time were we here?"

"After ten. I didn't have a gig that night. I was fixing to go out when I heard you and Pearl raising a racket in the hall. I came out to see what was going on."

"We were fighting?"

"No, laughing. You fell on your ass and Pearl couldn't get you back up. Both of you were giggling like that was the funniest thing in the world. I carried your sorry self into her apartment."

"I got a bad foot," Bishop said. He raised his cane as if that explained everything.

"Shit."

"Then what happened?"

"I dumped you on the couch and you thought Lucille was the prettiest thing you'd ever seen. Couldn't stop touching her."

"Who the hell's Lucille?"

King pointed the shotgun at the dog.

"I thought her name was Jake."

"What kind of stupid motherfucker would name a girl dog Jake?" He trained the .410 back on Bishop.

"A hazy one," Bishop said. "What happened next?"

"You wanted a drink. Pearl had a bottle of Roses in her purse she said you stole from The Chez Amis."

Bishop winced. "Christ."

"Christ had nothing to do with you that night. That's a fact."

"So, we stayed here and drank?"

"One drink. That's all that was left in the bottle. Besides, you two were off to some fancy place. Pearl said she came back to pick something up before heading there."

"What'd she pick up?"

"She didn't say, and I didn't ask. Wasn't my business."

"So, we had one drink with you and then we left for a fancy place? What kind of fancy place?" Bishop asked.

"She said a friend's house. You insisted on taking Lucille with you. Pearl thought that was funny. Taking a dog to a house like that. She thought everything you said was funny. 'You're a funny man,' she kept saying. Said you'd protect her. I thought you were a damn fool. Still do. You couldn't protect shit. You couldn't even stand. Now Pearl's gone." King raised the gun higher. "You're worse than that other cracker she brought around."

"What cracker?"

"Some other white fool she was messing with. I told her to stay away from white men. Nothing good comes from that. But she wouldn't listen. She learned, though."

Bishop raised his hand, the palm facing King. "Listen, I'm going to reach into my pocket for a photograph. When I open my jacket, you'll see my gun. I'm not reaching for that. I want to show you a photo, all right?"

"That's all right with me. And it's all right if you go for your gun. I won't mind shooting you."

"I might mind. I'm getting the picture now." Bishop leaned his cane against the counter, then unbuttoned his suitcoat and pulled it open with one hand to show his holster. He dipped his other hand into his inside pocket and pulled Brandt's photograph out using his forefinger and thumb. "Is this the guy Pearl was seeing?" He held the photo out to King.

King nodded. "That's him."

"He come around a lot?"

"Enough for me to notice."

"When'd she start seeing him?"

"I don't know. There was snow on the ground. She run off with him?"

"No."

"He kill her?"

"I don't know."

"Did *you* kill her?"

"I'm trying to *find* her."

"So, you thought she was here? Hiding? That's why you broke in her apartment? Or you returning Lucille?"

"I didn't even know the dog belonged to her."

"Shit." King lowered the .410 until it pointed to the floor.

"Did she wear a blonde wig a lot?"

"She said the cracker liked it. She'd wear it for him. I told her a blonde wig on a colored woman wasn't right. She wore it to the house you went to."

"One last question," Bishop said, reaching for his cane. "What color evening gown was she wearing that night?"

"Blue dress with blue shoes. Said she had the Saturday night blues."

Chapter 10

Doris Slater sat at the Lafayette Hotel bar when Bishop made his rounds that night, an untouched martini in front of her. Her long legs crossed. She sat angled on her stool so she could watch the lobby entrance. Her eyes brightened when she saw him. He didn't head to her directly. Instead, he scanned the room, searching for faces that didn't belong. Everybody checked out—the salesmen with the loosened tie, the newlyweds honeymooning before the husband shipped out, the middle-aged couple not speaking to each other. Crawford stood behind the bar drying glasses, and nodded to him, his head so smooth and bald it reflected light. When Bishop looked again, Doris' skirt had inched higher. He hoped it wasn't by accident and wondered what game she was playing.

"Miss Slater," he said, sliding on the stool next to her. "This is a pleasant surprise. I'm hoping you have some information for me."

"Yes. Maybe. I don't know."

She rummaged in her purse for a cigarette. Bishop lit a match, and she bent to it. Her perfume smelled of gardenias. He liked it. Once her cigarette was lit, she sat back and blew smoke toward the tin ceiling. There were faint bruises on either side of her neck. Bishop waved out the match and tossed it into the ashtray. Crawford came over and asked him if he wanted anything. Like all the bartenders at The Lafayette, he wore a maroon jacket, white shirt, and black bowtie. Bishop thought he looked like an organ grinder's bald monkey. He ordered soda water before turning his attention back to Doris.

"So, what do you have for me?" Bishop asked.

"Probably nothing."

"I hope not, for your father's sake. What did you learn about the Krauts?"

"Definitely nothing."

"Then why are you here?" Crawford placed a glass of soda water in front of Bishop.

Doris waited until he walked away before she spoke. "I know something else. It has nothing to do with Germans, but it struck me as strange."

Bishop sipped the soda. "Yeah? What was that?"

"I work at city hall."

"For the War Council," Bishop said, nodding. "I know."

She touched his hand. "My office is in the basement. The Office of Permits and Planning is next door."

"So?"

"They do more than issue building permits there. They keep things on file. Blueprints. Architectural plans. Approved proposals. If a structure is within city limits, all that stuff is kept there."

"What does this have to do with Rhielman?"

She squeezed his hand. "Robert asked me to pull the blueprints for the Albright Art Gallery."

"What for?"

"They're expanding the gallery, and he said he needed the original blueprints from 1900 for some committee meeting."

"That doesn't sound strange to me, Miss Slater. They're about to break ground on the new wing. I read about it in the *Courier*. Maybe Rhielman does need them for a meeting."

"He's a councilman, Bishop. He could get the blueprints himself. Or send an aide or his secretary. But he asked *me*."

"You work right there," Bishop said. His voice was flat, unimpressed. "It would save him a trip if you grabbed them. Another excuse to meet you at some hotel and smack you around."

She squeezed his hand harder. "You don't understand. You have to sign blueprints out. I don't think he wanted anyone to know he has them. Don't you think that's suspicious?"

Bishop pulled his hand free and took hold of her chin. He guided her head gently to the right and saw the thumb-sized mark under her jaw and then to the left and saw four vertical bruises. "Did he ask you for the blueprints before or after he choked you?"

She pushed his hand away and touched her throat, trying to cover the marks. "Is that information worth something or not?"

"It's not, Miss. Slater, at least not to me. I don't care about the art gallery. Rhielman is probably too lazy to walk to the basement and get the blueprints himself. Choking women must be exhausting. I want to know what he's doing with those Germans you told me about. Unless you bring me some real information, I'm mailing that photograph to your dear old dad. He doesn't have a bad heart does he? Because mine races when I look at them."

"You look at them?"

"Sure."

"A lot?"

"Daily."

She lowered her head and took a deep breath. When she looked up, her eyes were half closed. Her hand touched his knee. "If the information about the blueprints is no good, maybe there's another way I could get the negative."

Her hand slid higher. How long had it been since a woman had touched him like that? If he'd slept with Pearl Saturday night, he didn't remember and that was the same as not being touched at all. Was Gia the last time? He remembered everything about that night. No amount of bourbon could wash that from his mind, but he didn't want to think of her at that moment. He wanted to think about Doris. Doris, with her legs uncrossed. Doris shifting close. Doris, with her hand, slender and manicured, rubbing his leg.

"There must be something I can do," she whispered, squeezing his thigh, releasing her grip, squeezing again.

He remembered the photographs he'd taken of her on her back and knees, her long legs black stockinged and gartered. It was a quick elevator ride to his room. No one would miss him. He could say he had a tip about another card game, that he'd been investigating, if Oliver asked. It was worth the negative. He had more he could hold over her.

"I think there might be several things you can do," Bishop said.

She licked her lips. "You're starting a list?"

"It's growing by the minute."

"I can see that. Maybe we should start working on that list."

"That's an excellent idea."

"Do you want me to start at the top and work my way down?"

"I think I'd enjoy that."

"I know you will. I'll make sure of it."

Crawford cleared his throat and leaned over, his head catching the ceiling lights. "Say, Bishop. Sorry to bother you, but there's a dame asking for you. Says she's a client."

Bishop looked in the direction Crawford pointed. Elizabeth Brandt sat halfway down the bar and raised her chin at him. She was wearing a mint-colored dress that looked like it would melt if he touched it. Her fingers were wrapped around a tall drink.

"God, not now," he said.

"When it rains, it pours, huh Bishop?" Crawford asked and laughed.

"You're not going to leave me, are you?" Doris asked. She dug her nails into his thigh.

"For a minute. Let me see what she wants, and then I'll get rid of her. Finish your cigarette. I'll be back before you're done with your martini." Bishop rose from the barstool, well aware of the pressure against his pleats. He drained the soda water and ordered another.

Bishop made his way to Elizabeth and sat to her left, his back facing Doris. He thought it best not to have both women in his sight at once or he'd turn to bourbon for sure. "Mrs. Brandt, what brings you to The Lafayette?"

"You, of course. It looks like you're working hard tonight, Mr. Bishop."

"You have no idea. What can I do for you?"

Crawford set the soda water in front of him and winked. Bishop reached for it and rubbed the glass across his forehead.

"I was hoping you could give me an update on my case. I drove by Mr. Weiss' office. The door was boarded. Did he go out of business? Not that that would surprise me."

"Nothing like that," Bishop said, and set the glass down. "He had another window broken."

Elizabeth straightened. "That's impossible."

"The broken glass says different."

"There was paint on the board. Was something written on it again?"

"Star of David this time."

Her face darkened. "That angers me."

"Ira wasn't too happy, either."

"Surely, the police will get involved now. That stupid kid."

Bishop's eyes narrowed. "What kid?"

"I thought you said a kid painted the window. The same one probably broke this one."

"Maybe. I told Ira I'd look into it for him."

"You can't."

"I beg your pardon?"

"I mean, that would take you away from my case."

"Your case is closed, Mrs. Brandt."

"What do you mean?"

Bishop sipped the soda before starting, already missing the smell of gardenia. "Your husband was having an affair with a colored woman named Pearl DuGaye. She was a singer, and a pretty good one from what they say. The affair had been going on at least since last winter, but he's no longer seeing her. She's disappeared, either skipped town or skipped life, probably the latter. Smart money says she's not coming back."

Elizabeth leaned back on the barstool, a small, amused smile curling her lips. "A colored woman?"

"Yes."

"Impossible."

Bishop squinted at her. "That's the second time you said impossible to cold facts. They were together for months."

"My husband wouldn't have an affair with a *colored* woman."

"You saw his self-portrait. Why do you think he named it *After Pearl*?"

"I have no idea."

"She was at your house the night she disappeared."

"*My* house? The only colored woman allowed in my house is our maid."

"Don't play blonde, Mrs. Brandt. You're too smart for that and you can't pull it off. She was at your house, and I was there, too, from what I hear. Funny you didn't mention that when we met."

Her eyebrows pinched. "When was this?"

"Last Saturday night."

"I was at our lake house Saturday night."

"Without your husband?"

"I was trying to escape the heat. I didn't know he'd had company."

"Do you always go to your lake house without your husband?"

"Not always."

"Who was there with you?"

"I was alone."

"I see." He took a swig of soda water.

"You don't really think I'd invite my husband's *colored* mistress to my house for cocktails, do you, Mr. Bishop? That I would *entertain* her?"

Bishop put the glass down. "I have no idea what you would or wouldn't do, Mrs. Brandt."

"What's your next step, Mr. Bishop?"

"There is no next step," Bishop said. "You hired me to find out if your husband was having an affair. He was, but Pearl's gone. Like I said, I'm betting she's not coming back. Ever. There won't be any photographs of them together, clothed or otherwise. There won't be any sworn testimony from hotel clerks or waitresses or from grease monkeys who pumped their gas at out-of-the-way places. There will be no evidence to file for divorce. The case is closed, Mrs. Brandt. I'll have Ira send our bill in the morning."

"It's not closed, Mr. Bishop. This colored singer…"

"Pearl DuGaye."

"…was *not* having an affair with my husband," Elizabeth said. "You have the wrong woman. Maybe she was posing for him, but they certainly were not lovers."

"They were," Bishop said. He softened his voice. "I'm sorry."

She took a long drink from her tall glass, the outside sweating with condensation. Bishop glanced over his shoulder at Doris. Her legs were crossed again, her hem even higher. She raised her martini glass to show him it was almost empty. He finished his soda water wishing it were bourbon.

Elizabeth put down her cocktail. "You need to keep investigating, Mr. Bishop. You need to find my husband's mistress."

"You're not listening."

"My husband would never sleep with a negress," she said, driving each word home with a tap of her finger against the bar. "We're not those kinds of people."

"Those kind?"

"And I don't want you wasting your time searching for kids who break windows and paint doors. I want you concentrating on *my* case. Do you understand me? Let parents deal with their children."

Before Bishop could answer, Crawford called his name and tilted his bald head toward the end of the bar. Bishop first looked at him and then traced his tilt to Gia. She waved at him from her stool.

"Good Christ," he muttered.

Crawford laughed. "It's pouring harder by the minute, Bishop. I wish it'd rain on me."

Elizabeth followed his gaze. "She's much too pretty to be your triggerman."

"She's much too pretty to be a lot of things. Excuse me for a moment." Bishop grabbed his cane and went to Gia. Sitting next to her, he could see both Doris and Elizabeth down the bar. Crawford served him another soda water without him asking.

"Soda. I'm proud of you," she said, and ordered a Sidecar.

"Don't be. I'm hoping to lose merit badges tonight. What are you doing here?"

"Well, it's good to see you, too, Bishop."

"Sorry. Doris and Elizabeth Brandt both showed up at the same time. The hotel is probably getting robbed while I'm babysitting them."

"What do they want?" she asked.

"Doris thought she had some information, but it was bupkis. It wasn't even about Krauts. I filled Elizabeth in on Pearl. She doesn't believe me."

"Why not?"

"Says her husband would never sleep with a Black woman. I told him he had been, but it was over, and Pearl was probably dead. She doesn't buy it and wants me to keep looking for his real lover."

"Is she dead?"

"Her closet's filled with clothes. I don't think she skipped town."

He didn't tell her about the two missing slugs from his gun. Christ, he needed a drink.

Gia looked down the bar at the two women. "So why are they still here?"

"They're both negotiating. I need to get back to them. How come you stopped in?"

"I just left Meyer."

"Now? I thought you met him this morning?"

"We spent the day together."

"That's swell." He rubbed the soda glass across his forehead again. "What's he like?"

"Boring. Not my type at all."

"He's a murder suspect."

"That's the most interesting thing about him. The rest is unbuttered toast."

Bishop looked down at Doris. She held up her empty martini glass. He told Crawford to mix her another and put it on his bill.

"You're buying her a drink?" Gia asked.

"We're not done negotiating."

"What, exactly, are you negotiating?"

"For the negative," he said. "What else?"

"You tell me."

"Tell me what you did with Brandt all day."

"He sketched me in the morning."

"Clothed?"

"Completely. Then we had lunch at a little bistro right near his studio."

"Still clothed?"

She hit his arm. "Don't be an ass."

"And after lunch?"

"After lunch we went to the art gallery."

"The Albright? Why?"

"To get out of the heat. He showed me his favorite paintings. I think he was trying to impress me. He's partial to nudes."

"Most men are. I'm glad you had a pleasant day. I had a shotgun pointed at me."

"By whom?"

Bishop started to answer but stopped as he watched Doris gather her purse to leave.

"Sorry, slugger," Crawford said, walking toward him. He set the Sidecar in front of Gia. "Swing and a miss. That tall broad says thanks but no thanks to the drink."

Bishop struggled to his feet as Doris approached.

"Looks like your dance card is full tonight, Bishop," she said, not slowing down. "You'll have to take care of your list by yourself."

She left Bishop sniffing gardenia as she breezed by.

"What list?" Gia asked.

"Krauts," he mumbled. "Possible Nazis."

Gia looked past his shoulder. "Here comes the other one."

Bishop turned and saw Elizabeth approaching.

She smiled at Gia. "Miss Alessi, it's good to see you again."

"Likewise."

"I assume as Mr. Bishop's associate you're up to date on my case?"

"I am."

"Excellent. I can speak freely then. I want you to keep investigating my husband, Mr. Bishop. You need to find his real lover and forget this nonsense about Pearl DuGaye."

Bishop raised his hand to stop her. "As I said—"

"I'm prepared to raise my fee, given the difficulty of the task and your reluctance. I don't think you'll object to a higher fee, do you?"

"I certainly won't. But you're wasting your money, Mrs. Brandt."

"It's settled then. And with the rate I'm paying, I expect to be your top priority. I don't want you chasing after children with paintbrushes. Do you understand me, Mr. Bishop?"

"Perfectly."

She looked at her watch. "I'm late meeting Meyer. You'll have to excuse me, but I do look forward to your next update, Mr. Bishop."

"So do I, but I doubt it will be any different from the one I just gave you."

"Think positively, Mr. Bishop."

"That's not his strong suit," Gia said.

"He has room for improvement, then."

"You have no idea," Gia said, and sipped her Sidecar.

Elizabeth shook Bishop's hand and left the bar. He sat back on the stool next to Gia. His kidneys ached and temples throbbed. He'd spent too much time on his foot today and thought of the bottle in his room.

"There's a woman who's used to getting her way," Gia said. "I like that."

"It's easy to get your way when you have money." Bishop took an unsatisfying sip of soda.

"Well, at least you'll get paid more. You need the money."

"The more time I spend with her, the more off I think she is. Maybe it's just rich people."

"I wouldn't know. There aren't any rich people on Seventh Street. What are you going to do about her husband?"

"I guess I'll track down hotel clerks and gas station attendants who'll swear they saw him with Pearl. Maybe then she'll believe me. What a waste of time."

"Why's it a waste?"

He looked into her eyes. "Because Brandt's already moved on to something better."

"You mean me?" she asked, leaning back on her stool to look at him. "Bishop, did you pay me a compliment? That's a first."

"It's the soda water talking."

"You should drink more soda then."

"He has you figured for the next Pearl on his string."

"Well, that's not going to happen," she said. She reached for her glass.

"I hope not. I'd hate to take dirty pictures of you two at some cheap motel."

Gia stared at him.

"You don't think I would?" he asked.

She sipped her drink and set it down before answering. "I think there's nothing you'd enjoy more than taking pictures of me, dirty or otherwise. But you wouldn't show them to Elizabeth or anyone else. You'd keep them for yourself."

"You're sure of that? I'm getting paid to do a job."

"I'm sure of it, but it's not going to come to that."

"It sounded like you had a swell date."

"Here's the thing, Bishop," she said, leaning in. "Guess what I was thinking about the whole time I was with Meyer?"

"Posing for him?"

"I was thinking about you. 'Would Bishop have asked that question?' 'Would Bishop think that was important?' 'How does Bishop know when people are lying?' 'What wisecrack would Bishop make if he heard that?' 'I wish Bishop was here to see this painting.'"

"You were thinking all that?"

"And a lot of other things, too."

"Like what?"

"Like I wish it was you who took me to that little bistro for lunch."

He smiled. "Yeah?

"Yeah, jackass. And all the while you were here *negotiating* with Doris Slater."

"I was working a case, like you," he said, trying to sound innocent.

"You were working something all right."

He swigged soda instead of answering. It only took a thigh squeeze and whiff of gardenia for him to play it wrong with Doris. She wasn't going to find any information about those Germans. Hell, she wouldn't even try now that she knew she had something he wanted. What all men wanted. She'd played him like a rube, and he knew it. Now he'd be forced to mail the negative to her father. He hated that it had come to this.

"Damn it, Bishop. I knew you'd be in the bar," Oliver Prine said, heading toward him in a straight line.

"I'm working, Oliver. See?" he said, gesturing around the room. "No hookers. No jailbait." He held up his soda water. "No booze."

"We have complaints about a dog barking in one of the rooms. Guests are furious. *I'm* furious. You need to get that dog out of here."

Bishop sighed. "Fine. Another exciting case for the house dick to solve. The Case of The Barking Dog. Which room?"

"Yours."

"Since when does my goldfish bark?"

"Go!"

Bishop told Crawford to put Gia's Sidecar on his tab, and the three of them walked into the lobby. Benny The Junkman was standing at the front desk, his cart parked inside the door.

"Bums are wandering in off the street now? How did he get past the bellman?" Oliver asked.

"Benny's harmless."

"I don't care if he juggles knives. Our guests don't want to wait in line with a hobo. Get him out of here."

"I'll take care of it," Bishop said. Bishop hustled to the front desk as fast as he could. "Benny, what do you know? What do you hear?"

Benny faced his friend. "I know things, Bishop."

"Yeah? Good things?"

"I know where your green car is. I saw it."

"Where did you see it, Benny?"

"Here."

"What do you mean?"

"Right here. At the hotel. Parked in back in its usual spot."

"You sure it's my car, Benny?"

"I know your green car, Bishop. I saw it. Keys are in it."

"I'll be damned," Bishop said, and opened his wallet. He pulled out a five spot and passed it to him. "You did good, Benny. Real good. You're a better detective than I am. Go to that deli around the corner and get yourself a sandwich."

"Okay, Bishop. You need anything else, let me know."

"Will do."

Bishop watched to make sure Benny and his cart left the lobby before joining Gia and Oliver at the elevators. They were holding a car for him. He'd have to wait to check the trunk.

"Did you give that bum money, Bishop?" Oliver asked. "Is that what I saw? That encourages them, you know. He'll be back panhandling tomorrow, looking for more."

"That's no bum, Oliver. That's the finest detective in the city. A war hero. He's working undercover. He broke our stolen car case today. Isn't his disguise aces?"

"Jesus Christ, Bishop."

The bronze elevator doors shut, and they rode up in silence. A few minutes ago, he thought he'd be taking this ride with Doris. He shook his head. Nothing turns out the way he hoped. Maybe hoping was the problem.

They heard Jake barking as soon as the elevator opened. Oliver stepped off the elevator first. "That better not be the same dog I saw you with in the lobby the other day, Bishop," he said.

"I don't have a dog, Oliver. That's against the rules. You know that."

They hurried down the hall. Bishop pulled out his room key but tried the knob first. It was unlocked.

"Are you sure you locked it before you went downstairs?" Gia asked.

"Positive. The house detective is unreliable. They say he drinks. I always lock it." He unbuttoned his jacket and drew The Fitz. "You two stay here."

He stood off to the side and pushed the door open, hoping to find Doris in her garters waiting for him, but he didn't smell gardenias. He smelled rot and decay. Before stepping inside, he covered his mouth with his handkerchief. The room was dark. He reached for the light switch. Jake was shut in the bathroom, barking and jumping against the door, her nails scratching against wood. Bishop let her out and she ran to the bed. The barking deteriorated to crying. He followed her, Gia and Oliver trailing a few feet behind with their hands over their mouths.

"Christ," Bishop said, and holstered his gun. It wasn't Doris Slater waiting for him in his bed.

Pearl DuGaye was tucked under the covers.

Chapter 11

Darcy had Bishop sitting on the floor in the hotel hallway, his hands cuffed behind him forcing him to bend forward. Two bulls stood over him, one a head taller than the other, both making him feel small. Jake rested her head on his thigh, whimpering and trembling. Coroner orderlies carried Pearl out of Bishop's room on a stretcher. Kerchiefs covered their faces.

"For God's sakes, use the service elevator!" Oliver yelled. "Go out the back, not the lobby."

Darcy sauntered behind, his hat pushed back on his head, his smile growing wider when he saw Bishop. "You're fucked," he said. "You won't weasel out of this one. You're getting the chair for sure." He reached down, opened Bishop's jacket, and took his gun from his holster.

"So, she was shot?" Bishop asked. "How many times?"

"You tell me, Weasel. Put it in your confession."

"How would I know that?"

"Because you pulled the trigger."

A flashbulb popped, blinding Bishop so he only saw stars. When his vision cleared, he saw Timothy Flynn holding the camera.

"Anything for a story, right Timothy?" Bishop asked.

"Sorry, Bishop. You're frontpage news. You got a quote for me?"

"Make something up. Make me sound innocent. Spell my name right."

"Nothing'll make you sound innocent," Darcy said. "There's a dead girl in your bed, last seen alive with you. I'd start thinking seriously about your last meal. I recommend pork chops."

"Do you really think that if I killed her, I'd hide her body in *my* bed?"

"You're a sick fuck, Bishop," Darcy said. "A twisted boozehound weasel who steps in front of taxis. Who knows what you do when you're drunk? I asked the M.E. to check her for recent sexual violation."

The elevators opened and Gia hurried from the doors. Darcy, the bulls, and Bishop all watched her stride toward them, a small notebook in her hand. Flynn took her picture.

"Did you call Ira?" Bishop asked.

"He's on his way."

"That fat shyster can't help you," Darcy said.

"What'd you find out?" Bishop asked.

Gia read from the notebook. "At eleven a.m. the maid cleaned your room. No body was in your bed then. At three-thirty p.m. you had a bottle of bourbon sent up, which we'll talk about later. The porter says there was no odor and only the dog was on the bed. At five o'clock you reported downstairs for work."

"That gives you ninety minutes to sneak down to your car and lug that stiff up," Darcy said. "Plenty of time."

"My car's been missing a week. I didn't even know it was here until a few minutes ago."

"Did you report it stolen?" Darcy asked.

"No. Talk to Benny. He was looking for it."

Darcy laughed. "The junkman? He's out in the alley yelling about mustard gas. I don't think he'll make a good witness."

"Well, ask the Gospels, then. I saw one of them driving it."

"Which one? Mathew, Mark, Luke, or John?"

"Christ, I can't tell them apart. Interrogate them all."

"I'll get right on that, Bishop," Darcy said.

"Lieutenant, let me ask you something. Think hard, all right?" Bishop said. "Here's the question. Have you ever seen me walk?"

"Sure, if you call that walking."

"Correct. I limp. I use a cane. My foot is garbage. Explain to me how I carried a corpse up the stairs with one hand on the railing and the other holding my cane."

Darcy shifted his weight. "Who said you took the stairs? Maybe you used the service elevator."

"Again, how did I carry her? Slung over my shoulder? How could I do that without toppling over? Besides, she's stiffer than you are, literally dead weight."

"Maybe you had an accomplice. Maybe Ira helped you."

"A three-hundred-pound man and a cripple carried a corpse, and nobody saw?" Bishop shook his head. "Not likely. Even a crack lawman like yourself would notice that."

"I don't know how you did it, but I know you did it. The DA will figure out the rest."

"Somewhere in a dark corner of your small cop brain you know I didn't kill her. Ira will have me out on bail by breakfast." Bishop switched his attention to Oliver. "I'll need a new room. This one smells like a morgue with bum refrigerators."

"A new room?" Oliver said. "You're out of your mind. This is terrible for the hotel. A murder? A dead body? The house detective arrested? Bishop, you're not getting a new room. You're not getting *any* room. You're *fired*!"

* * *

When Darcy was called to another crime scene, Bishop told the taller bull he wanted to kill himself. He'd been in the county tombs before—public drunkenness, vagrancy, trespassing—and knew what it was like to be held in the tank with the other unwashed who found themselves in Dutch. He wanted his own cage. The tall cop was familiar with Bishop and how his foot had been crushed. He thought it possible that he'd might try hurting himself again. He locked him in an observation cell and told him not to do anything stupid. A paper-pushing guard sat in full view and checked if he was still among the breathing when he remembered to, which wasn't very often. They'd taken his cane so all he could do was sit or lie on the metal bunk; they considered its pewter-handle a weapon. He wondered if they were worried that he'd use it on the guard or to beat himself to death.

Bishop knew he was in trouble when the headache started, a dull throb that originated at the top of his skull then expanded until it pressed against his temples. He wished he'd gotten his flask in with him, but the cops had taken that along with his other possessions. The sweats and chills came after the headache had grown to a vise. He asked for a blanket, but the paper-pusher denied him without looking up.

"Wouldn't want you to hang yourself with it on my watch," he said, a hint of Cork in his voice. "I'll give you one when my shift ends. You can kill yourself after I leave, Weasel."

Bishop's heart raced in intervals as he shivered. One minute it would pound like it was trying to work itself free, the next he'd wonder if it was beating at all. He thought of the bourbon in his room, but imagining tipping the bottle down his throat didn't ease him. He waited for the nausea to hit, and, when it did, it came out swinging, curling him on his cot, knees to chest, his face pressed against the stained mattress.

Every nerve felt raw and exposed, stripped bare like an arcing wire. His bruised kidneys screamed when he breathed. His foot blazed, the crushed bones afire even when he didn't move it. He'd gone through this before and knew promises would come next: to quit drinking, to be stronger, to make amends. The same promises he'd made and ignored for years. But he swore them aloud again, curled on his cot between dry heaves, bartering with Jesus that he'd keep these vows if the nausea would end. His words fell heavy from his dry mouth, landing on the cement floor next to drops of sweat, tears. Bishop ignored the voice inside him that whispered that only the guard had heard his prayers. He didn't give a shit either.

His head jerked to the side like one of the Gospels was kicking his skull again. Sometimes the kicks were violent, and his head would snap, and other times it barely twitched. In either case, he couldn't control it. The urge to move, to pace, to run again gripped him, but he couldn't take two steps without his cane. Instead, he squirmed on his cot and the poor substitute frustrated him more. On different occasions he yelled for water, a blanket, a doctor, and each time was told to fuck off in an Irish lilt. He begged for sleep, but that prayer went unanswered, too.

* * *

Bishop stepped out of the Erie County Holding Center four days later, his tie loosened, his suit wrinkled and smelling of sweat and vomit. He palmed the perspiration from his face and took deep breaths, his heart still galloping. Ira's Hudson was parked in front. Leaning hard on his cane, not trusting his shaking limbs, he walked toward the car. The passenger door opened, and Gia went to him, her arms wide. He held her close, breathing her in, trying to remember the last time he held something that felt and smelled so good. Then he remembered the night they'd spent together. It seemed like centuries ago, something so distant he wondered if it was all imagined. He tried not to cry. She held him by the biceps, pushed him to arm's length, and inspected him.

"I've seen you worse."

"I feel like aces," he said, his throat raw from retching, his voice raspy.

"You look like deuces. You're shaking."

"You got me aflutter. Is that a new perfume?"

"Ivory soap. Let's get out of this place."

Bishop slumped in the front seat, and Gia climbed in back. Ira stuck out his thick mitt. Bishop shook it but didn't have the strength to return the squeeze.

"Thanks for springing me."

"It took longer than I thought," Ira said. "I'm sorry."

"It couldn't have been easy."

"The dead body in your bed complicated things."

"They always do," Bishop said.

"Who put her there?" Gia asked.

Bishop swallowed a few times before he answered, wetting his lips and mouth, trying to get his throat and tongue to work. "I thought it strange that both Elizabeth and Doris showed up at The Lafayette. Doris came on way too friendly considering she hates me. I knew it that night but chose to ignore it. That was a mistake."

"You think it was an act?" Gia asked.

"Unless I'm more charming than I thought."

"That must be it," she said, and squeezed his shoulder.

A tremor rippled through him, and he sagged against the door. His face glistened with sweat.

"God forgive me," Gia said, and held out a bottle.

Bishop waved it away and continued talking with his eyes closed, his head leaning out the window. Rushing air cooled his face. He wondered if he still had a fever. "I figured Doris was keeping me busy at the bar while her friends snuck Pearl up to my room. Maybe they gave her the high sign when they were done. Maybe that's why she left so suddenly. I don't know. I'm not sure why Elizabeth was there. Maybe she was backup if Doris couldn't keep my attention. Not all the pieces fit yet. Or I'm not thinking straight. It's hard to concentrate. Maybe Doris just wanted the negative. Maybe Elizabeth just wanted to talk about her case."

"Elizabeth called me after your arrest," Ira said.

Bishop opened his eyes. "To extend her condolences?"

"To have me send the final bill. She said with you incarcerated she needed to find another detective and, by extension, another lawyer. She was very curt. Evidently, she wants nothing to do with me."

"She won't believe any shamus or mouthpiece who tells her that her husband had a colored mistress," Bishop said.

"Maybe she'll rehire us when she knows you've made bail."

"The case is solved, Ira. He was having an affair with Pearl."

Ira shook his head. "She doesn't think so. Just keep an eye on Brandt. He'll cheat again. They always do."

"That's what I'm afraid of."

"Don't start, Bishop," Gia said.

Ira curved around Niagara Square to Court Street.

"Where are we headed?" Bishop asked.

"Your hotel," Ira answered. "I thought you'd want to clean up and change your clothes. You look like you should sleep."

"The Lafayette? I was fired and evicted," Bishop said. "Evidently, they have a No-Corpse policy I wasn't aware of."

"Miss Alessi's fixed all that."

Bishop shifted around to face Gia, the effort exhausting him. "How? Oliver wanted my head."

"I explained to him that it would be good publicity for the hotel if they stood by you. They should take the high ground and publicly state that you've been wrongly accused of murder and that you vow to clear your good name as well as the good name of the hotel. Everyone is confident you'll do so. Afterall, you're Nicholas Bishop, the house detective who uncovered a city councilman's salacious affair and an illegal gambling game involving the same councilman. Nicholas Bishop is not a murderer. He protects our city."

"And he bought that bunk?" Bishop asked.

"Not a bit," Gia said. "But Flynn added it to his article anyway and quoted Oliver. It painted him in a corner. He couldn't retract it without looking like a heel. You've become a bit of celebrity."

"Flynn did that for me?"

"No, for Gia," Ira said. "I think Mr. Flynn is sweet on her."

"I'll need to talk to him about that. So, I still have my room at the hotel?"

"A new one," Gia said. "Same floor down the hall. I moved all your clothes and files yesterday when they were done with the crime scene."

"And my job?"

"You're on a leave of absence to concentrate solely on the murder and restoring the good name of The Lafayette. At least that's the official story."

"With pay?"

"Don't be greedy. You'll be quietly fired after this blows over. Or in jail. Either way you won't be living at The Lafayette much longer. And don't expect a Christmas card from Oliver. He's not happy with any of us."

"You did good, Alessi," Bishop said.

"Damn right I did. I'm giving myself a raise as soon as you rehire me."

"Where's Jake?" he asked.

"At my mom's. I didn't know how long you'd be locked up."

"Good. I was worried about her."

"You were worried about something other than yourself?" Ira asked. "Jail does change a man. Now, what about Elizabeth Brandt?"

"I'll talk to her. If she wants to waste her money and rehire us, I'm not going to stop her."

"It's not all good news, though," Gia said. "You're stuck with me as your driver. Darcy impounded the Packard as evidence. Evidently the body was in your trunk."

"Christ," he said, trying hard to sound annoyed. "Did they find Pearl's wig?"

"They found her blue dress in your car. It'd been ripped. No wig, though. Is the wig important?"

"She was wearing it the night she disappeared, but she didn't have it on when we found her in my bed."

"I'll ask Flynn if he knows anything about it," she said.

"No, *I'll* ask Flynn. You stay away from him. One drunk in your life is enough. Anything else I should know about?"

"Hand him the paper," Ira said.

She passed him the front section. The headline announced Rhielman's resignation from the city council. Below the fold was an article about Pearl that carried Flynn's byline. Bishop couldn't focus his burning eyes. The newsprint blurred.

"Give me the short version," he said, pretending to read.

"The coroner announced her cause of death," Gia said.

"Let me guess. Gunshot wounds. Two slugs from a .38."

"No, a nine-millimeter."

* * *

Gia offered to stay with Bishop, but he sent her home with the bourbon and his suit to be dry cleaned. He hoped the crying, praying, and heaving was behind him. He didn't want her around if it wasn't. The idea of soaking in a hot bath appealed to him, but he wasn't sure if he'd have the strength to haul himself out of the clawfoot tub when he was finished. Instead, he washed himself as best he could at the pedestal sink, avoiding the puffiness and pallor in the mirror. The kidney bruises were fading, and his piss was no longer pink. He leaned on the sink with both arms and let out a breath he'd carried all week. He hadn't shot Pearl DuGaye.

He crawled into bed naked, the sheets and pillowcase crisp. Every part of him—the heavy lids, the tired muscles—cried for sleep, but it still wouldn't come. The new bed wasn't comfortable, but he couldn't decide if it was too hard or too soft. He tried different positions to find the sweet spot but couldn't. When he was on the verge of drifting off, his eyes would snap open, convinced there were voices outside his door or in his room. Each time he checked, the room and hallway were empty. When he did slip into sleep, it wouldn't last. He'd gasp and sit straight up, convinced a faceless man was by his bed or Pearl's naked corpse was lying next to him, the rot still fresh in his nostrils.

That was enough for him. He got up and took another sink bath and dressed in a light-colored suit with a baby blue tie and socks that matched. He slapped his face a few times for color and then called Gia. He needed a ride to Elizabeth Brandt's house.

Chapter 12

The Brandt's lion doorknocker was as big as Bishop's face. He grabbed the ring in the lion's mouth and rapped it against the oak. The rocking chairs lined along the porch sat motionless, the air heavy and still as he waited. Gia had dropped him at the corner, and he'd struggled to the house by himself. He didn't want Brandt seeing them together.

A maid opened the door. Her eyes widened when she saw him. He wasn't sure if fear or surprise caused it. "I'd like to see Mrs. Brandt, please," Bishop said, trying to make his voice gentle, kind.

"Who is it, Dinah?" Elizabeth called, from inside the house.

"Mr. Bishop," she answered.

"Mr. *Bishop*?"

"Yes, ma'am."

Elizabeth came to the door. She wore a cream-colored tennis dress. A matching belt cinched her waist and the wide pleated skirt fell to tanned thighs. Her cheeks were flushed, and her arms shone with perspiration. She held a tall glass of lemonade, the cubes rattling when she walked.

"Mr. Bishop," she repeated, her face wide with astonishment. "You're out of jail."

"I am," he said, forcing a smile. "I hope you don't mind me stopping by unannounced. I was hoping we could talk."

"Of course. I only have a minute, though. Let's sit on the porch.

Maybe we'll get lucky, and a breeze will kick up," she said. "Dinah, bring Mr. Bishop some lemonade."

"Water, please," Bishop said, and followed her to the rocking chairs. He sat to the left of her, and everything felt familiar—the hardness of the chair, the rocking motion, the angle to the street.

"What did you wish to discuss, Mr. Bishop?"

"Ira mentioned you let us go."

"I didn't think I'd be seeing you again. I thought I'd need to retain another investigator."

"As you can see, I'm back amongst the living. I was hoping you'd consider rehiring us. Ira's certain the charges against me will be dropped soon."

"Can't I just rehire you? I'm not particularly fond of Mr. Weiss."

"I'm not in private practice anymore. I work for Ira. It's both of us or none of us."

"If that's the way it must be," she said, though her voice and eyes remained flat. "I'm not dealing with him anymore. I'll deal with you from now on. Or perhaps your associate, Miss Alessi. I like her. But I'm done with Mr. Weiss."

"What did Ira do to offend you?"

"Let's just say I'm used to a different type of attorney."

"I'm certain that's true, but our fee remains the same."

"Of course. And our understanding is the same, as well."

"Understanding?"

"That my case is your priority. You won't be wasting time looking for delinquents who deface windows."

"Right."

"Then we're back to business as usual, Mr. Bishop."

"Ira's assuming he'll represent you if this investigation leads to divorce proceedings."

"I'll make that decision once you bring evidence of my husband's infidelity."

"There won't be any photographs, just the statements of people who saw Pearl and your husband together—bellboys, hotel clerks."

Dinah brought ice water. She avoided looking at him.

"Thank you," he said.

Dinah nodded, pressing her lips together into something like a smile.

Elizabeth waited until the maid had disappeared into the house before she spoke. "I've already told you, my husband is incapable of having an affair with a colored woman."

Bishop drank half the glass. His throat was parched. "I'm afraid I have to disagree, Mrs. Brandt."

"Can we agree that Pearl DuGaye is dead, Mr. Bishop?"

"Since I found her body in my bed and was arrested for her murder, we can most certainly agree on that."

"So, she's dead, but my husband is still behaving like he's having an affair. I'm no detective, but I would say there's another woman involved."

"How's he behaving?"

"Whispering on the phone. Away from the house hours at a time with no explanation of where he's been. Smiling as if he's remembering a delicious dessert. I've seen it before, Mr. Bishop. I don't even know where he went this morning."

"When did this start?"

"Right after you were arrested."

Bishop's stomach clenched. He pictured Gia whispering on her mother's hallway phone or stretched out on his new hotel room bed, smiling into the receiver, and wondered how many times they'd seen each other while he was sick and locked away. He finished the water.

"So, as you can see, this case has not been concluded," Elizabeth said.

"It seems that way," Bishop agreed. "If he's cheating again, I'll catch him at it. I'll catch both of them. I'll get you photographs."

"Excellent. I'll expect an update in a few days." She looked at her watch. "You'll have to excuse me. I need to shower."

"Of course," he said, and started to rise.

"No, sit. Rest a bit. Dinah can bring you more water. You look exhausted. Jail must've been awful for you."

Bishop forced another smile. "It was all right. I got a little sick in there. Prison food must not agree with me."

"You'll feel better in a few days. For now, enjoy the porch as long as you wish. Hand me your glass."

"Thank you," he said, and passed it to her. He heard her call Dinah's name as she stepped into the house.

Bishop closed his eyes and rocked. The motion was calming as it had been the first time he'd sat on this porch. He wondered if he fell asleep in this chair the night Pearl had disappeared, because now, with the sun warm on his face, he felt himself drifting under. How long had it been since he'd slept? He couldn't remember.

"Your water."

His eyes fluttered open. He stopped rocking. Dinah was close enough to touch him. He wondered how long she'd been standing there. He took the glass. "Thank you," he said. "Have a seat."

"I'm working. Mrs. Brandt wouldn't like it if I was sitting on her porch."

"I'm working, too," he said. "I'm a private detective. I have a few questions for you."

"I need to get back inside."

"What do you do here?"

"Cook. Clean. Answer the door and telephone." She shrugged. "The usual."

"You recognized me when you opened the door."

She didn't respond.

"You knew my name when you announced me."

Dinah stared at him.

"You were working the night Pearl DuGaye disappeared, weren't you?" asked Bishop. "That's when you first saw me and learned my name. I was here with her. Were the Brandt's having a party that night?"

She shot a glance at the door before answering. Her voice was low. Bishop leaned forward. "It wasn't a real party with singing and dancing and folks having fun," she said. "It was more like a meeting with Mr. Brandt and a few others sitting around talking seriously, hushing when I came in with drinks."

"Was Mrs. Brandt there?" Bishop asked.

She shook her head. "No. There weren't women there until Pearl showed up."

"Where was Mrs. Brandt?"

"I don't know. She doesn't tell me her business."

"Did Pearl always come to the house when Mrs. Brandt was away?"

Dinah's eyes glistened. "Only one time before that."

"When was that?"

"February eleventh."

"You remember the exact date?" Bishop asked. "Why?"

"That's my birthday. She came to see me."

"You were friends?"

"Pearl's my niece. Was my niece," she said, her voice breaking.

"She came to wish you a happy birthday?"

She pulled a handkerchief from her pocket and dabbed her eyes. "Brought me a cake. I wished she never did that. I wished she forgot all about my birthday. That she never came to this house."

"Why?" Bishop asked. "What happened that day?"

"That's when she met Mr. Brandt. He came in the kitchen. He liked her right off. Started talking about her coloring and cheekbones. I told her after to stay away, but she liked him, too."

"Why'd you warn her off?"

She waved a hand. "He's married. He's white. He's rich. How much trouble did that girl need?"

"So," Bishop said, trying to piece it together. "He invited her to the party the night she disappeared, and she brought me along."

"I said it wasn't a party and she wasn't invited. She just showed up wearing a blonde wig and holding your drunken self up. Everybody got mad when she walked through that front door with you and Lucille."

"Mad?" Bishop asked. "Why?"

"Why you think?"

He sipped from the glass, swishing the water in his mouth before swallowing. "Did Pearl bring something with her?"

"Besides you?"

"A box or a gift? Something for Mr. Brandt?"

"She had something under her arm, but I couldn't tell what it was."

"No guesses?"

She shook her head. "Couldn't see it clearly."

"Okay, what happened next?"

"Mr. Brandt ordered me to stay in the kitchen, but I cracked the door a bit."

"What'd you hear?"

"Everybody asking why she was there. Yelling. Some were mad because she was wearing the wig. Thought Pearl was making fun of them somehow."

"Was she?"

Dinah shrugged. "I don't know. Maybe. Never saw her wearing it before. Didn't look natural. But she'd been drinking. I could tell that right off. Not as much as you, but too much for her."

"Who did Mr. Brandt say she was? How did he explain her?"

"Said she was his model. That he was painting her. That part was true. Pearl told me about her portrait."

"Then what?"

"Then she introduced you as the famous detective Nicholas Bishop. Said you were front page news. Always solving crimes. Her protector. You took off your hat and bowed deep like you were meeting the queen of England, and you fell right over. Made a big crashing sound. Lucille started barking her head off. You and Pearl thought that was the funniest damn thing. Laughing like fools. Nobody else was laughing. Made everyone madder is all."

Bishop shut his eyes, trying to remember, glad he couldn't.

"Couple men picked you up and took you outside. They handled you rough, but they weren't gone long enough to hurt you much. They came right back."

"I'm pretty sure they dropped me in this rocker," Bishop said, patting the chair arm. "I remember rocking. I don't think anyone hit me. What happened with Pearl?"

"I don't know. Mr. Brandt came to the kitchen and said I was done for the night and could go."

"You left?"

Dinah brushed a tear. "I should've stayed. I should've waited out front for her, but I was scared. I tried calling her apartment later. I called all night."

"Why were you scared?"

"Everybody was so mad. You could see it on their faces. Like she'd walked in on something she wasn't supposed to." Dinah lowered her voice, talked through clenched teeth. "This skinny little man was the angriest. Didn't look old enough to shave. Kept calling her *Schwarze*."

Bishop leaned closer. "He called her that? A *Schwarze*?"

Dinah nodded. "A couple times."

"Was his name Krieger?"

"Don't know. Never seen him before. Never seen any of them before except the one."

"Which one?"

"Councilman Rhielman."

"Rhielman?" Bishop said. "You sure it was him?"

"I'm sure. He's here a lot. He left before you got here."

"You mean today?"

"You must've passed him on the street."

"Why was he here?"

"He was playing tennis with Mrs. Brandt."

* * *

Bishop sat in Ira's Hudson. The seat was broken, frozen in place, forcing him to sit too far back from the steering wheel. He wanted a cigarette but wouldn't risk having a striking match or glowing Chesterfield spotted. He was parked in eyeshot of Rhielman's house, and it occurred to him that he'd spent much of his life waiting. Waiting to tail a suspect. Waiting with his camera for a motel door to open. Waiting in his window for his mother to come home.

Practice had made him patient, able to sit still for hours in a car or stand shadowed in an alley, the only movement his arm raising a flask. Tonight, he didn't move at all, a statue behind the wheel, a living advertisement for the Hudson Motor Car Company. Incarceration had forced him to dry out. He didn't even bring a bottle.

He liked the quiet of waiting, the solitude. He never felt alone. Instead, he felt part of something—part of the car, or alley, or night. If the *Courier-Express* published a list of the best detectives in the city, his name wouldn't be included. He knew that. It wouldn't even appear on the second page, but he prided himself on his ability to surveil without being seen, to become a pair of hidden eyes, watching and waiting, blending in with his environment like some camouflaged predator in the wild. The farthest damn thing from a weasel.

Ten years ago, Teddy Thurston's name would have been near the top of that list. Bishop was sure of it. Lucky Teddy had survived the Great War unharmed except for a strong taste for brandy and an unlucky bout with venereal disease, which he often referred to as 'that unfortunate Paris incident'. After being discharged, he joined the Buffalo Police Department but quit after a few years to become a private investigator.

He'd found it difficult to enforce the Volstead Act while carrying a hip flask. One day while staring at a display window and deciding whether to enter the store, he felt a hand reach for his wallet. He grabbed the thin wrist of a boy with dirty fingernails and frayed shirt cuffs. Bishop was no more than fifteen, and smelled of bootleg whisky, but there was an intelligence about him and a face that no one would notice. He was perfect for an operative that Teddy could groom and become his eyes and ears on the street.

"Lesson one," Lucky Teddy'd said, still holding his wrist, "only pick pockets when sober."

Teddy would've liked Gia and would've scolded Bishop for borrowing the Hudson and not asking her to drive tonight. She'd have been eager to do it, excited to be in the field again. And Bishop wouldn't deny that he liked the idea of spending hours next to her, listening to her banter, looking at her as often as he wanted. But he'd asked Ira if he could borrow his car instead. Maybe Elizabeth Brandt was right, and her husband had started seeing someone. Maybe that someone was Gia. She'd told him at The Lafayette that she wasn't interested in Brandt, and he'd hoped that was true. But for all he knew, she was with him tonight and it was his own fault. He'd pushed her toward Brandt. He'd have to start following her soon.

At quarter to eleven, Rhielman's Ford pulled out of the driveway. Bishop waited until the Ford made a left at the corner before starting his engine and snapping on the headlights. He rushed to the stop sign and made the turn, but it was easy to spot the Ford. Bishop had broken one of the taillight covers while it was parked in Rhielman's driveway. One side shown red, the other fractured white.

Rhielman drove at a steady clip, neither speeding up nor slowing down. There were no unexpected turns, no accelerating through traffic lights. If he knew he was being tailed, he didn't show it. Bishop wasn't taking chances and hung back as far as he could, following the broken taillight through the city. Five minutes into the drive, he got a hunch where Rhielman was headed. He'd driven this route, drunk and sober, more times than he could remember. The Hudson made turns like it was driving itself, a migratory steel bird heading home. Bishop pulled to the curb a half block from Ira's office and cut the engine. He watched Rhielman park in front of Krieger's. The taillights went dark. The councilman exited the Ford and strode into the hardware store. He was carrying a three-foot, cardboard tube. The door opened as he approached.

The maroon Cadillac pulled up next and parked behind the Ford. Bishop was surprised to see Brandt climb out, instead of Elizabeth. She didn't strike him as a woman who shared her toys, especially with an unfaithful husband.

A silver Mercury with wide whitewalls drove up next. Bishop didn't recognize the car, but Joey Bones hopped out of the back. Joey wasn't taking chances tonight. All four Gospels were with him, looking up and down the street, hands inside their jackets, ready to pull roscoes. Bishop slid further behind the wheel and wondered what kind of trouble they were expecting at a hardware store at eleven o'clock at night. Everyone slipped inside except two of the Evangelists, one who stayed slouched against the doorway and another who circled to the back of the building.

Bishop waited to see if anyone else would arrive. No one did, but he heard rattling metal and a squeaking, wobbling wheel. Benny The Junkman was pushing his cart toward the hardware store. It was too dark, and Bishop was too far away to make out the items in the wagon, but he could tell it was half full. Benny had either discovered a late-night trove of salvage items or hadn't been able to pawn the day's haul. He stopped in front of the Gospel in the doorway and pulled out items one at a time, holding them up for inspection, trying for a sale. The Gospel—Mathew? Luke?—yelled at him to move along and opened his jacket to show him the heater holstered there. The gun didn't scare Benny a bit, and he yelled right back.

Bishop got out of the car and eased the door shut as the junkman screamed that the Gospel wasn't carrying a regulation sidearm and demanded to know what happened to his Enfield. Bishop used the distraction to hobble to the side of a building. He pressed himself against the brick and could still hear Benny and the Gospel arguing, so he figured he'd made it unseen. Limping down the side street, he came to an alleyway that ran behind Ira's office. It was unlit and full of shapeless shadows, and he wished he had a gun. He didn't move fast down the alley. Instead, he checked for lugs who might jump out and roll him; he gripped his cane tighter in case he had to swing at someone's melon.

A calico was perched on a metal ash can and hissed as he approached Ira's backdoor. The fat man had never given him an office key, so Bishop pulled his lockpicking tools from his coat pocket and went to work. His hands wouldn't obey him, but eventually the tumblers fell into place. He stepped into the office, keeping the lights off. The binoculars still rested on the birding books, and he grabbed them. The front door remained boarded. It cut down on the light seeping from the street. He stood at the front window and trained the field glasses on Krieger's Hardware.

The Gospel stood in front with hands on hips watching Benny push his cart down the sidewalk. Bishop shifted his gaze to Krieger's window and worked the thumbscrew to sharpen his focus. Rhielman and Joey Bones stood next to each other, leaning against the counter. Krieger and his son stood in the middle of the floor opposite Brandt. Two Gospels lingered by the door. There was a tall man with round glasses wearing a wrinkled suit standing off by himself. It took Bishop a minute to recognize him as one of the card players from The Lafayette.

Old Man Krieger seemed to be in charge of this meeting. He jabbed his finger at the artist as he spoke. Brandt shook his head, raising his shoulders and turning his palms upward. Even from this distance, Bishop could see how his face was begging to be punched. It looked like everyone in the room was waiting for a turn, except the tall man with round glasses who stood with arms folded, his face unreadable, watching it all.

Then the tall man pushed off the counter and walked toward Brandt, stopping inches in front of him. He, too, jabbed his finger when he spoke, except he poked Brandt in the chest. He must've felt he wasn't getting his point across because he grabbed Brandt by the lapels and shook him to help him understand. The artist's head flopped backward and forward like a ragdoll's. Bishop nodded in approval. He wouldn't mind giving the artist a shake or two himself.

The man shoved Brandt away. Brandt recovered his footing and pleaded his case, following the tall man with his arms stretched wide. Erik Krieger stepped in front of him, blocking his path. The slender punk didn't bother jabbing his finger. Instead, he drove each point home with a slap across Brandt's face.

Rhielman stepped forward then, holding the cardboard tube in the air, drawing everyone toward him. Krieger stopped slapping Brandt and watched as the councilman opened the tube and shook out a length of rolled paper. Rhielman walked to the counter and unfurled it. Everyone gathered around except Brandt, who stood in place rubbing his cheek. Bishop couldn't tell what they were looking at. It might've been a map, but he was betting that it was blueprints to the Albright Gallery. Maybe he wouldn't mail a negative to Doris' dad after all. At least not this week.

Everyone leaned in to see the councilman tracing his finger across the unfolded document, tapping his nail at certain points along the way. Bishop could see them all nodding. When Rhielman finished and straightened to full height, they all focused on Brandt, who raised his arms and let them fall the way a man does when he has run out of options. If there was a weak one in that bunch, one to lean on who'd crack and start singing, it was Brandt.

Bishop wondered who the tall man was and how he fit in with the rest of them.

Chapter 13

The next morning, Bishop parked the Hudson in front of the New Genesee. He glanced up at his old window, half expecting to see a ghost of his younger self staring back. What would he have thought if one morning while he waited for his mother's return, he'd looked down and saw this older, crippled version of himself, hobbling on the sidewalk and squinting back at him? Would he have been terrified if their gaze had met and he'd peered into his older bloodshot, perhaps jaundiced, eyes and saw how his life had turned out? Would that've been enough to make him finally raise the window and jump? It was only a two-story fall, but he always figured if he went headfirst the height wouldn't matter. He shoved that thought away like he always did. There was no ghost gazing down, judging him. Morning light shone on the windowpane, revealing only dirt and grime kicked up from years of Genesee Street traffic. The specters that haunted him were from within.

The restaurant was noisy with the breakfast crowd when he entered. Tables were filled with wartime workers who'd finished their shifts at Curtiss Wright and Bell Aircraft and had stopped in before heading home to sleep. The counter was lined with truck drivers hunched over cups of coffee or plates of eggs and hash, fueling up before starting their routes. Tamis stood behind the counter, coffee pot in hand, and nodded when he saw him as he always did. Sal sat at his usual table. A folded newspaper rested next to his orange juice.

"Silver dollars on your plate...," Bishop started, as he walked closer.

"...silver dollars in your pocket," Sally finished. His jacket was draped over the back of his chair. The red suspenders matched his tie. "I was going to visit you in jail today."

"No, you weren't."

"I didn't know you were out until I got your message."

"Ira sprung me yesterday."

"You need a bellboy to carry those bags under your eyes."

"You look handsome, too, Sal."

Bishop sat across from him. It felt good to sit. His foot wasn't bothering him too much, but he was tired, a weariness that ached in his knees and shoulders and lower back. He needed sleep. The two men didn't shake hands. A waitress came over. She was a pretty redhead with green eyes. Her skin was so fair Bishop bet she never tanned but skipped right to burning. He ordered tea. Sal's maple syrup's sweet smell nauseated him.

"Tea? Aren't you proper?" Sal said. "They stick you in the women's cell?"

"It settles my stomach."

"When's the last time you ate anything that needed settling?"

"I don't have much of an appetite."

"You should try the pancakes."

Bishop watched the redhead walk toward the counter. "Do you remember Faye?"

Sal put down his napkin. "Faye who?"

"The waitress who worked here when I was a kid. She'd come upstairs when you ran card games."

"The whore? Yeah, I remember her. She was pretty until she wasn't."

"Whatever happened to her?" Bishop asked.

"I don't know. The same thing that happens to all whores when they get old. Why are you asking about her?"

"That redhead reminded me of her."

Sal balanced the chair on its back legs. He looped his thumbs under his suspenders and grinned. "Thinking about your first time?"

"What are you talking about?"

"Faye. Coming to your room Christmas Eve."

Bishop sat back in his chair as if pushed. "You knew about that?"

"Who do you think sent her?"

"No."

"It was my Christmas gift to you. Peace on earth and all that. You never even thanked me."

"I thought she did that on her own."

Sally laughed a true, hard laugh. "All these years and you thought *that*? That she *gave* it away? Or did it because she *liked* you? Whores fuck for money, Nicholas. That's their job, even on December twenty-fourth. She didn't want to do it. Said you were just a kid. Begged me to get somebody else, but I saw the way you looked at her. I had to pay extra. But what the hell. It was Christmas. It was the best present I could give a kid with no friends who sat alone in the window all the time."

Bishop palmed the sweat from his face. "Jesus."

Sally slid *The Courier-Express* across the table. "You didn't come here to talk about losing your virginity, did you? You got my money?"

Bishop picked up the newspaper and opened it on his lap, keeping it out of sight. Folded inside was a modified Colt .45.

"I don't know why you like these Fitz Specials," Sal said. "Knives are quieter."

"Is it a clean piece? You're not selling me someone else's trouble, are you?"

"It's cleaner than Faye ever was."

Bishop holstered the gun and took some folded bills from his pocket. He placed them by Sal's plate. His uncle picked them up and counted.

"It's all there," Bishop said.

"Sure it is."

"What do you know about Erik Krieger?"

Sal pocketed the money. "I told you last time. He's a nobody. He didn't have a seat at the table. He emptied ashtrays and poured drinks."

"Is he a nobody who wants to be a somebody?"

"Aren't we all?"

"He runs with Joey Bones and The Gospels."

"Well," Sal said, shrugging. "Joey needs his ashtrays emptied, too, I guess."

"Think he's got the moxie to shoot someone?"

"Maybe. Seems like a hot head."

"What about that tall guy with glasses who was playing cards that night? What do you know about him?"

Sal started to answer but stopped when he saw Gia enter. "Here comes your secretary."

Bishop looked at her then at his cracked Bulova. "She's early. We're supposed to catch up on things."

Sal stood when Gia approached. "Remember what I told you, kid," he said, hurrying to shrug on his jacket. "They never do it out of sympathy or love."

She stopped next to Bishop's chair. "Hello, Sal."

"Always good to see you, Gia. When are you going to leave this bum and come work for me?"

"Never, Sal. Never in a million years."

"And why is that?"

"Because I can't stand the sight of you."

Sal laughed. "You'll come around."

"Don't bet on that."

"I can spot a sure thing a furlong away. Until then, thanks for buying me breakfast, Nicholas." He patted his nephew's arm as he walked past. He called over his shoulder. "Oh, and Merry Christmas!"

Bishop heard him laughing until the door closed behind him.

"Merry Christmas?" Gia asked, taking Sal's seat. She pushed his plate away. "What was that all about?"

"Nothing. We were reminiscing about childhood memories."

"I don't know why you still talk to him or why you come to this place," she said, glancing around.

"I was getting information out of him until you scared him off."

"I didn't realize he scared so easy."

"He doesn't like talking to people who don't like him. Especially dames. He folds early."

"He talks to you."

"That's different. We're family. Sometimes you got to talk to family even if you don't like them."

The redhead placed a cup and saucer in front of Bishop. "I've never seen you drink tea in my life," Gia said.

"It settles my stomach. Besides, no one boils water like the Greeks."

"I don't think it's working. You look worse today than yesterday."

"Stop sweet-talking me and order something. Sal recommends the pancakes."

"Then I'll have coffee. I hear the boiled water is excellent." The redhead rolled her green eyes and headed to the coffee urns.

Bishop studied Gia, trying to spot if anything had changed about her—a new hat, a different shade of lipstick, brighter eyes.

"What are you gawking at?" she asked.

"You've been seeing Brandt?"

"He sketched me a couple times. He calls them studies. We went to the Albright again."

"And you've talked on the phone?"

Her eyes narrowed. "Did you tap my party line while you were in jail?"

"Elizabeth thinks he's still seeing someone."

"And you suspected me."

"I wasn't wrong."

"Jesus, I was working the case, Bishop," she said, leaning back and crossing her arms. "He's our only suspect. Proving he killed Pearl seemed like a good way of getting you cleared. Maybe Ira should've let you sit in jail a little longer. Maybe that would've smartened you up a bit."

"So, you're palling around with him as part of the job?"

"Yeah, genius. He thinks I want my portrait painted. What the hell would I do with a portrait on Seventh Street?"

"The last girl he painted ended up dead."

"I can take care of myself. Besides, I'm not sure he's even interested in me. He flirts and says things that are out of line and makes passes, but I think he does that with every woman. He's conceited that way. Maybe he really is only interested in my bone structure."

"His only interest in your bones is jumping them. He's playing the long game. Don't let him fool you. That guy's no gentleman, and he doesn't have gentle friends." He filled her in on last night's meeting at Krieger's Hardware Store.

As he talked, the waitress brought Gia's coffee. She added cream and sugar and stirred while she listened, the coffee swirling and lightening. When he finished, she tapped her spoon against the cup's rim, and rested it on the saucer. "Jesus, I attract the winners, don't I?" she asked, and raised her cup and sipped.

"You attract them all. But here's the thing. You got close to him. We can use that."

She set the cup down hard. Coffee sloshed on the table. "You *want* me to keep seeing him? Is that what you're saying? First, you're mad because I was spending time with him and now you want me to go on with it? You're sending mixed signals here, Bishop."

His stomach cramped. "You're on the inside now. I don't like it, but you're undercover like a real detective. You did good. Maybe you'll learn something. Hear or see something you're not supposed to."

"Apologize."

"What?"

She leaned across the table. "You heard me. Apologize. Apologize for not trusting me. Apologize for thinking I'd be attracted to that spoiled mug. Apologize for never even *considering* that I was trying to help you."

Bishop felt his entire insides cramping, not just his stomach. "I'm sorry."

"What are you sorry for?"

"Jesus, you don't let up."

"What are you sorry for?" Gia demanded.

"I'm sorry for not trusting you."

"You damn well better be. You need to start trusting me if we're going to be partners."

"Who said we're going to be partners?"

"We already are. You just don't know it yet."

"Let's talk about that later. Much, much later. When do you see Brandt again?"

She looked at her watch. "In an hour."

"At his studio?"

"Hoyt Lake across from the gallery. He wants to draw me in natural light."

"How long do these posing sessions last?"

"They vary. An hour, usually. They're getting shorter and shorter, though. He has a big art project he's working on that takes up his time. He won't talk about it. It's real hush-hush. All he says is the deadline's coming up and he won't have time to start my portrait until it's over."

"An hour's enough."

"For what?"

"While you're showing off your cheekbones, I want to look around his studio and see what I can find. Maybe a blonde wig'll turn up. Maybe a murder weapon."

"Why would he kill Pearl?"

"Jealousy? A crime of passion? Maybe she was blackmailing him? Who knows, but we'll find out. Sooner or later, we'll find out."

"He seems harmless."

"Or cold-blooded."

* * *

Bishop dropped off Ira's car at his office. Gia followed, parking behind the Hudson. The door was still boarded but it was unlocked. He held it open for her. It was already warm inside, the ceiling fan pushing around hot air. Bishop's shirt began to stick. Ira was at his desk. His tie was loosened, his jowls spilling over his unbuttoned collar. A bottle of schnapps and a book on regional birds were both open in front of him.

"It's a little early for German juice, isn't it?" Bishop asked, closing the door behind him. "Are you celebrating because Elizabeth Brandt rehired us?"

"She did?" Ira asked, his dull eyes brightening.

"I talked to her yesterday. She didn't look too happy to see me, but we're both back on her dime."

"Grab some glasses and join me then."

"I'm abstaining these days and Gia needs to be sober for her natural light date," Bishop said. He and Gia sat in the chairs opposite Ira. "What's the real reason for drinking your breakfast? Not that I ever needed one."

"Timothy Flynn just left."

"I usually celebrate when he leaves, too. What did he want?"

"He wanted to know about Nazis and my broken door and vandalized window."

"I thought stupid kids did that," Gia said.

Ira shook his head. "He's investigating *local* Nazis."

"In *Buffalo*?" she asked. "I'd like to get my hands on one of them."

Ira refilled his glass. "Maybe you'll get your chance. I knew they were here, but no one would listen. Until today."

"Hold on," Bishop said, wiping his face and neck with a handkerchief. "I planted that Nazi seed in Flynn's gin-soaked brain so he'd do the legwork for me. We promised to share information. He has big dreams about it becoming a major story. He's probably kicking Kraut tires to see if any goose steppers fall out. Maybe some did, but I doubt it. I'll check with him later."

"In the meantime," Ira said, "I'll sit here and wait for them to attack me again." He opened his desk drawer and pulled out Bishop's .38. The snub nose looked small in his hand. He set it next to the schnapps.

"Drinking and handling firearms isn't the best idea, Ira," said Gia.

"She's right," Bishop said. "That combination makes you worry about what's rolling around in your trunk."

"You're tiresome when you're sober, Bishop. Has anyone ever told you that?"

"No, but I've never been sober before. It's all new to me."

"Well, you *are* tiresome. Leave me alone with my schnapps. Don't you have any windows to peep through?"

"Not this morning," Bishop said. "Today is breaking and entering day."

* * *

Gia let Bishop off a block from the Buffalo Art Institute then drove the rest of the way by herself. He watched as she parked on Elmwood Avenue and entered the institute. She didn't glance back at him. He tottered down the sidewalk and then ducked into the barbershop across the street. Sitting in the shoe-shine chair, he had a clear view of the avenue through the shop's front window. George The Shine Man cuffed his pants. Bishop craved a Cuban instead of a Chesterfield the way he always did when he got a shine, but he felt too nauseous for a cigar. He made small talk about trotters and baseball. George applied polish and snapped the cloth across leather.

George was spit polishing the second shoe when Brandt and Gia stepped outside. Brandt carried a satchel in one hand, which Bishop assumed contained art supplies, and a picnic basket in the other, which he assumed contained fresh bread, French wine, and plump grapes he planned on hand feeding her. Gia carried a blanket, her smile wide and bright even from across the street and through a dusty window. Bishop dug his nails into the chair's leather arms as they drove off.

He waited until George finished buffing his wingtips before he left the shop. Ideally, he'd have liked to have searched the studio at night when no one was around, but he knew Gia would keep Brandt occupied. They wouldn't return unexpectedly unless Brandt had forgotten something for their picnic—a corkscrew, wine glasses, prophylactics. He imagined swinging his cane and the satisfying sound of pewter connecting with bone.

Gia had told him the location of Brandt's studio, and he entered the institute with all the briskness of somebody who belonged there. He went up the stairs, forcing himself to place one foot on each step instead of two. It'd be easy for a witness to remember the cripple who'd labored up the staircase, so he tried to make it look normal and effortless. By the time he reached the landing, his foot and ankle were firing bolts of pain. He wanted to rest, but he pushed on to the second floor, his pace slowing. At the top of the stairs, he was lightheaded, his heart hammering.

The hallway smelled of paint and varnish. There were four rooms on the second floor, former bedrooms converted to studios, and the doors were closed. From the room closest to the stairs, classical music played, the cello and woodwinds seeped through the door. There was no sign or nameplate indicating that the last studio on the left was Brandt's, but Bishop stopped in front of it and pulled out his lockpicking tools. The door was old but there were two locks, both new and sturdy and not what he expected. He wondered what Brandt kept in there that warranted double locks. His hands shook and his fingers were sweaty. The bottom pins eluded his pick, refusing to be pushed into the top set. He was taking too long to get inside, but the hall remained deserted except for the music. He worked the pick and screwdriver with closed eyes. When both locks finally yielded, he stepped inside and shut the door behind him. That old feeling of fear and excitement washed over him like a shot of bourbon.

He'd never been in an art studio and wasn't sure what to look for. An oak drawing table was pushed close to the windows, its top covered with sketches, palettes daubed with paint, and charcoal pencils like the one he'd found in the men's robe hanging in Pearl's apartment. Bishop flipped through the drawings—street scenes, still lifes, Gia. Some were of her profile, others of her straight on. A few were of her lounging on the fainting couch in the studio corner. One was of her hands—he recognized the birthmark on her left wrist. His favorite was a sketch of her with half-closed eyes and parted lips, her hair swept across her forehead. He folded it carefully into his breast pocket. He took a drawing of a speckled bird for Ira as well, knowing he'd like it.

Three easels were lined up in the center of the room. The first two were empty, but the one on the far right was covered with a sheet. He tugged it off. Propped on it was a formal portrait of a Black woman against a gold background. Her hair was piled high in victory curls, framing her delicate features. She faced forward, but her head was tilted to the left, revealing a cord of muscle running along her neck. One earring, a cluster of pearls, was visible. They matched the double strand encircling her throat. Her eyebrows were rounded, following her eyes' natural curve. She wasn't smiling, and Brandt somehow had captured in her countenance the sorrow of a woman who'd perhaps witnessed too much, or loved too hard, or maybe lost what little she had. She wore a blue strapless evening gown gathered at the bust. A handwritten note was taped to the easel: *Pearl In Blue.*

The memories came then, fragmented and fractured like he was looking through the bottom of a cracked lowball glass: Pearl on stage at The Chez Amis; Pearl driving his Packard, her blonde wig strands blown by the wind; Pearl tilting her chin, closing her eyes, letting him kiss her. Each image was a surprise, both foreign and familiar, that took his breath each time they appeared. His heart machinegunned into a gallop again. He reached for the fainting couch and sat on its edge, his cane planted between his knees, and stared at *Pearl In Blue*. Guilt pumped through him with every irregular heartbeat. Maybe he hadn't killed her, but he hadn't protected her either. And he sure as hell hadn't saved her.

When no more memories oozed back and his pulse had slowed, he looked around the rest of the studio. A floor radio, an expensive one with standard broadcast, police, and shortwave bands, stood near the fainting couch. Its walnut top marred with paint smudges and rings from forgotten water glasses. A wooden cabinet stood adjacent to the window. He pushed off the couch and stumbled to it, pulling open every thin drawer. Some contained paper of varying weights and stocks while others held different sized paintbrushes. Another cabinet, this one taller, steel, and padlocked, took up most of the far wall. He went to it.

The padlock was easier to pick. When he pulled the shackle from the lock's body, he yanked open the metal door and peered inside. There were five identically sized canvases all on the same shelf. The rest of the cabinet was empty. He wondered why a lock was needed and was reaching for one of the rolled canvasses when he heard the door open behind him. He dropped the canvas, pulled The Fitz, and pivoted on his good foot. Erik Krieger stood in the doorway, his eyes growing wide as he stared at the gun barrel aimed at his chest.

"Erik, what do you know? What do you hear? Shut the door and grab some air."

Krieger kicked the door closed and raised his hands. "Where's Brandt?"

"Eating grapes. Open your jacket. Slow."

Krieger unbuttoned his suitcoat and opened it. He wasn't packing.

"Not even a paintbrush? I'm disappointed," Bishop said. He kept The Fitz pointed at him.

"Certain people aren't going to like you poking around here," Krieger said.

"Oh, yeah? Who might they be? Joey Bones? The Gospels? Rhielman?"

The muscles in Krieger's cheeks twitched.

"Did they send you to slap Brandt around some more or did you think that up on your own?"

"I don't know what you're talking about."

"You don't, huh? Well, what about her then?" Bishop asked, gesturing to Pearl's portrait with his gun. "You know something about her?"

Krieger's eyes darted to the easel then back to Bishop. He hitched a shoulder. "How would I know her? She's some colored girl. I don't pal around with coloreds."

"Just another *Schwarze*, huh? That's what you call them, right?"

Krieger's lips pressed together in a bloodless line.

"You called her that at Brandt's house."

"Like I said, I don't know what you're talking about."

"Sure, you do," Bishop said. "You called her that right before you shot her."

"You must be drunk again."

"On the contrary," Bishop said. "I'm horrifically sober. Why are you looking for Brandt?"

Krieger smirked. "I thought I'd get my picture drawn."

"That'll look aces hanging in your cell."

"I'm not going to jail, Weasel. I didn't kill Pearl."

"I think you did. I think you're a little Nazi shit that doesn't like Blacks or Jews," Bishop said. "You graduated from painting windows to murdering awfully quick. Was that part of your graduation from the Hitler Youth or were you just trying to impress Rhielman? He's running this show, isn't he?"

Krieger's forehead wrinkled into rows. "You talk a lot for a cripple."

"It's my foot that's ruined, not my mouth," Bishop said. "Your best way out of this is to start talking. Tell me what happened the night Pearl was killed."

"You tell me," he sneered. "You were there."

"I'm a little short on details."

"Well, here are some details for you, Weasel. You were blotto. Barely conscious. Falling down and shooting your mouth off like you usually do. You and Pearl were fighting."

"About what?"

"About how drunk you were. How you were embarrassing her and were going to make her late getting back to the club."

"Yeah? That sounds possible. Then what?"

"Then you shot her. We tried to stop you but couldn't."

"Nobody could stop a drunk cripple?" Bishop asked, his voice an octave higher. "A guy barely conscious? And falling down, too? I must be stronger than I thought. A real Jack Armstrong, all-American boy fighting off a bunch of Nazis. What happened next, Brother Grimm? Go on. You tell a good fairy tale. You should be a writer when you grow up."

"Brandt didn't want trouble. He's got that society wife and Linwood Avenue neighbors. He didn't want a dead colored girl in his living room."

"Nobody does."

"Exactly," Krieger said. "So, we put the body in your trunk, and you behind the wheel, and sent you on your way, hoping you'd drive off a bridge or into a tree or something. Next thing I know, I'm reading in the *Courier* you got the stiff in your bed. I guess weasels will fuck anything."

"We draw the line at corpses. But, like I said, you tell a good story. Except there's one problem. I saw you and an Evangelist joyriding in my car."

"Who's going to believe a weasel?" Krieger asked. "The body in your bed, her dress in your trunk. It doesn't look good for you."

"It never does, but I have no motive for killing Pearl. You do with all your master race crap."

"Christ, you got the shakes. Put the gat away before it goes off and kills me."

Bishop looked at the gun trembling in his hand. The Fitz was wavering from side-to-side, occasionally bouncing toward the ceiling. He lowered it, not wanting another dead body linked to him. Krieger, young and fast, rushed him then, hurtling his thin body through the air. It didn't take much to knock Bishop off his bum foot. He fell backward, still holding onto his cane but dropping the .45. Krieger landed on top of him but scrambled to grab The Fitz that had clattered across the floor. Bishop rolled over and pushed up to his knees as Krieger got hold of the gun.

The pewter handle first came down on Krieger's thin wrist, knocking The Fitz from his hand. The second blow landed on the back of his skull. His body sagged to the floor and lay so still Bishop was afraid he'd killed him. He crawled to the boy then felt a pulse butterfly in his neck. Krieger weighed no more than a lightweight, but Bishop struggled to roll him on his back. When he did, he lifted his wallet from his suitcoat and opened it. His old man must not pay him well. It only contained twelve dollars and his driver's license. His address was listed as the apartment above the hardware store. He tossed the license and wallet aside but pocketed the cash.

There was nothing of interest in his other pockets—a pack of Lucky's, a matchbook from The Chez Amis, some loose change. In his shirt pocket, however, was a business card:

Dr. Andrew C. Ritchie, Director
Albright Art Gallery

Chapter 14

The old sadness draped Bishop when he entered The Kitty Kat. There was still nothing happy, nothing hopeful about this bar during daytime. The early crowd, bent over glasses and mugs, leaned away from the sunlight that streamed through the opened door. When it shut and the tavern darkened again, they craned to see who had entered. Some looked disappointed, others angry, when they recognized Bishop. His drunken history of vulgar comments, picked fights, and sloppy passes made at friends' wives must have all been spectacular to turn a barroom of rummies against him. Or maybe these transgressions had stacked one after the other for so long they'd exhausted the patience of even the most alcoholic in the bunch.

It was too early in the day for the Bisons to be playing, so Crosby crooned on the radio about being careful with his heart. Other than Bing and the rattle of ice and the raspy calls for one more, the bar was quiet.

"Jesus Christ, Bishop," Frank said, drawing a Lang's from the tap. "What'd I tell you last time? You're not wanted here. Charlie chewed me out good when he heard you came in again."

Bishop raised a trembling hand like he was stopping traffic. "I need to talk to my good friend Flynn over there. Give me five minutes and some soda water. Then I'm gone."

"Five minutes and that's it. I don't need Charlie yelling at me again. At least you didn't bring your damn mutt this time."

Flynn sat at the end of the bar and lifted his head when he heard his name. A worn leather satchel rested near his empty gin glass. He smiled his half smile as Bishop shuffled toward him. His eyes were glassy, and the right side of his face sagged almost as much as his nerve-damaged left. Bishop wondered if he'd started day drinking with Ira and kept going. Sometimes that happens to Bishop, too. He never planned it. He'd have a drink or two with a friend, then find he couldn't stop. A liquor undertow would catch him, until he woke lying across railroad tracks or stepping in front of taxis, wondering how he'd gotten there. Booze is funny that way, he thought. One thing he knew for sure, not much news would be reported today, at least not by Timothy Flynn.

"What do you know, Timothy? What do you hear?"

"Heard you made bail, but I didn't believe it. Heard you were still on the wagon and believed that even less."

"Here I am, partly clean and mostly sober."

Flynn stuck out his hand and Bishop shook it before climbing on the stool next to him. Frank slid soda water in front of him. "Five minutes, Bishop."

Bishop ignored the bartender. "I appreciate you adding that bit at the end of your article about the hotel sticking by me. A retraction would have made them look like louses. You embarrassed them enough to keep a roof over my head."

Flynn wavered on his barstool. "Oliver wasn't happy, but I was glad to do it. How's Gia?"

"Let's not talk about her. What do you hear about Pearl?"

Flynn tried to sip out of his empty glass. He looked surprised that the gin was gone and gestured to Frank for another before he answered. "Not much. Shot twice at close range."

"Raped?"

"No. But they found sand."

"Sand?"

"Yeah, on her skin, in her hair, all over your bed. There was a bunch in your trunk, too. They figure you two drove to the beach and you killed her there. You remember anything about going to the lake?"

"No, but I didn't have any sand on me or in my shoes when I came to. Who are their suspects?"

Flynn closed one eye and pointed at Bishop. "Well, there's you. And you. And there's also you. Nobody else."

"Christ."

"Did I mention they pulled your prints from her apartment?"

"Meyer Brandt's fingerprints should be all over the place, too, especially by the Murphy bed."

"Elizabeth Brandt's husband?"

"He and Pearl were lovers."

Flynn let out a whistle that was too loud for the quiet bar. People looked his way, some startled and others annoyed at being disturbed.

Frank placed a Gilbey's in front of the reporter then crossed his thick arms. "Four minutes, Bishop."

"Your Cracker Jack watch is running fast, Frank. You better get it fixed. Or buy a Bulova. Mine's cracked, but it keeps perfect time."

"My Hamilton runs fine, Bishop, and it's going to run you out of here in exactly four minutes," he said, over his shoulder as he walked away.

Flynn leaned in too close the way drunks do. "You sure about Brandt? Him and Pearl?"

Bishop leaned away. "His wife hired me. I did some digging and that's what I found. It'd been going on for a while, right up until she was killed. Did the cops find her blonde wig?"

"I didn't know there was a wig."

"She was wearing it the night she was murdered."

He whistled too loud again then sipped his gin. "I'll look into it. Maybe whisper in Darcy's ear about Brandt and the wig. Not sure if he'll listen. He's ready to hang you. He wasn't happy you made bail."

"Buffalo artist. Society crowd. Has an affair with a colored nightclub singer and murders her? That would make headlines," Bishop said. "That would sell a lot of papers with your byline."

"A lot more than if the murderer was a drunken detective who no one cared about."

"That's true," Bishop said. "No matter how handsome he is."

"Three minutes!" Frank yelled, from the other end of the bar. He popped a toothpick in the corner of his mouth to show he meant business.

Bishop nodded at him. He remembered when he liked Frank. That seemed like a long time ago. He said to Flynn, "There's something else."

"What?"

"The night she was killed she was at Brandt's house. She brought him something."

"What'd she bring?"

"I don't know. I was hoping you'd tell me."

He shook his head. "This is all news to me."

"I'm going to lean on Brandt next. Maybe he'll sing." Bishop took a sip of soda. "I heard you talked to Ira."

"Never had schnapps before," Flynn answered. "Those Krauts are on to something. Nice way to ease into the day."

"You don't think there's really Nazis here, do you?"

Flynn gulped his gin then reached for his satchel. He rifled through it with clumsy fingers before pulling out a yellowed pamphlet and pushing it toward Bishop.

"What's this?" Bishop asked.

"Directory of Buffalo Ku Klux Klan members, circa 1924."

"They had a directory? Like a phone book?" Bishop thumbed through it. The booklet was organized alphabetically by occupation—city employees, clergy, dentists. "There's a lot of names here."

"Thirty pages worth. They started with eight-hundred members and grew from there."

"What happened to them?"

"There was trouble. That directory was stolen and displayed at the police station for everyone to see. The newspapers published names. A lot of members quit after that. The church crowd and politicians didn't like everyone knowing they wore hoods. People started protesting in front of their offices on Chippewa Street, peacefully at first then things got violent. You know how that goes. Bricks and bottles were tossed. People got shot. One person died. The cops and papers wouldn't let up on the Klan after that. The ink slingers wrote daily articles and editorials, always listing names. Cops arrested them in front of their families and neighbors for breaking laws that didn't exist. People boycotted Klan businesses. It got too much for them. It's tough being in an Invisible Empire when it's not invisible anymore. They faded away in '25 or '26."

Bishop tossed the directory on the bar. "That was seventeen years ago. What's this got to do with Ira?"

"It was a place to start," Flynn said. "These people still live here, Bishop, the racists, the anti-Semites, former Klansmen. They still think the same way. At least some of them must. They don't wear sheets and burn crosses anymore, but that doesn't mean they've changed. Some could be sitting in this bar right now."

"This crowd isn't ambitious enough to join the Klan."

Flynn pushed the directory back to him. "Flip to *Hardware* and check the names."

Bishop flicked pages then stopped and ran his finger down the list, pausing halfway down the page. "Dewey Krieger."

"Ira's neighbor."

"I just left his son. You think Dewey's a Nazi?"

Flynn shrugged. "It's not farfetched that some of the Klan fell in line with the goose steppers. Maybe Krieger's one of them. Maybe the Klan is back. Maybe he just doesn't like Ira."

"Maybe he raised his son to believe the same crap," Bishop said. "I think that little shit painted Ira's door and window. What else did you find out?"

"That's it. The schnapps derailed me."

"Times up, Bishop," Frank called. "Take a powder."

Bishop ignored him. "One last thing. The poker players at The Lafayette who got arrested. There was a tall man with round glasses. You remember him?"

"Sure. He has a Kraut name. Hans Schrieber."

"Who is he? He looks like a Sunday school teacher."

"He's an art dealer. Has a gallery in New York. I forget which one."

"Bishop!" Frank yelled. He pulled a night stick from under the bar and slapped it against his palm, wood against skin, wood against bone.

Bishop struggled to his feet. His bad foot had numbed. It felt as though pins were jabbing him from heel to toe. He tossed some bills on the bar. "Make yourself useful, Frank, and get Flynn a drink on me. He earned it."

"Thanks," Flynn said. "Let's talk in a few days. See where we are."

"Sure, but let's pick a friendlier place. The bartender here's worse than a cop."

"Maybe you'll be off the wagon by then."

"It's looking fifty-fifty."

* * *

Bishop stepped outside The Kitty Kat and lit a cigarette. He tucked his cane under his arm and cupped his match, shielding it from the breeze. Squealing brakes made him look up from his Chesterfield. A Mercury screeched to a stop at the curb. The suicide doors swung open, and two Gospels scampered out, a third sat behind the wheel. Bishop didn't try to run, not with that foot. He waved the match and tossed it aside then pulled the cane from under his arm and gripped it tight.

"Hello, boys. What do you know? What do you hear?"

"Shut up," the shorter Gospel said.

They closed in, one on either side, to grab him, but he swung his cane with both hands, their heads fat targets. The pewter handle struck the first Evangelist hard above the ear, and he crumpled to the sidewalk. Bishop hit the second Gospel—Mark?—on the backswing, a glancing blow but enough to break skin at the brow. The next shot, a clean cut, caught the gunsel square in his mouth, shattering teeth and puncturing gums. He howled and dropped to his knees, his hands clutching his bloody maw. Bishop hurried to the Merc as fast as he could, drawing The Fitz from its holster as he flung himself in the backseat, the Chesterfield still clamped between his lips. He shoved the .45 against the wheelman's skull and cocked it.

"Drive."

The Gospel put the car in gear and pulled away, leaving the others bleeding in front of The Kitty Kat.

"You're dead, Weasel."

"Worse. I'm sober. Pull your gun out with your left hand and pass it back to me. And do it slow, Mathew. I got a loaded .45 and jittery hands, so avoid sudden movements, potholes, or annoying me in any way."

"I'm Luke."

"You're whoever I say you are, Mary Magdalen. Hand me that piece."

The Gospel reached inside his coat and passed his gun to Bishop. "Do you know what Joey's going to do to you when he hears about this?"

"Hire me."

"You're crazy or drunk."

"Neither. I'm crippled and laid out two of his top torpedoes then got the jump on the third. He'll thank me for showing how remarkably incompetent his goons are. Make me his personal driver. He'll pay me more than he's paying you. You're out of work, Mary. Hang a left at the corner."

"Where are we going?"

"To see a lawyer," Bishop said. He flicked ash on the seat. "You're in trouble, pal. Deep trouble. I'm not even sure a mouthpiece can save you. Say, this is a nice ride. Did you steal it, or do you only boost Packards?"

"It's my brother's."

"Which brother? The one with the cracked skull or the one with the cracked mouth?"

"I'm going to kill you slow, Weasel."

"I've been trying to do that for years, and it can't be done. I'm indestructible. Make a right then cut down the alley on your left. Let's keep this fine automobile out of sight, or someone might steal it."

The Mercury pulled down the alley until it reached Ira's backdoor. Bishop told Luke to park, cut the engine, and hand over the key. "Get out and get those arms up," he ordered. The Gospel did as he was told. Bishop trained The Fitz on him but kept his distance. "Knock on that door."

Luke knocked but no one answered.

"Knock again. Harder. Pretend you're hitting some old lady who owes Joey money."

"I'll pretend I'm hitting you," he said, and pounded the door.

Ira opened it this time. His hair was disheveled, and his ballooning suit wrinkled like he'd been sleeping in his chair. He held the .38 and leveled it when he saw Luke with his hands raised.

"Is this a Nazi?" he asked, thumbing back the hammer.

"He's dumb enough. Let us in."

Ira stepped aside and the two squeezed past. He closed and locked the door. "As your attorney, I must point out that this has the earmarks of a kidnapping."

"Mary isn't a pressing-charges kind of gal, are you, Mary?"

"I'm going to smash your other foot with a ball-peen hammer, Bishop. I swear to God I will."

"That's not the proper use of hand tools, is it? Sit in that chair and put your mitts on your pointed head."

The Gospel sat in the chair in front of Ira's desk. He locked his fingers and placed them on his slicked hair. The schnapps bottle on the desk was three quarters empty.

"Why is he here?" Ira asked.

"He and his brothers came after me. I dropped two of them and grabbed this one to see if he'd talk."

"I'm telling you nothing, Weasel," The Gospel said.

"You better sing, or the fat man'll sit on you. And I'll be honest, I think he's bigger today than yesterday."

"It's this suit that makes me look bigger," Ira said. "I need something more slimming. Or a better tailor. Why did Joey send The Gospels after you?"

"I think because I laid out Krieger."

"Dewey?"

"No, his kid. Erik."

"What did he do?"

"Long story, but he surprised me at Brandt's studio."

"You've had a busy day," Ira said. He ticked off with his fingers. "Three assaults, one breaking and entering, and one count of kidnapping, and that's if I'm adding correctly. That also, of course, doesn't include the murder charge."

"When you put it like that I sound like a criminal."

"I think I may need a new private investigator soon."

"Hire Gia while you can afford her," Bishop said. "She'll be on top of everyone's list soon enough. Even the goddamn Pinkertons."

"In the meantime, what are we going to do with him?" Ira asked, gesturing to the Gospel with the .38.

"Is there a basement?"

"A small one."

"He doesn't need to be comfortable," Bishop said. He nodded toward the door. "Go across the street and buy some rope. The sturdy kind. You better hurry. My trigger finger's jumpy. I'd hate to accidently pump a round or two in his ball-peen swinging arm."

Ira shoved the snub nose in his suit pocket and hurried out the door without his hat. Bishop sat in his leather wingback across from Luke, placing his cane next to the schnapps. He studied the gunman. Together, the four Gospels looked identical, but up close, Bishop noticed differences. This Evangelist had a more pronounced widow's peak and a small, vertical scar across his forehead. The nose was thin and straight with flared nostrils, giving it an arrow shape. His beard was darker, heavier—one of those gorillas who needs to shave twice a day, three times if he's catching the midnight show at The Chez.

Bishop could feel his foot pulsing and swelling inside his brogan. He wanted to elevate it. And he wanted to drink the schnapps, remembering the way it'd warmed and dulled him the day after Pearl Harbor. He needed some dulling. Instead, he picked up his cane and smashed the bottle, spraying The Gospel's shirtfront with glass and schnapps. Luke glared at him.

"Tell me about the last time you were here," Bishop said.

"I've been here before? When was that?"

"When you tossed this place and stole Rhielman's file. What's in that folder that's so important?"

"I don't know what you're talking about, friend."

"No? Let's talk about the day you saw me at The Chez Amis then. You must remember that. Why'd you tell me to forget what I saw then kick me in the head?"

"I couldn't help myself. You have a kickable head," The Gospel said.

"What did you think I saw?"

"After I kicked you? Stars. Before I kicked you? Pink elephants, ya drunken weasel."

"You're a funny guy. A real radio comedian, but that weasel talk's getting old. What do you think I saw the night Pearl DuGaye was murdered?" Bishop asked.

"Her eyes rolling back. You shot her."

"I was drunk on the porch. Someone inside the house killed her. Were you there?"

"Where?"

"Brandt's house when Pearl was killed."

"I don't know Brandt."

"Sure, you do. You were with him the other night."

"Yeah? Where?"

"Across the street at Krieger's with your Nazi pals. Or are they Klansmen? I always get you racists confused."

The Gospel didn't answer.

"What was that meeting about? The Albright?"

"You know too much."

"Me? I'm nothing but a drunken weasel, remember?" Bishop said. "What's Hans Schrieber doing in town?"

The Gospel didn't answer.

Bishop slapped the desk. "Was he at Brandt's house when Pearl bought it? I know he was playing cards with Rhielman at The Lafayette."

The Gospel didn't answer.

"How does Joey Bones fit in all this? Is he just providing the muscle or is he in deeper with these Krauts?"

The Gospel didn't answer.

"You sure are quiet for an Evangelist," Bishop said. He leaned back in the lopsided chair.

Ira returned with the rope. His face was flushed, his forehead shiny with sweat. "What'd I miss?"

"Nothing. We were dancing, but he wouldn't let me lead," Bishop said.

Ira sniffed the air and then saw the broken bottle and The Gospel's stained shirt. "What happened to my schnapps?"

"Spontaneous combustion. That Kraut juice is explosive. Where's the basement?"

"By the bathroom," he said, pointing.

"Follow the fat man, Mary. Keep those hands on your head. My gun will be pointed at your spine so act smarter than you look or paralysis will be your new best friend. Ira, bring his chair."

Ira led them to a narrow door. He had to turn sideways to fit through the opening. The Gospel and Bishop followed. At the bottom of the stairs, Ira pulled the chain to a bare bulb. A puddle of yellow light cut through the gloom. The basement was small and damp. Water dripped somewhere in the darkness.

"Set the chair in the light and take a seat, Mary," Bishop said. "Tie him up, Ira. Make sure those knots are tight."

Ira was breathing hard after he'd tied Luke to the chair. He pulled out a handkerchief, dainty in his large hand, and wiped his face. "His boss will be looking for him."

"Good," Bishop said. "Let him worry. Shove that handkerchief in his mouth. We'll check on him later. Maybe a few hours down here with the rats will improve his memory about the murder and his Nazi pals. Douse that light when you're done."

Bishop holstered The Fitz and climbed the stairs. He went to the window to check for trouble, and spotted Benny pushing his cart on the other side of the street. He opened the boarded door, stuck his thumb and forefinger in his mouth, and whistled. The junkman looked up, and Bishop waved him over. His cart rattled, filled with dented pots, a car fender, tin cans. Even Benny was doing his part for the war effort by collecting scrap metal. Ira came up from the basement, locked the door and fell heavily into his chair. He shook his head when he saw the shattered schnapps bottle again.

"Benny, what do you know? What do you hear?" Bishop asked, when he stepped on the curb.

"Hello, Bishop. You whistle loud."

"It's a gift. Say, you know how to drive, right?"

"You want me to drive your green car?"

Bishop dug out the key and handed it to Benny. "No, there's a silver one in the back. I need you to get rid of it for me."

"I haven't driven in a long time."

"It'll come back to you. Keep off the sidewalk and you'll be fine."

"Where do you want me to drive it?"

Bishop thought for a moment. "Linwood Avenue. You know where that is?"

"Fancy street. Big houses."

"That's right. Park it in front of 288. There are rocking chairs on the porch." Bishop pulled out his wallet, looked inside, and frowned. "Here's a fin for gas except it doesn't need gas. Buy lunch instead."

"What about my cart? Someone might steal my cart," Benny said, taking the money.

"Leave it in the alley. I'll keep my eye on it."

"Okay, Bishop."

"You remember the house number?"

"288."

"And the street?"

"Linwood Avenue. Fancy place. Big houses."

"Good man. Carry on, soldier."

Bishop watched Benny push his cart toward the corner.

"Not sure parking a stolen car in front of our client's house is good for business," Ira said.

"She's paying us. Her husband isn't. I want him rattled. To know I'm onto him."

"About what?" Ira asked.

"Pearl's murder? Whatever he's doing with Joey and Krieger? I don't know. He's mixed up in something. I want him jumpy when I pressure him. And I don't want that car outside your door."

"When are you planning on pressuring him?"

"Tonight."

Chapter 15

Before Bishop left Ira's office, he called Gia. Her mother answered and didn't sound pleased to hear his voice. She told him that Gia wasn't home, and he assumed she was still at Hoyt Lake with Brandt. He left a message for her to meet him across the street at the Albright and wondered if her mother would tell her.

Ira drove him to the gallery in the Hudson, but Bishop thought it might have been safer if he caught a ride with Benny. The fat man drove slowly, trying to be cautious. He'd drunk too much schnapps. A line of cars honked behind them.

"Are you rationing gas?" Bishop asked.

"What do you mean?"

"I mean step on it, Ira. I could walk there faster on my bum foot."

Ira grunted but didn't accelerate. He gripped the steering wheel like he was choking it. Bishop slid down in the passenger seat and pulled his hat brim low. Joey would be looking for him and not to offer him a job. He'd have to be careful and stay out of sight as much as possible until he figured out who killed Pearl and what Rhielman and the others were planning. Ira dropped him on the Lincoln Parkway side of the gallery then drove off at ten miles an hour, weaving slightly through Delaware Park.

Bishop watched for Gia behind a chestnut tree. From this vantage he could keep an eye on the main entrance so he wouldn't miss her. He wondered if she was still posing for Brandt with a few blouse buttons opened and her face tilted toward the sun. He thought of walking across the parkway to see if they were still picnicking by the lake. Instead, he kept his hat and shoulders slouched and tried to blend with the tree as he waited, imagining their conversations, their laughter, her angling her body as the artist wanted. He thought of them together until he wanted to drink bourbon, then he stared at the art gallery and tried to block her from his thoughts.

The Albright was all marble and columns. It looked like it had slid off Mount Olympus and skidded to a halt at the corner of Elmwood and Lincoln. Bishop had never set foot inside. The thought of spending the day with Picasso, Cezanne, and Matisse had never occurred to him. The closest he'd come had been passing out in the doorway one rainy November night. He remembered telling the copper who'd rousted him that he was trying to stay dry. The copper wasn't interested and shoved him into the downpour.

Bishop had four crushed cigarette butts by his feet and a crumpled pack of Chesterfields in his pocket when he saw Erik Krieger marching toward the entrance. The boy wore gray woolen trousers and a matching jacket. Bishop hadn't recognized him at first, mistaking him for a skinny soldier, but the bandage on his wrist where Bishop had struck him gave Erik away. The badge pinned above his breast surprised him.

Bishop watched him climb the marble stairs and enter the gallery like he owned the joint. "I'll be damned," Bishop said, aloud.

Five minutes later, Gia pulled to the curb. Bishop watched her from behind the tree. She must've gone home after she posed for Brandt. She'd changed outfits and was now wearing a sleeveless white dress with blue polka dots. Her peep-toe sandals slapped against the sidewalk as she made her way to the gallery. He waited until she was close before he stepped from the tree and called her name.

"Bishop. You startled me. Why were you hiding behind a tree?"

He took her arm, turning her around, and quick-limped her back to the curb. "I'll tell you in the car."

"We're not going inside?"

"I think that Krieger kid works as a security guard here. He'd spot us."

"Are you sure?" she asked. "He's awful thin for that kind of work."

"It's not boxing, Gia. There's no weight classes for watchmen."

In the car, Bishop slouched down again.

"Are you embarrassed to be seen with me?" she asked, starting the engine.

"That'll be the day. Let's get out of here."

"Where are we going?"

"Ira's office."

"Tell me what's going on."

He told her all of it: Flynn and his theory about the Klan, the two Gospels trying to grab him at The Kitty Kat, the third locked in Ira's basement. He saved Krieger surprising him at Brandt's studio for last.

"After I knocked the kid out, I pulled this from his pocket." He showed her the Albright director's business card.

"Andrew Ritchie? What's he got to do with this?"

"I don't know. We were going to chat with him but then Krieger showed up. We'll have to call him."

They parked in Ira's alley. The Merc was gone but Benny's cart was still there, the scrap metal inside untouched. Ira answered the door on the first knock. His jacket was off, his sleeves rolled to the elbows, revealing pale, hairless arms. Sweat shone on his face and darkened his collar.

"Don't tell me you've been exercising," Bishop said, following Gia inside.

"I was interrogating the prisoner."

Bishop frowned. "What'd you find out?"

"He says he's not a Nazi."

"Of course, he's not a Nazi. He's one of Joey's goons."

"I'm not convinced."

"How did you interrogate him?" Bishop asked, noticing Ira's reddened knuckles.

"The way I've wanted to interrogate a Nazi since Kristallnacht," he said. "That's not true, actually. I wanted to beat him with a phonebook, but I couldn't tear it in half. The cops beat you with only half a phonebook, don't they?"

"I don't know," Bishop said. "Buffalo cops don't care if they leave marks." He touched Gia's wrist. "Fill Ira in on Krieger and Andrew Ritchie while I check on Mary Magdalen."

Bishop went down the cellar steps. The Gospel was still tied upright in the chair, but his head was slumped, his chin resting on his chest. He looked up when Bishop pulled the light chain. His left eye was swelling and would soon close, his upper lip split. Bishop pulled the wadded handkerchief from his mouth.

"You all right?"

He spit blood on the floor. "I'm going to carve up that fat bastard a pound at a time."

"That'd take a while. He thinks you're a Nazi."

"He's crazy."

"You pal around with Nazis—Dewey, his kid, Rhielman."

"I do what Joey tells me."

"How's Joey mixed up with those jackboots? What's in it for him?"

"Money." He spit out more blood. "What else?"

"What's the play?"

"I'm not telling you or that hippo anything," he said.

"You better think that over. There's no telling what'll happen when a fat man starts throwing his weight around."

"I'm going to let my brothers take care of you. Ira's mine."

"It's nice to be wanted. Let's talk again later." Bishop balled the handkerchief and forced it back into his mouth, then pulled the chain, dousing the cellar back to gloom.

He climbed the stairs as he normally did, placing both feet on the tread before pulling himself up to the next step. Every firing nerve reminded him that he'd been on his foot too long. At the top of the stairs, he closed the narrow door and locked it.

"What'd he say?" Gia asked.

"That he's not a fan of Ira's."

"He didn't tell you anything?" Ira asked.

"He didn't deny that the Kriegers and Rhielman were Nazis…"

"I knew it!"

"…but he didn't confirm it either. We know as much as we did before you smacked him around."

"He deserved it, and I enjoyed it." He slapped his belly like he just finished a satisfying meal.

"Don't do it again," Bishop said. "Not even with half a phonebook. You're the lawyer. Stick to the legal stuff. If anything shady needs to be done, either me or Gia will do it. That's our job. And that includes smacking Nazis who aren't really Nazis, so lay off."

"I'd like to smack a Nazi or two," said Gia.

"Everyone should be able to hit at least one," Ira offered.

"You two are going to win the war all by yourselves at this rate."

"So, what's next?" Gia asked.

Bishop dug out the business card. "You call this Ritchie guy."

"What am I supposed to say?"

"Find out if Krieger works there, when he started, stuff like that. Pretend you're a landlady and you're checking to see if he has a job before you rent to him."

"Okay."

"And don't sound sexy. Landladies aren't sexy."

"Wait until I own a house."

"I've had enough for one day," Ira said, rolling down his sleeves. "Beating Nazis is exhausting. Lock up when you leave."

"I don't have a key."

Ira pulled his jacket from the back of his leather chair and wrestled it on. He yanked open a desk drawer and rummaged until he found a key. "Don't lose it," he said, tossing it to Bishop.

"Thanks, and be careful. Check for tails and lock your doors. They know I work for you."

"Don't worry about me," he said, and patted his jacket where the revolver hung heavy.

"Be careful anyways," Bishop said. "And don't shoot yourself. Cut the lights and lock the door like you usually do when you leave."

The fat man tipped his hat, killed the lights, and locked the door behind him. Bishop handed Gia the candlestick phone. "Let's get Ritchie on the horn."

She dialed while Bishop listened in. They stood next to one another, shoulders brushing, and shared the earpiece. He could smell lilac in her hair and mint on her breath. He put his arm around her, resting his hand on her hip. She let him keep it there. When the receptionist answered, she asked for Mr. Ritchie, but her voice wasn't hers. It was her mother's and grandmother's, it was the voices of all the Seventh Street women who called to each other from front porches and open windows. The English was broken, with patterned tone changes and extra vowels tagged to the ends of words. He squeezed her hip and she leaned into him. When Ritchie came on the line, she told him that Erik Krieger wanted to rent a room from her, and she wasn't renting a room to no bum.

"Mr. Krieger has been working at the gallery about a month," Ritchie said, his voice thin and tinny on the other end.

"Yeah? What he do there? Sweep floors?"

"Mr. Krieger is the gallery's new night watchmen."

"He say he sleep all day and work all night. That I'll never even know he in my house," Gia said.

"Yes, I suppose that's true."

"He the only night watchmen you got?"

"Yes, he took over for a young man who joined the navy."

"Only one, huh? He must be some big cheese, this Krieger."

"We're grateful to have him. So many men are going into the service. It's hard to find people," Ritchie said.

"You right. So many. God bless. None of my business, but you pay him good? He can afford four-fifty a week for a room? It's a nice a room."

"He should be able to manage that without any problem."

"Okay then, a Mr. Ritchie. You a good man. I believe you. I rent him the room. Thank you much."

Gia hung up the phone and laughed. "That was fun."

"Forget about being a P.I. You should be on radio," Bishop said.

She pulled away from him, sat in Ira's chair and put her feet up, crossing her legs at the ankle. Bishop took a seat on the other side of the desk. He was sorry she was so far away from him. He could still feel his hand on her hip.

"So, Erik does work there," she said.

"The rooster guarding the hens."

"Maybe he needed an extra job."

"Smart money says he's the inside guy," Bishop said.

"Inside guy for what?"

"I'm not sure."

"What's our next move then?"

"We need to talk to Brandt," Bishop said. "These other mugs— Joey, Rhielman, that knucklehead in the cellar and his brothers—aren't going to talk. They're all tough nuts. Brandt's the weak one and the one most likely to have iced Pearl. How was your date?"

She glared at him. "It wasn't a date."

"How was your posing session?"

"It was fine."

"You got some sun," he said, her cheeks and nose already pinking. "When do you see him again?"

"He wants to paint my portrait at his lake house."

"Is that what you kids are calling it these days? 'Painting the portrait'?"

"Shut up, Bishop."

"You know he wants you up at the lake for other reasons, right?"

"I wanted to pose at his studio, but he said the light was different at the lake. The angle or something."

"When does he want to start?"

"Next week. The house should be done by then."

"What do you mean 'done'?" Bishop asked.

"They remodeled. Took out walls, added a room. They've been working on it all summer evidently. The painters should be finished in a few days. He was quite excited about it."

"He's excited about getting you there," Bishop said. He rubbed his chin. "Do they own more than one lake house?"

"I don't think so. Why?"

"Elizabeth Brandt wasn't home the night of Pearl's murder. She told me she went to their lake house for the weekend."

"So, she lied."

"She doesn't strike me as the paint-scraping type."

"Are you going to confront her?"

"We better drive out there and make sure this remodeling story checks out first."

"Why would Brandt lie?"

"All killers lie."

Before they left, he took Brandt's bird drawing from his pocket, smoothed it flat, and left it on the desk for Ira to find in the morning.

* * *

The late-afternoon sun burned low and hot as they wound their way on Lake Shore Drive. They'd left the city and the world seemed to unfold before them with Lake Erie's great expanse on one side and the open road ahead. Sailboats dotted the water, appearing still on the horizon as if painted in place. They passed beaches, clam shacks, and lakefront bars as seagulls cried above them. The tires' hum and the car's steady movement lulled Bishop until his eyes closed, and his head nodded. He was aware of Gia's voice and the radio playing and the seagulls calling, but every sound reached him muffled and distant. After a few miles, his head snapped up and he blurted, "Check for tails."

"I am. We're alone."

His head drooped again for another stretch until he dreamt that his cane had splintered, and he was falling from a great height. He jerked awake and checked the side mirror and then over his shoulder to be sure they weren't being followed. This is how he'd slept since he was released from jail: in brief snatches and never fully resting.

"I'm going to slip you a Mickey, so you'll sleep without twitching around," Gia said.

"I'd settle for a sock in the jaw."

"I can do that, too. You wouldn't even see it coming."

"How much further?"

"It's right up here, I think," Gia said.

They turned onto an unpaved driveway and rolled up the windows to keep the dust and dirt from coming into the car. They snaked their way to a clearing. A two-story home crowned a rise overlooking the shore. A stone staircase led down to the deserted beach.

"That must be it," Gia said.

"It's got to be. There isn't another house around."

"A bootlegger built it. There's a tunnel that leads from the basement to the beach. That's where they unloaded booze from Canada and brought it ashore."

"Brandt told you that?"

"He was proud of it."

"That's why it's in the middle of nowhere. No witnesses. Same reason he wants to get you out here alone," Bishop said.

"Not everybody thinks like you, Bishop."

"You'd be surprised."

They parked and climbed out of the car. Wide tire tracks crisscrossed through the dirt. Bishop pointed to them. "Trucks."

They heard the lake lapping against the shore as they climbed the front steps.

"I pictured a much smaller house," Bishop said.

"Meyer has money."

"*Elizabeth* has money. She lets Meyer play with it sometimes."

The front windows were coated with dust. Bishop wiped the pane with his sleeve. They stood shoulder-to-shoulder and pressed their faces against the glass, their hands shielding their eyes to cut the glare. The floors were covered with tarps and ladders, the walls half painted.

"Looks like Brandt was telling the truth," Bishop said.

"And Elizabeth lied."

"I'm beginning to think I'm the last honest person in this town."

"God help us."

They walked around the house, stopping to peer through each window. When they reached the backdoor, Bishop handed her his cane.

"What are you doing?" she asked.

He pulled the lock picking tools from his pocket. "We need to check the second floor. Those rooms could be finished. Maybe she was here decorating the night Pearl was killed."

"You don't believe that do you?"

"No, but we have to check. That's what we do."

He bent to the lock and worked quickly, wanting to impress her.

"How'd you learn to do that?" she asked.

"Sal taught me."

"Of course, he did. All uncles teach their nephews how to pick locks and pockets and winners at the track."

"I was never good at picking pockets," Bishop said.

"Still, he gave you quite the education."

"Wait until I tell you what he gave me for Christmas one year."

"Was it your favorite toy?"

"Something like that."

The tumblers clicked into place, and he pushed open the door. He bowed and extended his arm, ushering her in. She handed him his cane and entered with eyes closed and nose in the air, pretending to be royalty. He followed behind, a cocktail of fear and excitement hitting him as soon as he stepped across the threshold. It felt stronger, a headier rush than when he'd broke into Pearl's apartment or Brandt's studio. Having Gia with him increased the potency of everything.

The lake house smelled of plaster, turpentine, and yesterday's cigarettes. A few windows were cracked for ventilation, but the house was hot with retained heat. It'd be cooler when it was occupied and the doors and tall windows were opened, capturing the lake breeze, but for now the air was still and stifling. Bishop loosened his tie to breathe. He imagined the house decorated in a nautical theme with sea paintings and anchors and oars hung as decorations. The temperature increased as they climbed the stairs to the second floor. The three bedrooms had been painted light gray, sky blue, and turquoise. None of the rooms were furnished.

"Well, if she was here when Pearl was murdered, she either slept on the floor or on a tarp," Bishop said.

"She wasn't here, Bishop."

"The question is, where was she and why'd she lie about it?"

"She was someplace she shouldn't have been," Gia said.

"Or *with* somebody she shouldn't have been with."

"Maybe she was having an affair, too."

"Bingo."

* * *

They stopped at a cafe on their way back to the city. They sat outside at a small table covered with a blue and white checkered tablecloth and watched the water shimmer and the sailboats grow larger as they neared the shore. There was something about being near the water—the sound or smell or motion—that always calmed Bishop. He felt the same way staring into a wood-burning fire. Even his foot felt better.

"I want a cold beer," Gia said.

"Good, because you won't get a Sidecar in a joint like this."

"I don't want to drink in front of you."

"I'll be fine. Beer's for amateurs."

"When we were on the phone with Ritchie in Ira's office," she said, "you were standing pretty close."

"Close enough to touch you."

"You were touching me."

"Was I?"

"I didn't smell liquor on your breath."

"Maybe I wasn't standing close enough."

"Maybe you weren't, but I still would've smelled it," she said. "I'm proud of you, Bishop."

"The jury's still out," he said, but hearing her say that made him feel better than he had in a long time.

A waitress brought menus. She was a fresh-faced kid with fair skin and freckles. Bishop guessed she was the owner's niece or daughter, the sweetheart of some soldier or sailor she wrote to every night before falling asleep. He didn't think her face would be as fresh or eyes as bright by the time the war ended. He didn't think she'd ever see her soldier or sailor again either, then chided himself for letting his mood darken.

They ordered beer, soda water, and oysters. Even if the service was slow and she spilled the drinks, Bishop decided he'd leave the waitress a big tip, as if that would make up for the coming war years and what lay ahead for her, for all of them.

"When will you question Elizabeth?" Gia asked.

"Not right away. I think I'll tail her for a while. See how she spends her days and nights and with whom."

"Following your own client? Ira will love that."

"It won't be good for his blood pressure."

"And Meyer?" she asked. "His studio checked out except for that Krieger kid showing up?"

"I guess. I wasn't sure what I was looking for. Then Krieger came before I was done poking around. A couple things bothered me, though."

"What?"

"He has two locks on his door, the heavy-duty kind," Bishop said.

"Maybe he's very protective of his artwork."

"None of the other studio doors have locks like that. I checked on my way out. Did you ever see what he keeps in that big cabinet that takes up the whole wall?"

"The metal one?" Gia asked. "No. It's always been closed when I was there."

"Closed and padlocked?"

"I think so."

"I peeked inside," Bishop said. "It's empty except for five canvasses all the same size. Krieger walked in on me before I could unroll them and see what they were. After I knocked him out, I hightailed it in case anyone heard us rolling around and called the cops. That big cabinet and its five paintings have been nagging at me."

"Nagging you enough to go back and take another look?"

"I think so."

"When?"

"After we finish the oysters."

Gia ate most of the oysters and chased them with a second beer. Bishop's stomach clenched after the first one. He felt full even though he couldn't remember the last meal he'd eaten. He nibbled on salted crackers as he watched her slurp them down one after the other. By the time they drove back to the city, the art institute had closed for the night. They parked in the alley near the side gate leading to the backyard. The gate squeaked when they opened it. They froze for a heartbeat or two and waited to see if anyone'd heard. No one did so they cut across the lawn without speaking, their shoes dusty and sand-coated from the lake house.

The rear door had a simple lock. It didn't give Bishop any trouble. Once inside, they listened to make sure they were alone, his pulse already quickening. He imagined paint-smeared artists locked away in their studios, holding their brushes like foils and fencing with canvasses as they worked through the night. Maybe he'd gotten that idea from some B movie he'd seen at The Allendale or maybe they were early, and the artists and their muses hadn't arrived yet. The institute was as quiet and deserted as the lake house had been.

Bishop climbed the stairs at his own pace and rested when he needed. Gia stayed by his side. When they walked down the hallway, he pointed to the door locks with his cane. "They're as old as the house," he whispered. When they arrived at Brandt's studio, he pointed to the new hardware. "See? Like Fort Knox."

Gia nodded as he pulled out his tools. Like earlier in the day, he struggled with the locks.

"Want me to do it?" she whispered. "I know how."

"I remember. It was quite the job interview."

"A girl learns a lot on Seventh Street, including breaking and entering. Let me have a turn."

"Back up a few steps. You're too close. You're distracting me," Bishop said. Sweat trickled into his eye. He knuckled it away.

"It's my fault you can't pick locks?"

"Quiet. I'm working."

"Let me try," she said again.

"Fine," Bishop said, and handed her the picks. She bent to the lock. Her fingers—calm, steady—worked the tools without hesitation. Determination knitted her brows, set her jaw. Bishop found himself holding his breath, rooting for her, unable to stop staring at her face.

Her expression didn't change when the first lock opened. She just blew a wisp of hair out of her eyes and started on the second. When she opened that lock, they both laughed.

"Show off," Bishop said.

"Damn right," Gia said, and pushed open the door. They headed straight to the metal cabinet. "You want to pick the padlock? It looks easy."

"You do it," Bishop said. "You're on a roll."

Picking the padlock was simple after the door. She jerked the handle and pulled it free. The five canvasses were still lined on the shelf. Bishop grabbed the first and unrolled it. It was an oil portrait of a mother holding her child. The mother had a cloud of dark hair, almost black, while the child looked angelic with golden ringlets. They shared the same rosed cheeks and rounded blue eyes, their skin almost luminescent. There was a soft, fullness to the mother that hinted at comfort and warmth, her breast partially exposed. They wore silvery gowns, the fabrics—silk, perhaps—blended as if woven from the same thread, each fold and wrinkle distinct and shadowed.

"*Mere et Enfant*," Gia said.

"What?"

"*Mother and Child*. Renoir."

"How do you know that?" Bishop asked.

"It's Meyer's favorite painting. It's at the Albright. They acquired it a few years ago. We've stopped and looked at it every time we've been there. He'd stare at it for hours if they'd let him."

Bishop rolled the canvas and unrolled the next.

"It's the same," Gia said. "Mother and child."

And so were the third and fourth and fifth canvasses, all copies of Renoir's *Mere et Enfant*.

"Why five?" Bishop asked.

"Maybe he was trying to get it right."

"Why?"

"To improve his technique? To show he could do it?" Gia asked. "Wanting to be like his hero? My cousin tries to swing like DiMaggio."

"Your cousin's twelve. Brandt's a grown man, an accomplished artist from what I can tell."

"You're all little boys. You're all twelve years old."

"Why lock five copies away? Pearl's portrait is right there on an easel and there are sketches covering that table by the widow," Bishop said, pointing. "Any bum could snatch Pearl or stuff a couple drawings in their pocket and limp out of here. Those original pieces must be worth more than a bunch of copies of someone else's work."

"Let's lay them next to each other and see if we can spot the differences, see if he was trying to make each one better," Gia said.

They laid them side-by-side, then stepped back and compared them. They couldn't spot flaws or variations. To their untrained eyes, each was an exact duplicate of the others.

"Bishop," she said, staring from one painting to the next, "If you hung any of these next to the original in the Albright, I don't think I could tell them apart."

"Maybe that's the idea."

Chapter 16

Bishop wanted to swing by Ira's office to check on the Gospel. Maybe a few hours in the dark listening things skittering in the cellar had changed his mind about talking. They heard sirens as they approached, smelled smoke as they rounded the corner, and saw Ira's building engulfed in flames as they drew near.

"The man in the basement," Gia said.

"Ira."

"He went home."

"He could've come back," Bishop said, and white knuckled his cane.

The street was cordoned for emergency vehicles, so Gia pulled to the curb and parked. Bishop hurried from the car toward the fire, ignoring the shouts from police and firemen to get back. He didn't think of how he'd get past the flames or how he'd carry his friend if he found him unconscious on the floor. His only thought was of Ira. As he neared the building, the second-floor windows exploded from heat and black smoke billowed through jagged openings. Shards rained on the street, and Bishop had to turn and crouch, hunching his shoulders to protect himself from falling glass. A hand gripped his arm and jerked him toward the curb.

"You trying to get yourself killed, bub?" the patrolman asked. "Running into flames is a hell of a way to go."

"My friend might be in there."

"If he is, the firemen'll find what's left of him," the cop said and pushed him on the sidewalk.

A crowd had gathered to watch the building burn. Dewey Krieger stood crossed armed in his store's doorway, the inferno lighting his face. Haze and embers drifted over all of them. Bishop turned back to Ira's office. Flames leapt and darted inside, fueled by Ira's law and ornithology books, his crooked chair and old desk, all his possessions stoking the blaze. Bishop prayed—something he only did when drying out—that Ira was safe at home. Then he thought of the Evangelist tied in the basement, struggling to get free before the burning ceiling collapsed. Maybe the smoke would get him first. Maybe it already had. Either way, he was a poor dead bastard.

Lieutenant Darcy leaned against a lamppost watching the firemen aim a hose into a shattered window. When Bishop spotted him, he caned his way through the crowd. "Lieutenant," Bishop called, above another approaching siren.

Darcy looked over and his expression soured. "Not tonight, Weasel."

"Have you seen Ira?"

"No, and if he's inside, we'll never see him again. Nothing's going to survive in there. Those hoses are pissing in the ocean."

Bishop thought he might get sick in the street.

Gia hurried through the crowd to his side. "Are you all right? Jesus, what were you thinking?"

"I'm fine."

"Fine? You're crazy trying to gimp into that building," Darcy said. "Did you forget you're crippled? And what the hell was Ira up to, anyway? Did he have a still in the basement? That's a hell of a fire."

"It was arson," Bishop said.

"And how do you know *that*?" Darcy asked. "Are you confessing?"

"He was being harassed, and it was escalating—first they painted shit on his window, then smashed his door and ransacked the office, and now this."

"Who was harassing him?"

"I don't know for sure, but I'd start with Krieger and his kid across the street," Bishop said. He pointed to Dewey still standing in the doorway.

Darcy turned and stared at him. The hardware store owner uncrossed his arms and went into his shop. He turned the door sign to "Closed".

"They've had beefs with Ira in the past?" Darcy asked.

"Krieger doesn't like Jews."

"Christ," Darcy said. "Did Ira report any of this?"

"I doubt it."

"If he didn't report it because he thought you'd protect him, he bet on a lame pony. You know what happens to lame ponies, right? They put them down. One shot between the eyes."

"Let's call Ira," Gia said, tugging Bishop's arm. "See if he's home. He may not even know about this yet."

"See you around, Weasel," Darcy said. "Hopefully, in handcuffs."

"Me or you?"

"Scram."

"Talk to Krieger."

Darcy waved him away.

Gia and Bishop walked to the drugstore on the corner and went inside. No teenagers were flipping through comic books or seated at the soda fountain. No customers conferred with the pharmacist or shopped the shelves. The clerk stood at the window, craning his neck so hard to watch the blaze his crooked bowtie stood straight.

"Some fire," he said.

"Yeah," Bishop answered.

"Lousy for business. Everyone's outside watching it burn. Can't blame them."

Bishop fought the urge to cane him.

The phonebooth was by the magazines. They crossed the planked floor, past the racks of *Life*, *Look*, and *Photoplay*. Bishop left the bifold door open and dropped a nickel in the slot. The operator rang Ira's house. No one answered. He had her try again to be sure, but, still, no one picked up.

"Come on," he said, fishing his nickel from the coin return. "Let's drive over there. Maybe he hit the schnapps and the schnapps hit back."

"Has it ever hit you?" Gia asked.

"I'm learning to duck."

* * *

Ira lived in a cottage near the river, a few blocks west of Gia on Seventh Street. To Bishop, the house had always seemed too small for such a large man. He imagined him bumping into furniture and knocking over vases whenever he turned or rose from the couch. But Ira liked it there because of the variety of birds nesting near the water. He could sit in his small backyard with schnapps and binoculars and watch Sabine gulls, blue warblers, canvasbacks, and the other song and shorebirds who were his neighbors.

Ira's Hudson was parked in front of the cottage when they arrived, and Bishop was relieved. They pulled behind it, and the detective paused to touch the hood as they walked past. It felt cool. "It hasn't been driven in a while," he said,

"Bishop," Gia said, and pointed to the front door. It was ajar.

He pulled The Fitz and cocked it. "Wait here."

She followed him up the walk.

He called Ira's name as they climbed the three steps to the low porch. There was no answer. The jamb had been splintered when the door was forced open. Bishop toed the brass kickplate and the door swung wide, the hinges squeaking. Inside, chairs were overturned, lamps knocked to the floor. Colored heron and mallard illustrations, like the ones now ashes in Ira's office, hung askew where they'd been bumped and jostled. He called again, but the house remained silent.

"He put up a fight," Gia said.

"It's not easy moving a three-hundred-pound man who doesn't want to budge. Call the cops while I check the rest of the house."

The small kitchen showed no signs of struggle. A few dishes soaked in the sink. A bottle of schnapps sat in the middle of the table like a centerpiece. Ira's sport coat was draped over a chair. The .38 was still in its pocket. Bishop took it. The backdoor was locked and chained. He pulled back the lace curtain and peered into the yard. Birdfeeders hung from trees and bird houses were nestled on limbs snug against trunks. Birdbaths marked each corner of the property. He let the curtain fall and returned to the living room as Gia hung up the phone.

"Cops are on their way," she said.

"Here," he said, handing her the gun. "Stick this in your purse."

"And some poor girls only get roses."

"Insurance policies are better than flowers."

He climbed the stairs to the second floor, the risers creaking beneath him. Gia followed behind, gripping the .38. Like the kitchen, the bedrooms were undisturbed. Ira's bed was made, the bedspread smoothed and even. The mattress sagged in the middle, caved by the heavy man's weight. A wooden shaving mirror, a matching brush and comb set, and an ashtray overflowing with coins rested on his dresser. A silver-framed photograph of a dark-haired woman with a wide smile and bright eyes was on the nightstand next to an alarm clock, its ticking filled the room.

"Who's she?" Gia asked.

"No idea. He's never mentioned a woman."

"Maybe it's a relative. A sister? A kissing cousin?

"She's too pretty to be related."

They retraced their steps to the living room. Bishop checked the walls and floor. There were no blood drops on the rug, smudged on doorframes, or splattered on wainscotting.

"Whoever took Ira, grabbed him here," Bishop said. "He was still alive when they left."

"You sure?"

"It'd take six guys to carry him out."

"The neighbors must've seen something," Gia said.

A police siren grew louder as it approached, scaring the birds on the front yard, scattering them to flight. Bishop holstered The Fitz. Gia slipped the .38 in her purse.

"At least he didn't go back to his office," Bishop said.

* * *

After they gave their statements to the officers, Gia and Bishop shared a smoke on the porch, passing the Chesterfield after each drag. Ira lived on a quiet street. Few cars drove down it. Birds sang and called to each other from treetops as they talked. It was too peaceful a place for an abduction.

"Who would've taken Ira?" Gia asked. She handed the cigarette to Bishop. "Nazis?"

"Old Man Krieger was at the fire. It wasn't him."

"We still need to talk to Brandt and tail Elizabeth."

"Forget them. We have to find Ira." He offered the cig to Gia, but she waved it off.

"Where do we start?" she asked.

"No idea. But what I do know," Bishop said, "is we're being watched."

"Where? Who's watching us?"

"Brick house across the street. Front window. Look out of the corner of your eye like you're staring at something else."

"The curtain moved," Gia said.

"Yup."

"A nosey neighbor."

"They're the best kind when you're looking for a witness."

"Are we going to talk to them?"

"Yeah, before the cops do," he said, and flicked the butt into the bushes.

They crossed the street, and the front curtain was pulled closed.

"He must be shy," she said, as they climbed the front steps.

"Or scared."

Bishop rapped on the door. From inside, they heard muttering, locks turned and chains drawn. The door opened enough that Bishop could see the old man's face. It was lined and wrinkled like spoiled fruit. He had nervous eyes that darted between Bishop and Gia, never settling on either of them.

"My name is Nicholas Bishop. I'm a private investigator," he said, handing him his business card. "And this is my conscience, Giancarla Alessi."

"I know who you are," the old man said. "I seen your picture in the paper. You're that detective with the busted foot."

"You're famous, Bishop," Gia said. "Alan Ladd should play you in the movies."

"I'm taller than Ladd," he said, straightening. "Say, mister, we have a few questions we'd like to ask you. Can we come in?"

"No."

"It might be easier if we went inside. More private," Bishop said.

"No."

"All right. We'll talk right here. What's your name?"

"None of your business."

"Friendly type, isn't he?" Gia asked.

"He sure is. We'll call him Charlie Rainbow."

"This about the fat lawyer across the street?"

"His name is Ira Weiss," Gia said.

"I seen them take him."

"When was this?" Bishop asked.

"About an hour ago."

"Who took him?"

"I don't know. Never seen them before. They had a heck of a time getting him in their car. He didn't want to go." The man looked past Bishop as if he could still see Ira struggling with his kidnappers.

"Could you describe the men?"

"Too far away. Eyesight's not so good anymore. They all looked the same to me, though. Like they were related. Same build. Same hair. Nice suits."

"How many were there?" Bishop asked.

"Four."

"What about the car?" Gia asked. "Do you know the make? Ford? Nash?"

"I don't know cars. It was silver."

"Four mugs who look alike and a silver car," Bishop said to Gia. "The Gospels."

"All four? How'd the one in the basement escape?"

"Must've been a New Testament miracle."

"Maybe there are five of them," Gia said.

"A lost Gospel we don't know about?"

"Maybe."

"You two talk crazy," Charlie Rainbow said, squinting his eyes as if his head hurt.

"You should hear her when she's been drinking."

"Why didn't you call the police when you saw them kidnapping Ira?" Gia asked.

"I don't like talking to coppers."

"Nobody does, pal, but it's like going to confession," Bishop said. "Sometimes you just got to do it."

"I got nothing to confess."

"You must be a saint. Saint Charlie of the Rainbow. You got anything else to tell us, your holiness?"

"Yeah, that fat man was yelling about Nazis."

* * *

Gia and Bishop decided to search for the silver Mercury, hoping it would lead them to Ira. Brandt and Elizabeth would have to wait until morning. The sun had set, but the city was brightening with neon. Gia drove under the speed limit so Bishop could scan both sides of the street for the Silver Merc. When they turned onto Delaware Avenue, Bishop spotted Benny. The junkman dragged his left leg and leaned on his empty cart like it kept him upright.

"Pull over," Bishop said.

Gia cut off a delivery truck to get to the curb. The driver leaned on the horn and swore as he passed. She cursed back in Italian, gesturing out the open window. Bishop ignored them. He got out of the car too quickly and almost fell when he put weight on his injured foot.

"Benny," he called, righting himself, wincing in pain. "What do you know? What do you hear?"

Benny flinched as if a grenade had exploded nearby. He turned and Bishop saw it all at once: the bruised face, the bleeding mouth, the cut eyelid. "Benny, what the hell happened? Who did this to you?"

"I'm sorry, Bishop. I'm sorry."

"There's nothing to be sorry about. Tell me who hit you."

"I let you down, Bishop. I didn't finish the mission."

"What are you talking about? What mission?"

"I didn't park the silver car where you told me. I didn't park it at 288 Linwood, the fancy house with rocking chairs. I let you down."

"You didn't let me down, Benny," Bishop said. "Where did you park it?"

"Nowhere. The men took it from me."

"They took the car? What men?"

"The Gospel men."

"Sonofabitch."

"They made me pullover, Bishop. Came alongside and pointed guns. I got scared."

"How many Gospel men, Benny?" Gia asked. She opened her purse, pushed the .38 out of the way, and pulled out a handkerchief.

"Three. They dragged me out of the car. Two held me. The other hit me."

"I'll kill them," Bishop said.

Gia daubed at his bloody lip with the handkerchief. "Why'd they hit you, Benny?"

"They wanted to know where I got the silver car from. I wouldn't tell them."

"You should've told them, Benny. Right away. You don't have to take a beating for me. Not ever."

"I didn't want to let you down, Bishop. You always been good to me."

"You didn't let me down."

"I did. I told them. They hit me too hard. It hurt."

"What'd you tell them, Benny?" Gia asked, her voice soft and quiet. She worked on his eye, dabbing the lid like a cornerman in a prizefight.

"That I got it from the alley behind the fat man's office and you told me to park it in front of 288 Linwood Avenue. A big, fancy house with rocking chairs."

"So, they knocked you around, then went to Ira's office looking for me or him or both and found their brother instead. No New Testament miracle after all," Bishop said.

"They must've torched the place then went after Ira."

"I'm getting tired of these Gospels smacking people around," Bishop said. "First me, then Benny, now Ira. A cripple, a fat man, and a junkman who hasn't hurt anyone in twenty-five years."

"Not exactly your top three heavyweight contenders," Gia said.

"Maybe not, but guys like us can surprise you once in a while."

"With a lucky punch?"

"Or a bullet."

* * *

Bishop gave Benny what was left in his wallet. He'd wanted to take him home, wherever that was, but Benny wouldn't abandon his cart. Gia tried to convince him that no one would bother with it, that they could stash it an alley and retrieve it in the morning, but he wouldn't listen. The cart was his whole life, he'd said, and that made Bishop feel sadder than he had in a long while. When they pulled away, the junkman was standing on the sidewalk next to the cart still apologizing. Bishop stared out the window. Cars blurred by, their makes and models not registering. They could have driven by the silver Merc three times, and he wouldn't have noticed. His breathing grew deeper, more rapid as he inhaled and exhaled through his nose.

"Are you all right?" Gia asked.

He nodded, but he wasn't all right. Anger was growing inside him. It was white-hot, liquifying the numbness brought by months of alcohol and indifference to what happened to himself or others. He felt layers of skin and marrow dissolving, leaving nothing but exposed nerves. Benny was simple, harmless. Whatever meanness he'd possessed had been blasted from him during the war. He was the last person in this town who deserved a beating. Rage was overtaking Bishop.

They were driving down Delaware when a car sped past them.

"Didn't you break Rhielman's taillight?" Gia asked.

"Yeah," he said, barely hearing her. "The lens cover."

"And he drives a Ford, right?"

"Yeah," he answered, still staring out the window but seeing only Benny's bruised face and fearful eyes. He pounded the floorboard with his cane.

206 – STEPHEN G. EOANNOU

"I think he passed us."

"Who?"

"Rhielman."

"What about him?"

"Christ, Bishop," Gia said. "Wake up. Is that Rhielman ahead of us or not?"

Bishop looked out the windshield and saw Rhielman's Ford two car lengths ahead, his broken taillight a beacon. "Yeah, that's him. That bald fuck is either too lazy or too stupid to get his light fixed," Bishop said. "I wonder where he's going. Hang back a little. You don't have to follow close. That busted cover is a target. Keep your eye on that and you won't lose him."

"You sure you want to tail him? The Gospels grabbed Ira, not him. We might be wasting time that Ira doesn't have."

"We have no idea where they're holding Ira. He could be anywhere. Rhielman seems to be involved in everything. Last time I tailed him, he led me to Krieger and Joey Bones. Let's see where he goes tonight. Maybe he'll take us right to those piece-of-shit Gospels."

"He has passengers," Gia said. "One in the backseat, and one up front."

"Keep with him."

Gia tailed the Ford, staying far behind but keeping her eyes on the cracked lens cover and the seeping white light. Rhielman drove straight down Delaware to The Chez Amis. He parked in front of the entrance. Gia pulled to the curb and doused her lights. They watched as Rhielman hurried to the passenger side. He opened the door and extended his hand. Elizabeth Brandt stepped from the car.

"What the hell?" Gia said.

"I told you there was something off about her."

"What's she doing with *him*?"

"He goes to her house a lot. They're tennis buddies," Bishop said. "The maid told me."

"I think they're more than that."

"You thinking he's sleeping with both Doris and Elizabeth?" Bishop asked. "I should've voted for him last election."

Rhielman opened the rear door next and two long legs swung to the curb. Bishop would have recognized those pins anywhere; he'd stared at them in photographs and through motel curtains long enough. The blonde stepped from the Ford onto the sidewalk, her red dress vibrant under the marquee lights. She glanced around, her chin high, as if waiting to be swarmed by photographers and blinded by flashbulbs.

"Doris Slater," Bishop said.

"Three on a date. Nice."

"Don't judge. I have a new respect for Rhielman."

"Why'd she go back to him?" Gia asked.

"Maybe she's trying to find out information about the Krauts for me. Maybe that negative scared her."

"If that's true, you should be ashamed of yourself, Bishop. He hits her."

"I am ashamed but not about her," Bishop said.

"Jesus, is she wearing Pearl's wig?"

"Maybe Rhielman feels like smacking a blonde tonight."

"Maybe Elizabeth hits her, too."

"I told you she wasn't right."

The trio walked to the club, the women on either side of the former councilman. The doorman, Albert, ushered them inside. Rhielman nodded at him but didn't palm him a tip.

"Are we going in?" Gia asked.

"We'll have to order water. I gave all my scratch to Benny."

"I have a little of my first communion money left."

"Your grandparents would be proud of you spending it at a nightclub."

They exited the car and Gia took Bishop's arm. Albert didn't smile as they approached. Bishop swung his cane in circles like Chaplin when they neared.

"Here's trouble," Albert said.

"Don't talk about my date that way," Bishop answered.

"You two behave yourselves tonight. No skipping on bar tabs or passing out in bathrooms."

"I plan on passing out in the ladies' room in about an hour," Gia said.

"Say, Albert. Those three who entered ahead of us. Do they come here together a lot?"

"What three people?"

"The three that went inside."

"I didn't see no three people."

"You didn't, huh?"

"No, sir."

"Maybe a fin would buy you some memory pills. Help you remember things."

"Maybe it would," Albert said.

Bishop nodded at Gia's purse. She glared at him but pulled out a five-dollar bill and handed it to the doorman.

"So, they come here a lot?" Bishop asked, again.

"They do but not together. And that's the first time that lanky one came as a blonde."

"Did it look like Pearl's wig to you?" Gia asked.

"I'm no dame. I can't tell one from another," Albert said and shrugged. "A wig's a wig."

"How about The Gospels? They been in tonight?" Bishop asked.

"I haven't seen none of them yet."

"Maybe they were wearing blonde wigs and you didn't recognize them," Gia offered.

"Those four as blondes? *That* I'd remember," he said, opening the door.

The Chez was alive with noise. The Johnny Martone Orchestra was swinging its way through "Well, Git It!," giving the drums, trumpet, trombone, clarinet, and piano all a chance in the spotlight. The crowd by the dancefloor was clapping along, urging the band to play faster, louder. Laughter and a din of conversation came from the revolving gold bar. Cigarette and cigar smoke hung over all of it. The energy made Bishop want a drink. His tongue felt swollen. He had to swallow, imagining Four Roses burning his throat, the heat spreading through him. He missed that feeling.

Amigone stood behind the host station. His maître d' smile dissolved when he saw them enter. He wore a white dinner jacket and a dark expression. Bishop thought this oval man was the only one in the city who could look rumpled in a tux.

"This is what I need tonight?" he asked. "Bad pennies turning up?"

"See that, Gia?" Bishop said. "Pennies. He looks at us and sees money."

"I always thought we looked like new dollar bills."

"What do you and your husband want, Bishop?" Amigone asked.

"An evening of fine entertainment."

"You don't have a reservation."

"I have many but seat us up in the balcony anyway. Somewhere in the middle would be swell. You won't even know we're here."

"I always know when there's a weasel in the house. There's a certain odor." Amigone snapped his pudgy fingers and a hostess hurried over. "Seat these two upstairs. Tell the waiter they pay for their drinks upfront."

"Thanks, Phil," Bishop said. "You're a peach."

"Stagger one inch over the line tonight, Bishop, and you're getting tossed in the alley. I'll personally break your cane to watch you flop around."

"You know how to make a guest feel welcomed, Phil."

"Seat him before I beat him," he said to the hostess.

She motioned for them to follow. "This way."

They trailed her toward the balcony staircase. "Say, doll," Bishop said, to her. "How about a seat on the rail in the middle?"

"You're in luck. There's one table left," she said over her shoulder.

"I'm dripping with good fortune." He whispered to Gia, "Scan the left side of the room and I'll scan the right. Try not to make it obvious. Move your eyes and not your head as much as you can."

"What am I looking for?"

"Joey Bones, The Gospels, any Nazis in the house."

"Nazis? How do I spot them? Will they be wearing swastikas?"

"That'd be too easy."

Bishop checked his side of the dinner club. Flynn was slouched at the bar, his suitcoat wrinkled, his hair disheveled. Bishop nodded, but the reporter had rested his forehead against the bar. Bishop wondered if he'd been drinking since he'd left him that morning. A red flash made him turn. Rhielman was leading Doris to the dancefloor. Elizabeth was left alone at their table, watching him take the phony blonde into his arms. Her face was expressionless. Bishop waited for a flicker of anger or jealousy, but none came. There was no sign of Joey or the Evangelists. He knew seeing Ira sipping schnapps at a corner table was too much to ask, but he asked for it anyway. He was used to ignored prayers.

The hostess led them up a winding staircase, but she had hurried and had to wait at the top for Bishop to finish the climb. She apologized for not going slower, her eyes dropping to his cane.

"No need to apologize," he said. "I had to go slow. My sister here isn't used to wearing heels. She was recently paroled."

Gia elbowed his ribs, quick and hard. "Sister?"

They were seated at a table on the rail, which gave them a clear view of the dancefloor and bandstand at one end and the revolving bar in the middle. Bishop nodded at Gia's purse. She shook her head. He nodded at it again. She sighed and took out a dollar and handed it to the hostess.

"Now I know why you're always broke," she said, snapping her purse shut.

"And you thought I blew all my money on booze." He watched as the hostess walked to the waiter and whispered in his ear. He looked over at Bishop and frowned. Pay as you go.

"I stand corrected. You blow eighty percent on bourbon. The rest goes to tips and bribes."

"All three make the world go round," he said. He peered over the railing. "Spot anything walking in?"

"Not really. Some familiar faces but nothing to do with this case. Or cases. What about you?"

"Rhieleman and his girls have a table near the bar. He and Doris are on the dancefloor giving it a whirl. See her in that red dress?"

"You can't miss her. She's a good dancer. Must be those gams."

"She's got gams?"

"Two of them, both long and shapely. I thought an unrepentant leg man like yourself would've noticed."

"Not me. I did notice Flynn blotto at the bar, however. Too much gin for Timothy Flynn. I'll talk to him later to see if he's learned anything new. Hopefully, he'll still be capable of speech at that point. No sign of Joey or his goons."

"Now what?" she asked, as the frowning waiter arrived.

"I order drinks, and you pay for them."

* * *

Gia nursed a Sidecar, Bishop a soda water. He found nothing satisfying about it. The soda didn't heat or burn. They watched the crowd from the railing. Rhielman and Doris danced three numbers in a row, including a slow one, before returning to their table. Elizabeth had ordered champagne and a waiter hurried over once they were seated, grabbing the bottle from the ice bucket and filling their coupes. Elizabeth chatted with the ex-councilman, occasionally touching his forearm for emphasis. She rarely acknowledged Doris and spoke to her even less. Doris didn't seem to mind. She was busy downing champagne. Bishop wondered if one of her long legs was hollow. He was certain Elizabeth only ordered top shelf. She frowned every time Doris' glass was refilled.

"They don't look like a happy menage," Bishop said.

"What do you know about menages?"

"You learn a lot peeking through windows."

A half hour passed before two Gospels—the one from Ira's basement and the one Bishop had smashed in the mouth with his cane—entered the club. They headed straight to the bar, giving Rhielman a slight nod as they passed. The only remaining empty barstools were next to Timothy Flynn. They slid onboard, hardly giving him a glance.

"Those two look pretty beat up," Gia said.

"They must be accident prone."

Bishop and Gia waited a few minutes to see if anyone would join them, but no one did. The Evangelists didn't look like they expected anyone either, as they sat shoulder-to-shoulder gulping drinks and nursing wounds. Bishop imagined it was bourbon. He could almost smell it.

"What's our next move?" Gia asked.

"I think we leave before they make us. We'll wait for them in the car and tail them when they stagger out. Hopefully, they'll lead us to Ira."

"If he's still alive."

"Yeah, *if*."

They left their table, this time going down the staircase farthest from the bar. Amigone was away from the host station, moving from table-to-table, greeting guests, and making sure everything was to their satisfaction. Albert opened the door for them.

"Making it an early evening?" Albert asked. "Good. Can't find trouble if you leave early, at least not here you won't," he said.

"Albert, you know I mind my own business," Bishop answered. "But trouble finds me."

"Uh huh."

The silver Mercury was parked behind Rhielman's Ford in front of The Chez. They hurried to Gia's car and waited. The streetlights and marquee illuminated the Merc. Bishop's gaze alternated between it and the front door. He wanted a drink more than he wanted a cigarette. He chewed a wooden matchstick, and tried not to think about all the other things he wanted.

The moon slipped from behind a cloud and the Merc changed to a lighter shade. After twenty minutes, the nightclub's doors opened, and Timothy Flynn was tossed to the curb. He lay on the sidewalk where he landed. Albert stood over him, prodding him with his toe, trying to get him to move along.

"We can't leave him there, Bishop," Gia said.

"He looks comfortable."

"He looks unconscious. Go help him."

"We're working."

"We're sitting in a car." She pushed his shoulder. "Go help him."

"Nobody ever helped me."

"How do you know? You wouldn't remember if they had. Go get him. He's your friend."

"He's not my friend. He's Timothy Flynn."

"Hurry. Albert's kicking him."

Albert *was* kicking him. Not hard, but light taps against his ribs to get him to move. The reporter wasn't budging. Bishop knew harder kicks would follow, the blows landing in the same spot. Tomorrow it would be painful for Flynn to breathe and agony if he coughed or sneezed. He remembered his own pink piss.

"Fine," he said.

He got out of the car and crossed Delaware Avenue, calling Albert's name. The doorman stopped kicking Flynn and looked up.

"Figures he's your friend," he said, when he saw Bishop.

"He's not my friend. He's Timothy Flynn. Help me get him to his feet."

Flynn was conscious, and rolled on his side, singing "It's A Great Day for The Irish."

Albert crouched and grabbed him under his arms.

"Come on, Timothy," Bishop said. "Help Albert."

Flynn stopped singing. "Bishop?"

"What do you know? What do you hear?"

"Let's go inside and drink," he slurred.

"I have gin in the car," Bishop said.

"No, no, no. Let's go back inside."

"Gia's in the car."

"Gia? I like Gia."

"Everyone likes Gia. Stand up and I'll introduce you."

Flynn pushed as Albert hoisted him to his feet. Bishop put his arm around his waist, and Flynn slung his arm over his shoulder and leaned on him. The detective braced himself with his cane. They were locked in place. If Bishop took a step and moved his cane, they'd both topple.

Albert crossed his arms and laughed. "You are two sorry-ass drunks."

"Are you going to help me?"

"Help my least favorite customers? Hell, no. I got him upright. You're on your own."

"Come on, Albert. Be a stand-up guy for once."

"No, sir. You two drunks cause me nothing but trouble."

Bishop grimaced, his foot starting to hurt under the additional weight. He looked toward Gia, jerked his head, and whistled. Her headlights snapped on and she wheeled the car in front, leaving it idling next to the Merc. She left the driver's door open.

"Help them," she said, to Albert.

"Gia?" Flynn asked.

She opened the rear door. Albert was still standing with folded arms and a full smirk.

"Are you going to help them?" she asked.

"No, ma'am. This is like watching Laurel and Hardy or maybe two drunk stooges. Look at Curly and Moe here."

"I wish I was drunk," Bishop said.

"This is funny to you?" she asked Albert.

"Funniest thing that's happened all night. I want to see who's gonna fall first. I'm pulling for Bishop to topple."

Gia leaned into the car and opened her purse. She pulled out the .38. When she turned, she leveled it at Albert's nose. "Are you going to help them?" she asked, again.

Albert uncrossed his arms and took a step back. "You're crazy."

"Damn right." Gia cocked the hammer. "Are you going to help them?"

Albert swore but hurried to Bishop. He grabbed Flynn and shifted most of his weight toward him.

"Gia?" Flynn said, his drooping eye almost closed. "You're pretty."

"Shut up, Flynn, and walk."

Flynn moved like he was waist deep in mud, but they maneuvered him to the car and pushed him in. The reporter sprawled on the back seat, and Bishop made sure Flynn's legs were inside before slamming the door. The detective leaned against the Merc, his foot throbbing. "Sink or swim with Timothy Flynn," he said, breathing hard and needing a drink more than ever.

"You're a crazy broad," Albert said. "A damn crazy broad. I'm telling Mr. Amigone you pulled a gun. None of you are gonna be allowed back in here. Not over my dead body."

"Dead body? I can make that happen," she said, still aiming the gun at him. "Now smooth your skirt and go back to your door. Keep your mouth shut about this or I'll come back with two heaters."

Albert walked to his post, muttering under his breath.

"I may have made a mistake giving you that roscoe," Bishop said, still leaning against the Merc.

"I like it. It's heavy though."

"I'll buy you a smaller one so you can threaten doormen more easily."

"No, I like this one. You'll need to teach me how to use it."

"Just point and shoot, Gia. Point and shoot."

* * *

Gia drove around the block to make it look like they were leaving. She parked diagonally from the Merc, the car's rear fender closest to them. They had a clear view of Albert and The Chez' entrance. A half hour passed. Alcohol began oozing through Flynn's pores.

"Smells like a bootlegger's bathtub in here," Gia said, cranking down the window.

Bishop had been staring at the Mercury for the last few minutes. He could see the entire length of the car from this new angle.

"Do you know where Flynn lives? He can't sleep in my car all night."

Bishop didn't answer. He bent forward, his hand on the dash, and squinted, wishing he had Ira's binoculars but remembering they'd gone up in flames.

"Did you hear me?" she asked.

"Look," he said, pointing.

"What?" Gia asked and turned toward the nightclub. Albert held the door for a Marine in dress blues and a redhead in a black dress. "That's not the Gospels."

"Look at the car. The Mercury."

"What about it?"

"Look at it."

"I've been looking at it since we parked here. It hasn't changed."

"Look at the back of it. What do you see?"

"A pretty car. I like the color."

"Look closer. Is the rear hanging low or do I need a bourbon to see straight?"

Gia leaned toward the windshield, her hands on the steering wheel. "Maybe it's sagging. Not much, but maybe it's a little lower. What would cause that?"

"Maybe a fat man."

Bishop pushed open the door and stepped into the street. A horn blared.

"Look out!" Gia yelled.

Bishop stepped back as a cabbie swerved. He didn't remember much from the night months ago when another cab had crushed his foot. He was too drunk for that. Fleeting fragments remained: the yellow taxi, the chrome fender, somebody, like Gia just had, yelling 'Look out!'. Those pieces hurtled back at him, and he felt his stomach clench. He sagged against the car, the color drained from his face.

Gia hurried around the front of the car. "Are you all right?"

"Aces," he managed.

"I thought that cab was going to hit you."

"Lightning doesn't strike twice."

"You're shaking."

"There's a chill in the air."

"It's summer."

"Let's check the trunk."

Bishop crossed Delaware, leaning heavily on his cane, checking traffic in both directions even though the avenue was deserted. The other side of the street seemed a mile away. His breathing was loud and labored when they reached the Merc. He glanced at The Chez. Albert was still chatting with the Marine and the redhead and hadn't noticed them. Bishop rapped the trunk and called Ira's name. There was no response, so he pounded harder. Albert yelled to get away from the car.

"Maybe he isn't in there," Gia said.

"Maybe he's gagged. You got any bobby pins? I need two."

She pulled two from her hair and handed them to Bishop. He grabbed them and propped his cane against the fender. The cylinder lock wouldn't be much trouble, but Albert and the Marine were heading his way.

"That ain't your car, Bishop!" Albert yelled, coming up to him. The Marine was at the doorman's side, looking Parris Island-hard. Everything about him was square—his head, jaw, shoulders. A fresh private's stripe was sewn on his sleeve. The red head walked a step behind.

"I need to look in the trunk," Bishop said.

"It ain't yours to look in," Albert yelled.

"This is none of your business," Bishop said. "Go back to your door. I think a midget with a monkey is trying to sneak in."

"It *is* my business. You can't mess with our customers' automobiles. You know who this belongs to?"

"Those fine Biblical fellows drinking at the bar. The ones all busted up."

"That's right, and there's going to be trouble if they come out and see you fooling with their crate. I don't want trouble. Move along."

"Give me two minutes, Albert. That's all I'll need."

"The man said to move along." The Marine stuck out his chest to impress the redhead as much as to intimidate Bishop. "Don't you hear too good?"

"I hear fine," Bishop said. "Walking gives me trouble, but my ears are top notch."

"You're gonna have trouble breathing if you don't beat it," said the Marine. The redhead smirked at Bishop, waiting to see what he'd do. Bishop heard the gun cocked behind him.

"The man needs two minutes," Gia said, holding the .38 with both hands this time, pointing it at the Marine's deflating chest. "Start counting."

"What?" The private raised his hands.

"He needs two minutes. Count to a hundred and twenty. Count slow, like your life depended on it," she said.

The Marine started counting, and Gia shifted the gun to Albert. "Pointing a gun at you is becoming a habit tonight, Albert. I like it. Start counting."

Albert started counting at eight to match the Marine. The doorman's voice was low and tight, as if the numbers were struggling to get out of his mouth. She swung the muzzle to the girl. "You too, Red. Chime in with the boys. They need a soprano."

The redhead joined the count as Bishop twisted the first hair pin into a right angle. He pulled apart the second and bent one tip slightly. He inserted the angled pin into the lock then worked in the straighter one. The counting made it difficult to concentrate, but Gia was enjoying herself too much for him to quiet the counters. He closed his eyes and tried to slow his breathing, his heart, and especially his hands. They trembled. He wasn't sure if the near-miss with the taxi or lack of bourbon was causing it. He held the angled pin still as best he could and lifted the other, trying to catch the tumbler. The trunk popped open when the trio reached seventy-two.

Ira was crammed inside. His shirt was dark with sweat and blood. His nose was bent, and clear fluid ran from it. The trunk smelled of vomit. Bishop touched his neck. The skin felt hot and dry. He whispered 'please' as he searched for a pulse.

"Is he breathing?" Gia asked.

"Barely." Bishop straightened and almost lost his balance. He had to reach for his cane. "He broiled in there," Bishop said, then turning to the redhead, "Go inside and call the cops, then come right out. Don't tell anybody in the nightclub about this, understand?"

The woman nodded.

"Beat it, Red." Gia said, and the redhead rushed toward The Chez.

"We got to get him out of there," the Marine said.

Bishop lit a Chesterfield. "That's a lot of man in there, private. It's not going to be easy getting him out. Let's wait for reinforcements." He shook the match out. Gia still had the gun trained on the Marine's chest. "You can put the rod away, Tex."

"Do I have to? I like making tough guys squirm."

* * *

Bishop and Gia leaned against her car and watched the scene from across the street. A crowd had gathered on the sidewalk. Some had drifted from The Chez Amis, others had wandered by in shirtsleeves and stopped when they saw the commotion. Albert stood off to the side talking to Amigone, who shook his head every few seconds. Gia took a drag then passed Bishop the smoke. They didn't speak, afraid of jinxing the operation. Bishop filled his lungs and held the smoke before fogging the air. He passed the Chesterfield back. Sirens had been shut off, but a prowl car's revolving red light played across faces and building facades. Two ambulance attendants, the Marine, and a beat cop managed to get Ira out of the trunk and onto a stretcher without causing too much damage to the lawyer or the Merc. Flashbulbs popped. Beat reporters and photographers captured the scene for the early edition. Flynn groaned from the backseat. The attendants rested a moment, their hands pressed against their aching lower backs, before hoisting Ira into the ambulance. One hopped in and the other slammed the backdoor shut before walking to the driver side. Seconds later, the ambulance sped off, siren keening.

Four coppers brought out the handcuffed Gospels. The crowd's mumbling grew louder when they saw them. More flashbulbs popped. The bulls led them to the patrol wagon. Bishop caught the eye of the one he'd hit in the mouth and tipped his hat. The Evangelist spat in his direction and a cop gave him a shove. Flynn groaned again from inside the car. Bishop wondered if he was carrying a flask.

Chapter 17

They weren't allowed to see Ira that night and were told to return to the hospital the next day during visiting hours. Bishop listed himself as next of kin and gave Gia's phone number in case Ira's condition worsened. It'd been a long day, and he was tired. He needed a hot bath and a neat bourbon and was certain he'd fall asleep without either. The remaining two Gospels were certainly still looking for him. Bishop doubted it was safe to go back to The Lafayette. Gia's hand brushed his as they walked down the hospital corridor to the exit. Their fingers laced.

"Broken nose, concussion, dehydration, heat stroke. Poor Ira," she said.

"Could've been worse."

"Yeah, that cab could've hit you and you'd be lying in the bed next to him."

"Missed me by a mile."

"Inches more like it."

They didn't speak again until they were outside. The sky was clear and full of stars. Bishop had learned the constellations as a boy sitting in his window above The New Genesee with a book in his lap. He stopped and silently identified them: *Ursa Major, Ursa Minor, Lyra*.

"I need to ask you something, Bishop. Something we've never talked about."

"Conversations that start like that never end well," he said, still gazing at the heavens.

Hercules, Cygnus, Ophiuchus.

"I've been wanting to ask for a while. You almost getting hit by that cab earlier got me thinking about it again."

"About what?"

Aquila, Scopius, Sagittarius.

"About the night of your accident."

"What about it?"

"Was it an accident, Bishop? Or were you trying to get out of the draft like everyone says? Or were you trying to…do something else?"

He turned from the constellations and looked into her eyes. They shone as bright as any two stars. He wasn't sure what he saw there. Hope? Fear? Maybe both.

"Your guess is as good as mine, Gia. I don't remember much from that night. When I woke in the hospital, they told me I walked right in front of it."

"But tonight, you stepped back."

"As fast as I could."

She put her arms around his neck and kissed him long and slow, her body melding to his. Her kiss surprised him, but his arms shot around her, and he returned it, his heart pounding so hard he wondered if she felt it through his shirt. When it ended, she rubbed lipstick off his mouth with her fingertips. "Keep getting out of the way of those taxis, Bishop," she said, and walked away, leaving him stunned beneath a sea of stars.

* * *

Timothy Flynn was lying on Gia's hood, an arm covering his eyes as if Scopius was shining too brightly. One shoe was missing. His big toe poked through his sock.

"Looks like I got a new hood ornament," said Gia.

"He doesn't look too ornamental," Bishop answered, still off-balance from their kiss. He poked Flynn with his cane. "You alive?"

Flynn groaned but sat up, his hair sprouting in all directions. He blinked and took in his surroundings. The left side of his face seemed more uneven than ever. "Hospital?"

"They're handing out replacement livers," Bishop said. "I thought we'd pick up a pair."

Gia told him about Ira.

"I'm sure some sober reporter's already written about the arson and kidnapping," she added. "You missed that scoop."

Flynn rubbed his neck and shut his bloodshot eyes like he was trying to remember something important. "I was working a story," he said. "A different story. No, wait. The same story."

"Yeah?" Gia asked. "What's the headline, Ace? 'How To Get Thrown Out of a Bar'?"

"Why *did* you get tossed?" Bishop asked. "I'm hoping you took a swing at Amigone."

"No. Bothering a customer," he mumbled.

"A dame?" Bishop asked.

The reporter shook his head and opened his eyes, the left one drooping more. "Hans Schrieber."

"Who's Hans Schrieber?" Gia asked.

"Art dealer from New York," Bishop said. "He's pals with Brandt and Joey and Rhielman. He was at The Chez? I didn't spot him."

"Maybe Doris Slater dancing in that red dress distracted you," Gia said.

"He must've snuck in from the alley," Bishop answered. "Why were you bothering him?"

"Because," Flynn said, wavering in place and pointing a finger at Bishop, "he's a Nazi and I'm a drunk."

"Schrieber? A *Nazi*? A *real* one?" Gia said.

Flynn's arm shot in the air to give a Nazi salute and he almost fell off the car. When he righted himself, he patted his stained suitcoat, pulled a notebook from a pocket, and flipped through the pages. His eyes narrowed. He held the notebook close, then at arm's length, before handing it to Bishop.

"Helped Fritz Kuhn form the German American Bund in Buffalo '36," Bishop read. "Kids sent to Nazi summer camp on Long Island '38. Spoke at Nazi rally in Madison Square Garden '39."

"He *is* a Nazi," Gia said.

"You got a flask?" asked Flynn.

"I hid it for safe keeping." Bishop flipped to the next page, but it was blank. "What's Schrieber been doing lately?"

Flynn laid back on the hood and covered his eyes with his arm. "Nothing. Art."

"No Nazi stuff?"

"Kuhn's in Sing-Sing and the Bund went *kaput-kaput.*

"But what's he doing *here?*" Gia asked.

"Visiting family."

"No, it's more than that. He's an art dealer and chummy with Rhielman and Joey Bones. He's here to see a man about a painting," Bishop said. "I'd bet anything on it."

"The Renoir?"

"It has to be."

"What Renoir?" Flynn asked, his voice quiet and trailing away.

"Can't say yet, but you'll be the first to get the goods."

Flynn smiled, his arm still shielding his eyes. "There's more."

"What?"

"Schrieber, Rhielman, and Elizabeth Brandt."

"What about them?"

"Cousins."

"*Cousins?*"

"Mother's side. All of them."

"I'll be damned," Bishop said.

"Me, too," Flynn said.

"I guess Elizabeth and Rhielman aren't sleeping together then," Gia said.

"Maybe they're a close family," Bishop said.

"Wait, Flynn. Are *all* of them Nazis? Or just Schrieber?" Gia asked.

Flynn mumbled and drifted off. Gia shook his arm but couldn't rouse him. "Christ, can't any man in this town hold their liquor?"

* * *

Flynn lived in a basement apartment near *The Courier-Express Building* on Main Street. While Gia drove there and Flynn snored in the backseat, Bishop wondered how good a reporter Flynn would be if he could stay sober. How many other stories like Ira's had he missed because he'd been slouched over a bar, or sleeping it off, or too hungover to type? Would he be working in New York at *The Herald* or *Sun* or *World-Telegram* if he wasn't a drunk? Would there be a Pulitzer or two already on his shelf? Then he wondered how good a detective he could be if he stayed dry. Maybe good enough to rent another office and quit being The Lafayette's private dick. Maybe he'd get better cases and do more than peep through motel windows. Maybe he'd stop being called Nicky The Weasel. Maybe Lucky Teddy would be proud of him again, if he was still alive. Maybe it was all nice to think about.

"What do you make of all this Nazi stuff, Bishop? Do you think Flynn's right about Schrieber?" Gia asked, bringing him back to this case and reminding him how good a tumbler of Four Roses would taste.

"Flynn's a lush, but he's still a damned fine reporter," he said, swallowing his own desire for a drink. "I believe him. This is what we know so far. Krieger was in the Klan and his son is a punk who probably gets his kicks painting shit on Ira's door. He also works nights at The Albright. Brandt is an artist who's painted five copies of

Renoir's *Mother and Child*. His wife, who he cheated on with Pearl, is Rhielman's cousin, and he has blueprints to the Albright which *owns* the real *Mother and Child*. Rhielman's *other* cousin, Hans Schrieber, had ties to an American Nazi group in the Thirties, is currently a New York City art dealer, and happens to be back in town."

"They're going to steal the Renoir," Gia said.

"They're going to pull a switch. And if Brandt's forgeries are as good as I think they are, nobody'll notice. They could get away with it."

"But why five copies?"

"I don't know. Maybe he was practicing, and they'll use the best one."

"And Joey Bones?"

"He might be providing muscle or making sure no cops are anywhere near the gallery the night they make the swap. Or maybe Brandt or Rhielman shot Pearl, panicked, and called Joey Bones to get rid of the body. For a fee, of course."

"That still leaves the question of who killed Pearl DuGaye."

"Rhielman's girlfriend was wearing her wig tonight. At least I think she was. And since Pearl wore it the night she was killed, that's good enough to make him and Lover Boy Brandt tied at number one on Your Hit Parade as murder suspects. Besides, Rhielman likes smacking and choking women. Killing one doesn't seem too far a stretch."

"I still don't see how Elizabeth Brandt fits into this," Gia said. "Why hire you to investigate her husband if she knew he was painting forgeries? Wasn't she worried you'd find out?"

"She's an odd one, but I don't think she knows anything about the paintings. I think she's too worried about who her husband's screwing to think about anything else. Brandt and Rhielman. That's who we have to focus on."

They drove past *The Courier-Express*, a five-story Art Deco building made of brick and terra cotta. Bronze printer marks rose above the entrance, flanked by large sconces that lit the sidewalk below. The First Amendment was carved into the wall facing Main Street, reminding the city why *The Courier* was in business to start with. Statues of famous printers separated by a Celtic motif spanned the top story. Bishop recognized one of the printers—Benjamin Franklin—and asked Flynn if he knew the others. The reporter mumbled something incoherent from the backseat.

Flynn's apartment was a block down on the opposite corner. Bishop told Gia when to pull over. "Wake up, Walter Winchell," she said, and cut the engine. "You're home."

Flynn sat up and looked around. His confusion drained when he recognized his corner. He pushed open the door.

"I'll stay with Flynn tonight," Bishop said.

"You're worried about him?"

"I'm worried the Gospels are waiting for me at The Lafayette."

"You could come home with me."

"And where would I sleep?" Bishop asked.

"On the couch."

"Your mother would love that. She'll be guarding your bedroom door."

"The whole family will."

"Not Jake. She'll be on my side."

"My mother's taken a liking to her," Gia said. "She speaks to her in Italian."

"Italian? Isn't that poor mutt confused enough with one eye and a boy's name?"

"She seems happy."

Before Bishop could answer, Flynn vomited on the curb.

* * *

There were six steps leading down to Flynn's basement apartment. He held onto the railing and Gia held onto his other arm. Bishop followed behind.

"Do you have your key?" she asked.

"No key," Flynn said, and pushed open the door.

The apartment smelled damp and boggy. Flynn pulled away from Gia and stumbled toward his bedroom, shedding his hat, tie, and sport coat along the way. He fell face first on the bare mattress, his arms and legs sprawled wide.

"He's out already," she said.

"He'll be fine in the morning. Afternoon at the latest. By cocktail hour, he'll be knocking them down like Joe Louis."

Bishop pressed the push-button and the apartment filled with sallow light. A Remington typewriter sat on the kitchen table next to an overflowing ashtray and a Crosley radio. Dirty dishes filled the sink. Stacks of newspapers—*The Courier, The New York Times, The Plain Dealer*—were piled on the floor and strewn on the sagging couch. Clippings, most carrying Flynn's byline, were tacked to the living room wall. Empty bottles of gin lay on their sides throughout the apartment like the honored dead.

"Some place," Gia said. "I don't think many girls would set foot in here."

"The ones who charge don't mind."

"You sure you want to stay here? You'd be better off taking your chances with The Gospels."

"It'll be fine for one night," Bishop said. He toed an empty bottle by his foot.

"I'll make up the couch and leave a key under the mat in case you change your mind."

"You're a doll."

"I'm a sap. I wouldn't want Jake to spend the night here."

"Are you worried I'll catch fleas?"

"You'll be lucky if that's the only thing you catch."

He hoped she'd kiss him again before she left, but she only squeezed his arm on her way to the door. Flynn had no key to his apartment because his door had no lock. It did have a deadbolt, and Bishop slid that in place when Gia left. After killing the light, he cleared the couch of newspapers, and laid down facing the door. He pulled The Fitz, checked to make sure it was loaded, and placed it in easy reach next to his cane on the stained carpet. The only noise came from Main Street traffic and Flynn snoring in the other room.

Bishop felt the aching need for sleep in his back and foot. He tried clearing his mind of Pearl DuGaye, stolen art, and New York Nazis. He'd almost succeeded when he caught a whiff of gin. Maybe it came from a recent spill on the couch cushions. Maybe one of those dead soldiers wasn't quite dead. Maybe there was glass that Flynn had poured and had forgotten about, and now sat on a table or counter waiting for someone to limp along and down it. That whiff got Bishop's brain whirling again, and he wondered if there was a quart in a kitchen cabinet or a pint on Flynn's nightstand.

A drink would help me sleep, he reasoned.

It would calm me.

Dull my mind.

Take the edge off this goddamn foot.

Those were all fine reasons to get off the couch and rummage through cabinets and drawers looking for forgotten flasks and emergency bottles, an Easter egg hunt for alcoholics. The way he looked at it, he deserved a drink with the day he'd had. He'd toast to Ira's speedy recovery then turn on the Crosley and sip, working out his next move to catch Pearl's killer and foil the Renoir theft while listening to Benny Goodman or The Dorsey Brothers.

Swing and sway with Sammy Kaye.

Drown in gin like Timothy Flynn.

He grabbed The Fitz and holstered it and pushed off the couch. There was a bottle near the couch, but it was empty. So was the one by the Remington, and the bottle under the sink. He limped to Flynn's bedroom to check the nightstand. The reporter had rolled on his back.

His crooked face looked more crooked, like the left side had dropped another notch. His mouth was gaped and drooling. That big toe still poked through his sock. He groaned in his sleep like he was in pain, its origin deep inside him. The smells hit Bishop then—the vomit-splattered shirt, the alcohol seeping from his skin, the darkening urine stain on his trousers. They all triggered memories of when *he'd* been the one lying on the dirty mattress, or in the gutter, or curled on the drunk tank floor, smelling the same odors as now, but emanating from himself. Looking at Flynn was like looking at the ugly side of himself, the side that shamed him, the side he'd seen too often since his foot had been crushed. He almost expected the drooping face to rebalance itself, to raise the sagging mouth and eyelid and reform the features until it was like staring in a dirty mirror.

He didn't want to stick around to see if that would happen.

* * *

He woke on Gia's couch in his boxers and undershirt with Jake on his chest. The telephone's ringing had pulled him from dreamless sleep. Sunlight streamed through the living room windows. He checked the cracked Bulova. 6:45, much too early to be awake and sober. Jake's ears popped up when she heard Gia's mother muttering in Italian as she hurried to the phone, tying her robe around herself as she tottered in. Gia's bedroom door opened, and Bishop saw her framed in the doorway—hair mussed, face puffy from sleep. She wore a black peignoir. He couldn't remember the last time he'd woken to something that looked that good.

Her mother barked something sharp to Gia in Italian, and Gia barked back. Bishop didn't need an interpreter to know they were barking about him. The mother answered the telephone and her face darkened. She said something to Gia.

"It's for you," she said to Bishop

Jake jumped to the floor when he sat up. Gia's mother laid the phone down and headed back to her bedroom still grumbling. She didn't look at Bishop once. He grabbed his cane and was halfway to the phone when he remembered he wasn't wearing pants, but by then it was too late. He picked up the phone and answered by saying his name then listened, occasionally muttering "I see". The conversation ended with, "We'll be right down".

"The hospital?" Gia asked, as he hung up the phone.

"Ira's awake and yelling that he wants to see me. He wouldn't calm down until his nurse promised to call. He said it couldn't wait until visiting hours."

"I'll get dressed."

"Do you have a cigarette?"

"I think you put the pack in your jacket last night."

Gia reached for his sport coat hung on the back of a chair by the telephone. She slid her hand in the pocket and pulled out a folded piece of paper. "What's this?"

"Nothing," he said. He reached for it. "Give me that."

She unfolded it and stared at Brandt's sketch of her. "The face looks familiar. What's it doing in your pocket, Bishop?"

"You shouldn't be going through a man's pockets."

"I think I should go through them more often. Did you steal this in case you forget what I look like?"

No wisecrack came to him.

"Are you worried about amnesia?"

"I…"

"Yes?"

"…wanted it."

"Why?"

"You know why."

"Maybe I want to hear you say it."

Bishop was having trouble breathing, like there wasn't enough oxygen in the room. He leaned heavily on his cane, wishing he was wearing pants. "I stole it because I want to see that face all the time," he said, the words rushing out before he could stop them.

"All the time? You want to see my face before you go to sleep at night?"

"Every night."

"And when you wake up in the morning?"

"Every morning."

"You know what that would mean?"

"No."

"That would mean no more *negotiating* with the Doris Slaters of the world."

"I know," Bishop said.

"And no more drinking."

"I'm trying."

"And no more being a heel like last time," Gia said, her voice rising.

"That won't happen again."

"And no more being jealous of men like Brandt."

"I can't promise that."

"This would change everything. If we start up, there's no going back," Gia said. "We either move forward or we end. And if we end, you'll never see me again, except when you look at this sketch. You need to be all-in, Bishop."

"I will. I am," he said.

She looked at him long and hard and he looked straight back, holding her gaze and his breath. He felt like his whole life was about to be decided and none of it, or perhaps all of it, was in his control.

"Okay, Bishop," she said. "God help us, but okay. We'll give this a try. My family may disown me, but we'll give it a try. And for god's sake put your pants on. That's not your Fitz pointing at me." She folded the sketch and slipped it back in his jacket, leaving Bishop smiling, gasping for air.

* * *

Ira was too large for the hospital bed. He filled it from headboard to footboard and overflowed the sides of the mattress. The nurses had propped him on two pillows, a bandage covered his nose, his eyes blackened. He breathed through his mouth, the wheezing loud and labored, but he managed a smile when Bishop and Gia entered the ward.

"Ira, what do you know? What do you hear?"

"I know I've had better days," he said, his voice weak. He waved them closer. "At least you didn't bring that dog with you."

"She's with Gia's mom learning Italian," Bishop said.

"How are you, Ira?" Gia asked, taking his hand.

"I can vouch that The Gospels are very good at their job and leave it at that." The lawyer's eyes flicked to Bishop. "The office?"

Bishop shook his head. "Gone. Burned."

Ira nodded, the news not surprising him. "They told me they'd torched it. I'd hoped they were bluffing."

"Evangelists don't bluff," Bishop said.

"Indeed."

"You should be resting," Gia said. "Why'd you call us here so early? The nurse told us you wouldn't calm down until they agreed to let you see us."

"A man my size throwing a tantrum is hard to ignore."

"You got your way. What's the skinny, fat man?" Bishop asked.

"First, how'd they know I had their brother in my basement?"

"They saw Benny driving his car and they beat out of him where he got it. They drove to the office and found him, burned the place, then headed to your house."

"Did they burn that, too?"

"No, you'll need a couple new lamps, but the place is fine."

Ira shut his blackened eyes and let out a long breath. A single tear trickled down his swollen cheek and he brushed it away. "Thank god."

"The coppers pinched them when we found you in the trunk," Bishop said. "They'll be on ice for a while."

"Good," he said, opening his eyes. "Darcy's coming this morning to take my statement."

"I'd leave out the part about the Evangelist tied in your cellar," Bishop said.

"That's sound legal advice."

"So, what'd you want to tell us?" Gia asked. "What couldn't wait for visiting hours?"

"They worked me over pretty good and not just for slapping their brother around."

"What do you mean?" Bishop asked.

"They kept asking if you told me what you saw the night Pearl was killed."

"I only saw the bottom of a bourbon glass. I don't remember anything else."

"They think you do," Ira said. "Worse, they think you told me. They were going to off me and go after you next. They thought pinning Pearl's murder on you would end it, but Darcy's still sniffing around asking questions. Evidently, he doesn't think even you'd be stupid enough to hide a corpse in your bed."

"I didn't think Darcy held me in such high regard."

"I was surprised, too. But—and this is why he's probably still investigating—he doesn't think a jury'd buy it either."

"So, I get zotzed because they think I saw Rhielman shoot Pearl?" Bishop asked. "That's why they grabbed his file?"

"That makes Rhielman our guy, not Brandt," Gia said.

"They're planning to make your death look like a suicide," Ira continued. "They figured since you stepped in front of that taxi, everybody'd think you just tried it again and got it right."

"The Gospels are more creative than I thought," Bishop said. "They should be writing for the pictures."

"Why would Rhielman kill Pearl?" Gia asked. "What was his motive?"

"I don't know," Bishop said. "Brandt's got the motive. He's the boyfriend."

"He's the key to all this," Ira said.

"Who? Brandt?" Bishop asked.

"I overheard them talking. They said he's finished the paintings. They hit the Albright tonight."

Chapter 18

Bishop folded his gray pinstriped suit. He started with the jacket, tucking the sleeves behind the back, making the shoulders overlap, and then folded it in half from the bottom. The trousers were next, and he straightened and smoothed them after each fold, eliminating any creases before placing it on top of the jacket. The starched white shirt was set on the pants and the whole lot was put in the suitcase. His wingtips, belt, socks, underwear, and shaving kit were packed on either side. A maroon tie with gray diamonds was the last to go in the getaway bag.

"No bourbon?" Gia asked, watching him from a chair near his closet.

"No, and no gun or envelope full of money either."

"That's not much of a getaway bag."

Bishop closed the lid and pressed the clasps in place. "It's the best I can do for now."

"Have you ever had to use one?" she asked.

"Too many times."

"You don't think you'll need it tonight, do you?"

"I will if things go south," Bishop said. "The city won't be safe if a bunch of Nazis and hoods are after me. It's not safe now."

"I should pack a bag, too."

"You'll be fine. They think you're my secretary."

"Of course, they do." She lit a cigarette and blew smoke toward the ceiling. "Where'll you go?"

"Amigone says Pittsburgh's nice."

"When did you start keeping a getaway bag?"

"As soon as I had an extra set of clothes and enough money for bus fare."

"Teddy taught you?"

"Yeah."

"He ever use his?"

"Once that I know of. I was about twenty and came back to our apartment after tailing an embezzler for him. There was a note on my bed—*Had to use the getaway bag. See you soon, kid.*"

"Did you?"

"Did I what?"

"See him soon."

"I haven't seen him since," Bishop said.

* * *

Before the war, The Albright Art Gallery was illuminated at night. Spotlights lit the porticoes, caryatids, and Ionic columns, the marble taking on a ghostly hue. After Pearl, the lights were doused during blackout drills. Then it was decided to keep them off for the duration. At nightfall, the gallery became a hulking silhouette, its details lost in shadows.

Bishop, too, was hidden in the dark, sweating in his funeral suit and matching black shirt and tie. He once again stood behind the chestnut tree with a view of the entrance. The bells from a distant church chimed midnight. He'd been watching the gallery since closing. It'd been too many hours between cigarettes and too many days between drinks. He craved both. His foot felt numb in his wingtip, a dead appendage reminding him he'd been standing too long. Gia had wanted to come but he'd told her it was too dangerous. Now he wished she was here, whispering with him, maybe holding hands. Instead, Benny was somewhere close by waiting for the signal—unless the park had transformed into The Argonne and the junkman lay curled on the ground, his hands covering his ears.

Bishop heard the car before he saw it. It pulled in front of the gallery with extinguished headlights a few minutes after the church bells had faded. He recognized the cracked taillight as it braked near the gallery's marble stairs. The two Gospels were easy to spot getting out of the car, their size, and gait almost identical. A tall man climbed out after them carrying a small duffle. Bishop assumed it was Schrieber. The last person to emerge was the driver, Rhielman, his stooped shoulders giving him away. He carried a tube under his arm. The gallery door cracked open. Interior light escaped. Krieger, wearing his gray guard uniform, held it ajar, his wrist still bandaged. Three of the men jogged up the steps and hurried inside. The door shut, leaving a single Gospel by the Ford keeping watch.

Bishop tilted his head toward the park, listening for Benny. He heard nothing. His stomach felt like sour mash was gnawing through its lining. The moon slipped past a cloud brightening the gallery, and he worried the heavens were working against him. Maybe he should limp to Elmwood Avenue and flag down a cop or find a payphone and call Darcy. Maybe he should've done that in the first place. Then he heard the cart's rattle—the wobbling front wheel, the contents clattering against each other—and smiled as he pulled out The Fitz.

The watching Gospel heard Benny, too, and walked toward him, telling him in a loud whisper to get the hell away from here. But Benny kept approaching at a steady pace, still dragging his leg behind him. Bishop slipped from the chestnut tree as quickly and quietly as he could. Whatever noise he was making was drowned by Benny's cart and the Gospel's cursing. He was five feet away when he cocked The Fitz and told the Evangelist to reach for the planets.

The Gospel froze then raised his arms. "Bishop," he said, without turning, spitting the name out like it tasted bitter in his mouth. Bishop was close enough to see his back muscles bunching beneath his suit.

"You recognized my aftershave?" Bishop asked. "I'm flattered."

"I recognized your weasely voice."

"Let's not get personal."

"I'm going to kill you. How's that for personal?"

"I saw the car, Bishop," Benny said. "That was the signal. When I see a car pull in, count to a hundred and twenty and then come over. I counted to a hundred and twenty, Bishop. I'm pretty sure I did. Maybe I counted a little more. Maybe I counted a little less."

"You did good, Benny," Bishop said. "Real good."

"This is one of the guys that beat me, Bishop," Benny said, pointing. "I remember him."

"He's not going to hurt you ever again. I promise." Bishop poked the Evangelist with The Fitz. "Okay, Brutus, toss the gat into the cart. Do it slow."

"I'm going to kill you, Weasel."

"You already told me. Toss the gun."

The Gospel threw his revolver in the cart.

"Now your wallet," Bishop said.

"You're *robbing* me?"

"Consider it a donation to a war veteran."

The Gospel flipped his wallet into the cart.

"Okay, Benny," Bishop said. "Part two of the mission. Do you remember the second part?"

"Can I shoot him?" Benny asked.

"No. Do you remember the second part of the plan?"

"I'd like to shoot him. He hit me hard."

"I'll take care of him."

"How about if I hit him then?" Benny asked. "Maybe once or twice but hard like he hit me?"

"I said I'd take care of him. Go make your calls. That's an order."

Benny grunted then pushed his cart toward Elmwood Avenue, the wobbling wheel mixing with his mumbling.

"Now what?" The Gospel asked, his arms still raised.

Bishop answered by bringing his cane down on The Gospel's head, making sure he hit him with the wood and not the pewter handle. The Evangelist crumpled to the ground like he'd fallen from the cross. Bishop pulled handcuffs from his suitcoat and knelt by him. He pulled the unconscious man's arms behind him and locked the bracelets in place. The moon ducked behind a cloud, and Bishop thought his fortune might be turning.

His gaze shifted toward the gallery. The main portico was five columns wide. Fifty marble steps, the same width as the portico, led to the entrance. His foot swelled just thinking of the climb. He wasn't sure if he could make it. What if the thieves exited the gallery before he reached the top, catching him in the open? It would be better to wait for them at the bottom near the Ford, lost in the shadows. The best place, Bishop decided, was by the stair wall. He'd stay hidden until they descended with the stolen Renoir, then come up behind them. Then they'd all wait for the police to screech up, sirens wailing and lights flashing. He hoped Benny remembered to call Flynn after he called the cops. Hell, he hoped Benny remembered to call the cops. Not bringing Gia had been a mistake, he realized.

Bishop didn't have to wait long before he heard the door push open and muffled voices above him. His hand was shaking, and he tried to steady it. He pressed harder against the stair wall, hoping the marble would absorb him, keep him hidden. The thieves had stopped talking, and he strained to hear them getting closer. Bishop recognized Rhielman's voice cutting through the dark, but it still startled him. He hadn't realized they were already so close. Where were the cops?

"Where the hell's Luke?" the councilman asked.

"Must be taking a piss," someone answered.

"Christ."

They were halfway between the bottom step and Rhielman's car when Bishop stepped forward.

"That's far enough, ladies," he said, the strength in his voice surprising him. "Reach for the pistols in your jackets nice and slow and throw them under the car."

"Bishop," the councilman said.

"Everybody recognizes my voice. I feel like Bing Crosby. Toss those pieces under the Ford."

The guns clattered across concrete.

"Very good. Grab your hats and turn around slow so I can see your smiling faces."

The art thieves turned with their hands on their hats. Schrieber held the cardboard tube above his head.

"Okay, Herr Schrieber. Roll the Renoir toward me like you're trying to pick up a spare."

Schrieber's face was more amused than angry. "You know about the Renoir?"

"Sure, I do. I'm smart that way. Roll it over," Bishop said, still listening for sirens.

Schrieber rolled the tube. Bishop stopped it with his foot. He didn't bend down to grab it, fearing he'd lose his balance. Still no sirens.

"Having Krieger inside as a guard was pretty smart," he said, hoping he was buying time. "You could pull another switch as soon as Brandt whips up another forgery. Maybe steal a Monet next time. The whole gallery could be swapped out before anyone notices. You could've made millions. Who was the genius that came up with this plan? None of you look bright enough to draw this one up."

"Me," a woman's voice answered behind him. "Drop your weapon and turn around slowly, Mr. Bishop."

Bishop did as he was told. The moon again slipped from the clouds. He saw Elizabeth Brandt pointing a Luger at his funeral suit. The park behind her provided a shadowy backdrop. Bishop got the nauseating feeling that he was dressed appropriately for the occasion.

"I'll be damned," he said. One hand was raised, and he leaned on his cane with the other. "Mrs. Brandt. Where'd you come from?"

"Nearby. I like to keep an eye on things, make sure everything goes according to my plan." She gestured toward him with the gun. "You, sir, are not part of my plan."

"You're running the show? Not Rhielman? Sonofabitch."

"You don't think I'm capable, Mr. Bishop?"

"I knew something was off about you, but I didn't have you pegged as a common thief."

"Does this look like a common robbery? How've you muddled upon it is beyond me." Her eyes darted past Bishop to the men standing behind him. "Hans, get the Renoir."

Schrieber rushed forward and scooped up the tube.

"Tell me," Bishop said, still hoping for sirens, but fearing Benny'd lost his way in the French forest. "I understand about swapping out the Renoir, but what about the other copies your husband made? You're too smart to leave all that evidence laying around."

"We sell them, of course," she said.

"Sell them? All of them?"

"Certainly. Hans has many contacts here as well as in Europe, especially in Germany. He'll whisper in the wind that the *Mother and Child* has been switched and wallets will open all over the world for the original."

"You sell the original and four copies. Five times your money. Each buyer thinks they're getting the real Renoir but only one does. That's pretty good until one of the patsies catches on. Then you have four very angry people that want your head and their money back."

"The world, particularly the art world, is in chaos, Mr. Bishop. Money is changing hands. Wealth is changing hands. None of these private buyers will catch on. Each will think they have a masterpiece. The copies will be hidden away until peace comes. If it comes. Who knows if the buyers or forgeries will survive until after the world stops burning."

"It's still a gamble, but I guess Schrieber's the one taking that risk," Bishop said. "He's the one dealing with them. Tell me, who gets the original? Or does that make its way to the Fatherland? I understand there's a little man with a silly mustache who collects art any way he can."

"I've underestimated you, Mr. Bishop," she said. "You piece things together remarkably well for a falling-down drunk."

"I have my moments. Not many, granted, and few and far between, but I have them. I can see these nickel and dimers behind me doing it for the money, but you're already rich with your big Linwood Avenue house and new Cadillac. How much more money do you need?"

"One always needs more, Mr. Bishop. You of all people should understand that."

"I'm not robbing and killing people to get more bourbon."

"Not yet," she said.

"It's not all greed," Schrieber said. "Part of the money will go to the cause."

Bishop cocked his head slightly toward the voice behind him. "Ah. Yes. The glorious *cause*. You're resurrecting the old Bund or whatever you Nazis call it these days, aren't you? I guess sabotage takes money."

"You talk too much, Mr. Bishop," Elizabeth said, aiming the Luger higher on his chest. "That's always been your problem."

"That's only one of my problems." Bishop stared at the gun. "Lugers are nine millimeters, aren't they? That's the same size slugs they dug out of your husband's mistress. You should've planted the gun in my room when you planted Pearl in my bed. That would've framed me good. You didn't think that one through, sweetheart."

"She wasn't his mistress."

"That song again? What's with you? Is it beneath your master race mentality to accept that your husband had a Black girlfriend? Does it sicken you every time you picture them together? But I saw your husband's self-portrait at the art show, remember? *After Pearl*? It looked like he enjoyed the hell out of her."

"Shut up or I'll shoot you right here just like I shot her."

"And here I thought it was your husband who killed Pearl," Bishop said, shaking his head. "Why'd you shoot her? Jealousy? Or did you hate that your husband was crawling in your bed after crawling out of hers? Being Black isn't contagious, you know."

"You were so drunk you don't even remember," she said. "You're weak and pitiful. You *are* a weasel."

"Weak and pitiful aren't my best qualities, I'll admit. And my memory isn't very great either, especially of that night. What did Pearl bring to your house the night she was killed?"

"A copy of this," Schrieber said, raising the tube.

"So, there was a *sixth* copy," Bishop said. "Another one for you to sell. You are greedy Nazi bastards, aren't you? And poor Pearl figured out what you were up to and swiped one. Then she went to your house to confront your husband but walked in on a Bund meeting. That didn't go very well. Then you came home and shot her to shut her up. How close did I get?"

"Like you, the *Schwarze* knew too much," Elizabeth said. "I couldn't risk letting her live."

"You're a real peach, aren't you?" Bishop asked. "Shooting her was easy, but now you got a problem. What do you do with the body? So what happened next? The dirty councilman gets a bright idea and calls his pal Joey Bonesutto and asks for a favor—to get rid of the body. That's how he and the Gospels get involved. Until someone got the bright idea of digging her up and slipping her under my covers."

"How did you know that?" Schrieber asked.

"Lucky guess, plus the sand in my trunk and bed. Which one of you goose steppers did I shoot at the night of the murder?"

"You were passed out on the porch in a rocking chair," Elizabeth said. "You came to in time to see Robert carrying Pearl to the car and shot at him. You missed by a mile. By two miles. You shot at him twice. You're lucky you didn't shoot yourself."

"And you thought I'd write that down and put that in his file?"

"We didn't think you remembered anything but had to make sure."

"None of the neighbors heard the shots?" Bishop asked.

"Linwood Avenue families mind their business," Elizabeth said. "We don't like scandal."

"Especially over dead colored girls," Bishop said. His eyes cut to Rhielman. "I'm sorry I missed, councilman. I'd have enjoyed putting a couple holes in you."

"I'll be the one putting holes in you, Bishop," Rhielman said.

"That's a laugh. You only have the guts to slap dames like Doris Slater around. Besides, Elizabeth, Krieger, and a couple Gospels are ahead of you in line. Everybody wants to kill me these days. I'm popular."

"We should have buried you next to Pearl that night," Rhielman said.

"We'll bury him now," Elizabeth said.

"One last question before you break out the shovels and spades. Why did you even hire me? Why would you bring a shamus into your world when you were planning a heist?"

"I underestimated you," Elizabeth said.

"Most people do. At least the sober ones."

"You're a drunkard and a cripple. I thought you were only capable of following philandering husbands, which is all I wanted you to do. From all accounts, you're good at weasel tasks like that. It killed me to hire that Jew lawyer, but I did it to stay close to you in case, by some miracle, you remembered something about Pearl. I never imagined you'd stumble upon our art plans."

"Maybe you didn't underestimate me," Bishop said. "Maybe you overestimated yourselves. You Krauts tend to do that. You'd think you'd have learned from The Great War, but you didn't and now you're making those same mistakes all over again."

"You're quite the thinker, Mr. Bishop, but I've tired of you," Elizabeth said. "Get him in the car. And take his damn cane away before he knocks out another one of you idiots."

The Gospels stepped forward, one on each side, and grabbed Bishop, pulling the cane from his hand. He struggled, but their grip was too tight for it to matter. They squeezed his arms until it hurt to the bone. He realized he would die tonight. They'd shove him in the Ford's backseat and drive him out to the lake house. It would be dark and deserted like the night they buried Pearl. The last sounds he'd hear would be waves rushing ashore and the bark of the Luger. Yes, he would die tonight, he was sure of it, and he didn't like that very much, which surprised him most of all.

The gunshot shattered the night. It echoed off the marble and made Bishop and The Gospels crouch as if the bullet had whizzed by them. Elizabeth crouched, too, wondering where the shot had come from. She didn't have to wait long to find out.

"Drop the gun, sister," Gia said, coming out of the park's shadows behind Elizabeth, the .38 in her hand.

But Elizabeth didn't drop the Luger. She rose slowly, to her full height, the barrel was once again leveled at Bishop's chest.

"I said, drop the gun." Gia's voice was louder this time.

"Your triggerman has arrived," Elizabeth said to Bishop.

"She's my partner. She's been promoted."

"I better get paid like a partner," Gia said, then shouted, "Drop the damn gun."

"I have no intention of dropping my gun, Miss Alessi. But I have every intention of shooting your new partner."

For the second time, a gunshot shattered the night. Elizabeth screamed and crumpled to the ground, her right calf blossoming in torn flesh and spurting blood. The Luger clattered to the ground.

"Sorry, Bishop. Her leg won't be quite as shapely anymore. I think a chunk's missing."

"That's all right. Remind me to listen the first time you tell me to do something."

She swung the .38 toward The Gospels. "Let him go and then lie down next to your boss. You, too," she said, jutting her chin at Schrieber and Rhielman.

The gunsels let Bishop go and did as they were told. He grabbed his cane and took the tube containing the rolled *Mother And Child* canvas from Schrieber. All four men lay next to Elizabeth, who wailed and clutched her leg, blood seeping through her fingers. Bishop kicked the Luger away. He didn't want his fingerprints on any part of that gun. He tucked the Renoir under his arm and retrieved his Fitz.

"Hands on your heads and legs apart, gentlemen," Gia ordered. "And if anyone moves in a way I don't like, I'm shooting without warning. If you don't believe me, ask your boss with the bloody leg if I'm a kidder."

"I guess you figured out how to use that thing," Bishop said.

"You were right, Bishop. Just point and shoot."

The gallery door opened. Krieger poked his head out, took in the scene, then slammed the door shut.

"What about him?" she asked, tilting her head toward the gallery.

"We'll let the cops worry about Herr Krieger," Bishop said, moving toward her. "By the way, I thought I told you to stay home."

"Did you?" Gia asked. "I must have misunderstood."

Epilogue

Bishop sat at the last table at The New Genesee with *The Courier-Express* and a half-eaten plate of silver dollar pancakes before him. His hair was freshly cut, his face straight razor shaved. The shine on his shoes made his wingtips look wet. Jake sat by his feet, ears perked, eye wide, waiting for morsels to fall from the table. Uncle Sal wasn't with him, and Bishop wondered if Sally had decided to disappear for a while. Maybe his involvement with Schrieber and Rhielman went beyond arranging a poker game. Or maybe it didn't. He never could tell with Sal.

The headline read, "Nazi Art Thieves Foiled." The lead article carried Flynn's byline. Bishop wondered if the wires had picked up the story like the reporter had always hoped. The photograph accompanying the piece was of Bishop and Gia holding the saved Renoir. Neither was smiling. They stared into the camera with expressionless eyes and grim mouths, like two tough customers who were good at their jobs and knew it. The caption identified them as partners at The Bishop & Alessi Detective Agency.

The story was continued on page six and took up most of the columns. There was a photograph of The Brandts from happier days taken at some charitable event. She wore pearls and he a tuxedo, both looking every inch the attractive socialites they had once been. Next to that was a photo of Hans Schrieber from the Thirties speaking at a Bund rally. He wore round glasses and a black garrison hat cocked to the side. His fist was raised as if about to pound the podium and drive home some menacing point. Beneath that was Rhielman's picture taken from his last city council campaign. There was no mention or photographs of Joey Bonesutto. The Gospels weren't very bright, but they were smart enough to keep their mouths shut about who paid them. Erik Krieger was still at large, and The Albright was offering a reward for his arrest. Maybe there were Nazis in other cities, and he'd head to them. Maybe he'd disappear into Canada. Bishop doubted he'd ever see him again.

The final photograph was of Pearl's portrait. The grainy, black-and-white photo didn't do the oil painting justice. It didn't capture her sorrow or tired beauty and inherent grace like Brandt's brush had. But even in the newspaper you could tell *Pearl In Blue* was special. The subject was extraordinary. Bishop wondered if the painting was still resting on the easel at Brandt's studio. Maybe, after he brought Ira home from the hospital today and got him settled, he'd drive over and check. He was sure Dinah would want it, and he couldn't think of anyone who deserved it more. He touched his pocket to make sure he'd brought his lock-picking tools.

Tamis came over and refilled his coffee cup without being asked. He never said a word or mentioned the newspaper article, and that was all right with Bishop. Him coming over instead of a waitress was enough.

Bishop cut the remaining pancakes into small pieces, put the plate on the floor for Jake, and lit a Chesterfield. Looking out the restaurant window, he could see Genesee Street coming to life. Delivery trucks and trolleys rumbled past. Women in groups of three and four were either going to or coming from their shifts at Curtiss Wright and Bell Aircraft. Servicemen, some wrinkled and rumpled from last night's liberty and others as crisp as recruiting posters, walked by marching to their fates. Benny The Junkman stood on the corner counting a wad of bills, and Bishop wondered what in the world he could've sold for that much green. What Bishop didn't see, at least not yet, were the usual ghosts that haunted him—the faceless father, the returning mother, the yellow cab barreling closer—and for that he was thankful.

Then the trollies and factory workers and soldiers all disappeared, as if a lens had been focused on the only thing in the world that mattered. Bishop felt warm and full and more alive than he could remember as he watched Gia walk by the window, enter the restaurant, and hurry toward him.

Author's Note

I'm very lucky to have a dedicated team in place that has supported my writing career for over a decade. Carla Damron, Dartinia Hull, Beth Uznis Johnson, and Ashley Warlick have provided feedback, guidance, love, and friendship for nearly fifteen years. Thank you for letting me join your sorority. Special and continuing thanks to Andrew Gifford, Director of SFWP, for believing in my work, for pushing me to be excellent in all aspects of being an author, and for stocking cold Budweiser at all SFWP events that I attend. Thank you to my co-pilot Adam al-Sirgany, who edited both *Yesteryear* and *After Pearl*. I hear Adam's voice when I write and edit now. He's made me a better writer and for that I'm grateful. I'd also like to thank SFWP's cover artist Gunnar Jacobson for creating the cover art for both *Yesteryear* and *After Pearl*. His work is stunning. Countless people have told me that if *After Pearl* is half as good as the cover, it'll be a success. I know they're right.

Finally, I'd like to thank Nicholas Bishop, Gia Alessi, Jake the One-Eyed Dog, and all the characters in *After Pearl*. I started this novel during the COVID lockdown and finished a draft soon after. My goal when I started wasn't publication. It was escapism. I needed a project to distract me from the horrific pandemic news and the loneliness of sheltering in place with only a one-eyed dog for company. These characters provided me with a world where the things that can kill you—Nazis, greed, revolvers, and automatics—can be seen and touched. I don't have enough words to express my gratitude to them for pulling me through my dark times and into theirs.

—SGE

About the Author

Stephen G. Eoannou is the author of the novels *After Pearl, Yesteryear, Rook,* and the short story collection *Muscle Cars.* He has been awarded an Honor Certificate from The Society of Children's Book Writers and Illustrators, the Best Short Screenplay Award at the 36th Starz Denver Film Festival, and the 2021 International Eyelands Award for Best Historical Novel. Eoannou holds an MFA from Queens University of Charlotte and an MA from Miami University. He lives and writes in his hometown of Buffalo, New York, the setting and inspiration for much of his work. Find him at sgeoannou.com

Also from Stephen G. Eoannou

Muscle Cars

"These stories will transport you. Enjoy the ride."
— K. L. COOK, Author of *Love Songs for the Quarantined* and *Last Call*

"Part Richard Russo, part Bruce Springsteen, part OTB parlors and Cutlass Supremes, Eoannou's debut collection is all—all—heart. A fine first collection, and I look forward to the next."
— BRETT LOTT, author of *Jewel*, an Oprah Book Club Selection

"*Muscle Cars* is a magnificent debut."
— ASHLEY WARLICK, author of *Seek The Living* and *The Summer After June*

Yesteryear

"*Yesteryear* is a wild ride told in the style of radio dramas of the era: Fran is cursed by a madam, the gangsters keep tommy guns stowed in trombone cases...Eoannou gives readers a novel that is just as dramatic as it is fun."
— *Electric Literature*

"*Yesteryear* reads like a fever dream, but one in which 1930's Buffalo, New York, is resurrected in such specificity that you'll believe it never passed on, and what's more, it's brought to you in a voice that synthesizes the cadences of a sax solo, a radio play, and a comic noir."
— DANIEL MUELLER, author of *How Animals Mate*

About Santa Fe Writers Project

SFWP is an independent press founded in 1998 that embraces a mission of artistic preservation, recognizing exciting new authors, and bringing out of print work back to the shelves.

  @santafewritersproject | @SFWP | sfwp.com